THE
LABYRINTH
OF
MINOS

JC RYAN

VINCI
BOOKS

By JC Ryan

Carter Devereux Mystery Thriller Series

Nothing New Under The Sun
The Wolves Of Freydis
The Alboran Codex
The Nabatean Secret
The Labyrinth of Minos

Vinci Books

vinci-books.com

Published by Vinci Books Ltd in 2025

1

Copyright © JC Ryan 2018

A CIP catalogue record for this book is available from the British Library.

Paperback ISBN: 9781036703318

From the Historical Record

Myths of human-animal hybrids and the involvement of the gods in human affairs are common in folklore from all over the world. Myths and legends, we are told, are works of fiction, superstition, fantasy, or the vivid imagination of uninformed, over-religious, ancient peoples.

What gave rise to those myths? Was it only imagination? Lack of understanding? Could there be some veracity in every myth?

According to Homer's *Iliad*, the Greek king, Agamemnon went to war against the Trojans for abducting and keeping Helen, the queen of Sparta. Agamemnon's army besieged the city of Troy for ten years before finally conquering it. For millennia it was believed that this story was a myth. There never was a city of Troy nor a Trojan war.

That was until 1868, when the German businessman and archaeologist, Heinrich Schliemann, excavated a site at Hisarlik, Turkey and discovered treasures belonging to King Priam, the king of Troy. To this day there are still those who describe it as fantasy, but many archaeologists are now agreeing that there was a city called Troy and a Trojan war, pretty much as the poet, Homer, described it.

Archaeologist Manfred Korfmann, a modern-day excavator of Hisarlik, says the story of the Trojan War contains some truth. "According to the current state of our knowledge, the story told in the *Iliad* most likely contains a kernel of historical truth or, to put it differently, a historical substrate. Any future discussions about the historicity of the Trojan War only make sense if they ask what exactly we understand this kernel or substrate to be."

Another myth from the Greeks is that of King Minos of Crete and the Minotaur, and could very well be one of those that holds a kernel of historical truth.

Mention the name Minos, and two images immediately come to mind: One, of Minos feeding Athenian youths to the Minotaur in the Labyrinth. The other, of Minos becoming a judge of the Underworld as depicted in both Virgil's *Aeneid* and Dante's *Inferno*.

The Minotaur, a half-bull, half-human hybrid living in a labyrinth on the island of Crete is one of the most intriguing of the Greek myths.

King Minos, for whom the Minoan civilization, previously known as the Cretan civilization, was named, is regarded as the most important ruler of that civilization. His headquarters were in Knossos, the largest city on the island of Crete at the time. Today, more than three and a half thousand years after Minos, thanks to the discovery of the city in 1878, visitors can enjoy the mythical city's former glory again.

Minos was one of three children born from the union between the god Zeus and Europa, the daughter of the Phoenician king, Aginoras. The earliest references to King

Minos can be found in the epics of Homer, the *Iliad* and *Odyssey*, dating back to the 9th Century BC.

"For Zeus at the first begat Minos to be a watcher over Crete, and Minos again got him a son, even the peerless Deucalion, and Deucalion begat me, a lord over many men in wide Crete; and now have the ships brought me hither a bane to thee and thy father and the other Trojans." *Iliad* (Book 13.450)

"And Phaedra and Procris I saw, and fair Ariadne, the daughter of Minos of baneful mind, whom once Theseus was fain to bear from Crete to the hill of sacred Athens..." *Odyssey* (Book 11.321)

Minos had two siblings who rivalled him when he declared himself king and proclaimed that it was the will of the gods that he should be king. As proof of his claim, he offered a bull to the god of the Mediterranean Sea, Poseidon, and asked that the god would send him another bull also to be offered. According to the myth, Poseidon was pleased with the first offering and sent Minos a beautiful white bull from the sea. However, the bull was so beautiful and impressive that Minos and the citizens decided not to offer the bull but to set it free and sacrifice another in its place.

And that's where the problems started.

Poseidon was furious that his white bull was not offered to him, and as punishment he made Minos's wife, the goddess, Pasiphae fall in love with the white bull. She was so much in love with the bull that she asked the sculptor and engineer Daedalus to construct a hollowed out wooden cow. Pasiphae hid inside the wooden cow, and the white bull was mesmerized by the cow and coupled with it. The result of this union was the birth of a powerful creature with a human body and the head of a bull, the Minotaur.

The beast lived on human flesh and frightened Minos

and the citizens so much that Daedalus was ordered to build a structure, the Labyrinth, to contain the monster.

During this time, Minos, so the story goes, wanted to subject the city of Athens to his rule and asked the gods to bring plague and hunger to its citizens. The gods apparently obliged. The Oracle of Delphi advised the ruler of Athens that the only way to alleviate their suffering was to give in to Minos' demands: *"send seven boys and seven girls to Crete every nine years to be sacrificed to the Minotaur."*

Archaeologists distinguish between the historical Minos and the mythological Minos, selecting only those parts which have been verified by archaeology as true and everything else as myth. The question is if archaeologists can put their hands on their hearts and say, 'we've uncovered everything — there are no more discoveries to be made that might turn myth into fact'?

They've been wrong before, and they could be wrong again.

Although the story of the Minotaur is taken as a myth, it needs to be noted that a real Labyrinth cave was discovered on the island of Crete. Could this cave have been the inspiration for the story of Minos's Labyrinth and the fearsome Minotaur that resided within it?

Chapter One

It was early on a crisp but sunny September morning. Carter and Mackenzie were out on the deck of their log home on their idyllic Quebecois ranch, Freydis, each with a mug of steaming coffee in hand. Their children, Liam, almost nine years old, and Beth, just turned five, together with the five other kids making up the scholars of the Freydis homeschool were out on a field trip. They were under the watchful eyes of Steve Anderson, Mackenzie's dad, an ex-science teacher, and Carter's old friend Ahote. It would be their last fishing expedition of the year before winter would arrive.

The children had begged to go and see the new wolf pups as part of the field trip. Keeva had given birth about two weeks ago but had finally come out of hiding and showed the small litter, only two pups, to Mackenzie. Loki, Keeva's mate, kept them close to the den, though. Mackenzie wanted the children to meet the pups as well, but Beth and one of the other children were a bit of a handful, and the pups too young to be manhandled.

Mackenzie would trust her life to the wolves, whose special connection to her had once given her the strength to carry on in the face of the darkest days of her life. To Carter and other observers, this relationship between Mackenzie and the majestic animals could only be described as mystifying, incomprehensible, something akin to telepathy.

Mackenzie, though, knew that wild animals could revert to their natural behavior in a fraction of a second if their instincts were triggered, especially when their young were threatened. The pups would have to be older, or Beth more settled, before it would be a good idea to introduce them. And then she hoped the wolf pups would develop as strong a connection with her own young as their parents had with her. Carter agreed with her reasoning.

"Let's wait for Keeva to bring the pups to us when she's ready," she'd suggested to them. Though disappointed, the children knew that tone of voice. It meant no arguing.

So, instead of accompanying the kids on their field trip, Carter and Mackenzie were taking the rare moment by themselves to discuss their projects. They'd moved from the kitchen, where the family breakfast had created a mess neither wanted to tackle right then, to the deck. Carter set his mug down and leaned across the table to hold his wife's hand. Her fiery hair shone in the golden morning sun, and he counted his blessings for the millionth time since he'd engineered their meeting on campus more than a decade ago.

It had been a few months since they'd wrapped up their last mission for A-Echelon, a top-secret arm of the CIA. They'd both been recruited to the agency, whose mission was to investigate ancient mysteries for any truth that could be exploited in the interest of national security for the US and her allies. Carter, an archaeologist of mixed but growing repute at the time, and Mackenzie, a molecular biologist, had met on the campus of the university where they both taught.

His involvement with A-Echelon came first, when he was recruited by his grandfather's handler, James Rhodes, now recently retired as head of the agency. Mackenzie's had come later, when her exploration of ancient medicine in search for modern applications caught the attention of James Rhodes during one of his visits to Freydis. At the time, James was the deputy director of A-Echelon, and when he saw what she had uncovered and the potential it held, immediately convinced his director, Hunter Patrick, that Mackenzie had to be recruited.

Carter's last two missions had involved both of them, which meant Mackenzie's research project had to go on the back burner. Now, with the Nabatean secret society defeated and all of them who were not dead in custody, Mackenzie and Carter needed to discuss what had to be done to get her research project back on track. Mackenzie every now and then said she was eager to get back to it, and she was also regularly prompted by the new Director of A-Echelon, James Rhodes's replacement, Irene O'Connell, to resume the work. But for some reason or another she seemed to be dragging her feet to make a start.

It was about three months since they had returned to Freydis after a harrowing experience with the malevolent members of the Council of the Covenant of Nabatea, as well as the shady character of Russell McCormick, Assistant Director of the Counterintelligence Division of the FBI, and Kelly White, a misguided Counterintelligence Special Agent in the US Army Intelligence and Security Command, INSCOM. The actions of those two succeeded not only in turning President Grant and Bill Griffin, Director of the

CIA, both of whom had always been very loyal and supportive, against them, but very nearly landed Carter and Mackenzie in jail. Fortunately, with the help of their trusted friends of Executive Advantage, Sean Walker and Dylan Mulligan, the charges leveled against the Devereuxs by McCormick and White were short-lived, and they could proceed to smoke out the Nabateans and stop them from a power-grab which would have had ghastly consequences.

The whole nightmare started on March 15 and ended only three months later. No wonder Carter and Mackenzie were taking their time to enjoy the peace and tranquility of Freydis and spend every moment they could with their children, family, and friends.

Upon their return to Freydis in June, Carter immediately got busy with reorganizing and managing the translation work on the Library of the Giants and starting work on the newly acquired Library of the Nabateans, which he and his team had unearthed in Matera, Italy. He had to hire more translators, procure more computer equipment, and oversee construction of more offices and accommodation for the ever-increasing number of people working and living on Freydis.

Freydis, the ranch Carter's late grandfather, Will Devereux had willed to him, had once been a rustic place with a single log cabin and Ahote and Bly's smaller cabin a mile or so away. Over the past two years, however, it had become a thriving little village with close to thirty people calling it home these days.

For some time, Carter had sensed that Mackenzie had settled back into the Freydis rhythm, and that she was back in the emotional space where he could broach the subject of restarting her research, yet he also sensed some hesitation on her part.

"Mackie," Carter said, "I have been getting the impression lately that you've been wanting to get back to your research, but something is holding you back. Right?"

She smiled and looked at him. "You know me too well, Carter. Not that it's a bad thing, though. I like it. And yes, I am sort of ready to take it up again."

"So, what is it that's holding you back?"

"The children on the one hand," she said. "I've been away from them so much. Someone needs to tame Beth, and even a boy Liam's age needs his mother. On the other hand, I have to admit, I'm a bit scared as well..." she paused for a moment.

Carter started to ask a question, but she held her hand up. "I'm the one who talked you out of leaving A-Echelon after you rescued us from that hell-hole in Saudi Arabia. I'm the one who told you we can't back down, but you know what scares me when I look back over the past few years? It's as if when you and I touch anything from ancient times, there is an evil force just waiting to destroy us."

Carter nodded in silence. Those were thoughts that had passed through his mind often. He didn't interrupt her.

"The children and I have fallen into the hands of bad people, our family was attacked and almost killed here on Freydis, you and I almost landed in jail not long ago, assassins were hired to kill us in Italy...

"How many more times will we escape the evil forces bent on terminating us? That's what's worrying me and holding me back. My respirocyte research has already gotten me and the children locked up, and it almost destroyed Liu's life as well. We also know the Nabateans wanted to get their hands on my research work, and they were more than happy to kill us in the process.

"I'm convinced I'll find what I've been looking for in

one of those libraries, or a lead to it. The question is, at what price?"

Carter took Mackenzie's hand again and said. "I know Mackie. It's as if we're tempting fate every time we set out to investigate – as if we stir up a hornets' nest – but as far as we know you're the most knowledgeable person in the world about the concept of respirocytes in ancient times. There is no one else with access to the information you have available in those ancient libraries."

Mackenzie nodded and started smiling. "Yep, I know all of that, and I'm not going to hand over my work to anyone. I have to maintain what control I can over it. I'm going to finish what I started. I just wanted to tell you what's been troubling me."

At first Carter was stumped by her response. Then he started laughing. "Now that's my Mackie. For a moment there I thought you were trying to tell me you wanted out. See, I don't know you as well as you alleged earlier."

She grinned. "Well, at least you know enough to see when something is bothering me. So, now that my psycho-analysis is complete, and you know what's going on in my mind, I guess we need to start planning how to get my project kickstarted again?"

Before they'd gone much further in their discussion, they were interrupted. Carter was needed at the translation building, where a team of translators worked around the clock to extract the information about ground-breaking science contained in the ancient libraries of the Giants.

Mackenzie gave in to the inevitable and went to clean the train wreck she'd made of the kitchen earlier. She didn't mind cooking every now and then, but it was definitely not one of her favorite activities. She did her part in the kitchen when she had to but made sure to keep her dishes quick and simple. If the recipe said it would take more than fifteen minutes to prepare, she'd usually start looking for another one.

After seeing to the needs of the translation team, instead of using one of the electric carts, Carter decided to walk the two miles to the Executive Advantage training facility, Camp Tala. He loved the exercise, and besides, he needed some time to think. The name Tala, the Sioux word for wolf, was James Rhodes's idea, passionately supported by Mackenzie, of course. Originally, the name had been selected because of the relationship Mackenzie and the people of Freydis had with the wolves on the ranch. However, the name took on a new meaning when, a few days after the construction of the camp started, the entire wolf pack turned up at the site as if they were reporting for duty.

It turned out that was exactly what they did, reported for duty. At least the six young ones did. They seemed to be all very keen to be enrolled in an Executive Advantage training program conducted by one of the members, John Ruschin, who was an experienced military dog handler. Soon, six of the young wolves were trained as military "dogs" and they certainly showed their mettle when they were instrumental in protecting the inhabitants of Freydis against a murderous attack by a group of ex-Russian Spetsnaz mercenaries, hired by the Council of the Covenant of Nabatea.

Carter used the time he was walking to think about how fast his son was growing up, and what he wanted to teach him. Liam already showed signs of intellectual brilliance. His time as a prisoner in Saudi Arabia with his mother had given him a sweet bond with her and his little sister, and as a result he was almost as protective of them as Mackie was of him.

Carter wasn't jealous of the connection, but he needed one of his own to develop, and his frequent absences from the ranch made it difficult to establish more than the normal father-son relationship. He knew that to guide a brilliant child in emotional intelligence would require more than that.

Chapter Two

Carter's translation teams now had two libraries to translate, that of the Giants, which was housed on Freydis, along with a team of translators and computer experts who worked together to develop a program to translate the massive amount of data still unexplored. The Nabatean library was now housed near A-Echelon headquarters in DC, and translation on it had begun there. His and Mackenzie's ancient languages expert, Liu Cheun, traveled back and forth as needed.

The Executive Advantage team continued to train new recruits at their compound on Freydis. Sean Walker, the CEO of Executive Advantage once described the organization to Carter and Mackenzie.

"EA is a type of international mercenary force — much like a mini French Foreign Legion. Almost like the NATO of black ops — in other words, we are the free world's top-secret country-less antiterrorism organization with very little red tape or bureaucracy. Just a bunch of good guys hunting and eliminating the bad guys — agile and extremely effective, thus far. We are independent, apolitical, areligious, anti-dogmatic, et cetera, and therefore we have the support of intelligence agencies across the globe.

"EA was established when leaders of a few security agencies from around the world got together and agreed to form an independent, global Special Forces unit with a deep pool of expertise. We are officially part of the American black ops community, but we are funded by all the member countries. It's a unit of specialists who can assure swift and successful clandestine missions anywhere in the world. The result of this international interagency agreement is that Executive Advantage has access to the skills of former Special Forces members from around the globe. That means we recruit people from the Navy SEALS, Delta Force, Green Berets, AFSOC, British and Australian SAS, Canadian Joint Task Force 2 - JTF2, French Foreign Legion, Israel's Kidon — part of Mossad, Oman's Desert Phantoms, India's Gurkhas, and others.

"We're an organization of last resort, which means we're called upon whenever security and intelligence agencies find themselves with an intractable problem that must be dealt with when commercial, diplomatic, and political solutions have failed or are not an option.

"However, and I'm sure you can imagine, politicians of the member countries don't want to have any 'knowledge' about us or our activities — they want results and no links to them — plausible deniability."

Dylan Mulligan, second in command at EA, former SEAL team member under Sean Walker and his best friend, oversaw the training compound at Tala. He and Liu had married just two weeks after he and Sean, with a team of EA special forces operators, had helped Carter and Mackenzie wrap up the Nabatean affair. And although that was the end of the threat, another kind of busyness crept into their lives.

Liu and Dylan wanted to get married on Freydis. Carter and Mackenzie, with Bly's help with the catering, threw a lavish wedding reception for them. Then the newlyweds had gone to Boston to celebrate again with their friends and family there, and then departed on a month-long honeymoon.

While they were gone, Sean filled in for Dylan at the training compound, and one afternoon he'd gone for a horseback ride in the late evening sun with Samantha 'Sam' Rawlins, IT lead for the translation effort. They'd hit it off after her boyfriend, Rick Winslow, was killed. Rick had been abducted by hitmen working for the Nabatean secret society and refused to give up information about the dolphin research conducted by Carter and his team. After this incident, Sam moved to Freydis to help with the computer translations of the Library of the Giants. That was when she and Sean started spending as much time together as they could whenever Sean was visiting the ranch.

On the night in question, they'd come back engaged, which prompted another party.

In August, James Rhodes retired as he'd threatened, despite President Grant's request he stay on through the end of Grant's term the following January. James' second in command, Irene O'Connell, was promptly promoted, and James, with his wife, Carolyn, came to Freydis for a retirement party and long visit. At Carter's invitation, they'd selected a little west-facing plot about two miles from the homestead, on the side of a hill overlooking a beautiful, lush green valley. The mountains in the background would be snow-topped most of the year. They had built an ecofriendly log cabin, where they frequently stayed now.

Irene was also a frequent guest, but her visits were always work-related, or at least that was always her official reason for a trip to Freydis. Unofficially, she loved Freydis and the company of the Devereuxs, often saying that a day or two at the ranch, and in their company, was enough to energize her to face the politicians of DC and the demands of her job for a month to six weeks at a time. President Grant had encouraged her to name a new deputy director, but she hadn't yet done so. In addition, she refused to give up her duties as Mackenzie's handler, so she really needed the R&R breaks on Freydis every now and then.

Carter got tired just thinking about it all. In addition to all the parties and his frequent trips to DC, he had been needed at the Alboran dig several times. Once or twice, Mackenzie went with him to visit Merrybeth, the dolphin who'd helped recruit others of her species to help with the search for the sunken city of the giants and their library.

Carter realized she'd been right earlier that morning. She *had* been away from the children too much, as had he.

The next morning, after Carter's turn to make breakfast and clean the kitchen, the children were sent off to school, and the two of them were back on the porch, coffee mugs in hand.

"I have an idea," he said, thinking even as he spoke. "What if we build you a lab here and bring in anyone you need to help you?"

Mackenzie's jaw dropped. Yesterday had been busy, and the activities had swept their discussion to the back of her mind, so Carter's remark had come out of left field.

"Carter, that would cost millions!" she exclaimed, instantly catching up with his train of thought.

Carter had been a wealthy man in his own right, thanks to his discovery of the gold-laden Viking longboat off the coast of Florida during one of his university breaks, which put more than thirty million into his bank account. Apart from that, when his grandfather Will died, he'd left his only grandchild, whom he'd raised, his extensive land holdings and many more millions. Carter was able to cut a two-billion-dollar check that would not be dishonored. On top of that, Mackenzie had negotiated a contract with DARPA for the development and exclusive use of her respirocyte technology, when it came to fruition, that would make her a multi-millionaire on the spot. In short, Carter and Mackenzie were in the fortunate position that they didn't have the money worries that ninety-seven percent of the world population had. They could easily afford a state-of-the-art molecular biology lab, especially since they already owned all the land they'd need on which to build it.

"Where..." she began.

"We'll expand the translators' village," he answered, anticipating her question about where they'd house the scientists she'd need. What had started as a dormitory resembling a nice apartment building had been expanded by several single-family log cottages when some of the workers brought their partners and children with them. Others had inevitably formed couple relationships with co-workers or other residents on the ranch. There was still plenty of space for more cottages if the scientists Mackenzie needed were married, and some empty apartments in the dormitory if not.

"I'll need..." she tried to start again.

"Wait, let me get my laptop. Let's start planning it right now."

Morning briefing forgotten, Carter typed as fast as he could while ideas for Mackie's research facility flowed out of her mouth. They paused only for him to answer the phone and tell the lead translator to go ahead with the daily standup meeting without him.

At some point, Carter and Mackenzie moved into the home office to use the whiteboard there. A sketch of the building and its floor plan along with a mind map of the departments she'd want for support of her research grew there.

By the end of the day, they were mentally drained, but Mackenzie was too excited to sit still. While Carter and Liam went into the kitchen to cook dinner, she began a list of the scientists she wanted to contact and recruit. Ever practical, she knew not everyone would want to leave a university environment for a tiny compound on a vast ranch in the middle of the Québécois wilderness, no matter how sophisticated the lab was or how beautiful the setting. She therefore put at least five names under each category, the last of each being someone who could refer her to others if needed.

The dinner, fresh-caught trout, broiled to perfection with a lemon, onion, and tomato garnish, and served with a baked potato and broccoli from Bly's garden, was a big hit. Beth didn't want to eat the 'trees', but Mackenzie's make-believe enthusiastic enjoyment persuaded her to try them. Jeha also refused them when Beth tried to feed her the rest under the table. Beth declared that to be evidence that her mother and anyone else who liked them were weird.

Liam, who was assistant chef in preparing the meal,

took his sister's criticism in stride. "It's okay, Dad. She doesn't like anything green."

Carter refrained from reminding him that he hadn't either, at that age. He counted his blessings again as he and Mackie tucked the children into bed a little later. And he couldn't help when his mind wandered off as he started thinking about resigning from A-Echelon. He loved the work, but these last few days with the children made him think again about what was important. After a while, though, his sense of duty and patriotism brought his mind back to reality. He could not just walk away from A-Echelon. The world was still fraught with danger, and the libraries he had in his hands contained the solutions to many of the threats, if not to prevent them, then to overcome them.

Chapter Three

Six months previously

His name was Ahab. Educated in London, he'd always found it ironic to be named after the seventh king of Israel. The Bible depicts King Ahab as a wicked king because he followed the ways of his wife Jezebel, killing his subject Naboth, and leading the nation of Israel into idolatry. His modern-day namesake, who was not married and worshipped no god other than himself, was also a wicked man who would have done the ancient king proud. In fact, on the wickedness front he would probably outdo the king.

He'd been born in Saudi Arabia in a medical research facility to parents whom he never knew. He was told that his last name was Bashar. Growing up, he came to believe that he'd had the good fortune to be selected for an experiment that had given him near-superhuman strength and endurance. He was told, and he believed it, that it was only the very best and most brilliant who were selected for those experiments.

He knew nothing of those who'd been treated before him. If he had known, he might not have characterized his fate as good fortune. All who went before him died, one after setting a new record for a human being in a marathon. But that man's feat had gone unrecorded, as the race was not sanctioned. His record was known only to a few who'd been there, two of them scientists in the employ of a man named Algosaibi.

Ahab was the last, for Algosaibi had met the unfortunate fate of anyone who dared betray his country and his ruler. He'd lost his head one day, and the scientists he'd employed, those who didn't meet with the same fate as their employer, had scattered in fear for their lives.

Ahab, one of the subjects who had been regarded by the Saudi authorities as an innocent victim, was never examined for the experiments conducted on him, and set free. He was left to fully discover his abilities on his own with no one else knowing what he was capable of. He was also left without guidance as he grew from a teen raised in the institutional environment of an experimental laboratory to manhood. He was therefore unchecked in his antisocial behavior, an unexpected side effect of his treatment. Now a man in his mid-twenties, he was gaining a reputation in his chosen profession as an unconventional thinker. His profession was not known to be kind to unconventional thinkers.

Ahab was an archaeologist. He was also a sociopath and a serial killer but hid it well. Only his victims knew the truth, but that knowledge was always short-lived. He was disciplined enough not to take those of his colleagues who dared criticize him as his victims, though he was often tempted. However, he wanted to show them all that he was not the buffoon some thought.

Recently, his studies had taken him to Crete. Unlike the

archaeologists who'd searched for the Labyrinth of Crete before him, he had abilities that he felt would serve him well in searching deep in the earth. Crete had once been part of the mainland, the last vestige of a land bridge between Greece and Northern Africa that had formed when the Mediterranean had dried up in prehistoric times. The land had sunk, or the sea had risen. Both, according to his research. Previous archaeologists had searched only just below the surface of the island.

Based on his enhanced ability to go for long periods on only one breath, and to swim like a natural sea creature, he'd been exploring deep below the surface of the sea, miles offshore of the island. He therefore had no need to obtain permits for a dig, and no need for anyone to know of his interest, for that matter.

The story of the Minotaur had always intrigued him. As the result of the experiment on himself, he felt there might be some truth to the story that most thought of as just a myth. And if that were the case, there must be evidence, DNA perhaps, in the real Labyrinth. He was determined to find it, and if possible, to use it, not only to prove his brilliance to the naysayers, but in his secret life as well.

Ahab had only two goals in life. One was to make an enduring mark on the field of archaeology. In that regard, his role model was an archaeologist who had made a name for himself with discoveries of advanced prehistoric civilizations, Carter Devereux. A man who singlehandedly turned the modern version of human history on its head. Ahab reckoned that producing a living Minotaur would make that mark and put him in the cadre of revered archaeologists to which Carter Devereux belonged. Ahab's other goal was to extract all the pleasure he could from the physical pain and fear of others, until he was inevitably caught and killed. He reckoned owning a Minotaur would also assist in that goal. What better way to get rid of the evidence of his kills than to feed the bodies to a Minotaur?

He spent hours dreaming of the ways in which he could do it. After having his own fun, for example, he could watch as his pet monster made the kill. Or he could torture his victims by showing them the monster, telling them he would give them to the beast if they screamed, and then inflict pain in various ways while amusing himself by guessing how long it would take to wring a scream from them. He might even kidnap two victims at once and make one watch what was going to happen as he tortured the other. Oh, the joy it would bring him!

But first, he must find the DNA, re-engineer the monster, and raise it to adulthood. The scheme came to him while watching an old movie, *Jurassic Park*. In the movie, a wealthy man had used DNA found in samples of amber to recreate extinct animals – dinosaurs – for use in a theme park as entertainment. Of course, the experiment had gone horribly wrong. It didn't occur to Ahab that his own plan might have disastrous consequences. He was too arrogant to consider he might fail, or that a monster like the myth of the Minotaur described might be difficult or impossible to control. Might even destroy *him*. It was one of the typical traits of sociopaths – they got so hypnotized by the reward of achieving their goals that they ignored the risks and consequences.

From the moment he conceived the idea, he was obsessed with planning. He felt he was very close to seeing his dream fulfilled. All he needed now was the money to mount his expedition in search of the DNA. Once he found it, he'd need more funds to develop the technology to recreate the monster. Of course, nothing of the sort must be revealed in his grant requests. He'd financed his explorations so far by taking jobs on other archaeologists' digs, using any free time he had to explore on his own.

One of the archaeologists he'd worked under was a rebel like himself, his idol, Carter Devereux. The man had pulled off some frankly unethical moves and had come out smelling like a rose because of 'the greater good'. Ahab had studied him. Devereux kept a low profile on his background, but Ahab had discovered he was wealthy, and had met his wife, Mackenzie. Now that was a juicy morsel, but too old for his peculiar tastes. Though he was an equal-opportunity killer, he preferred children.

Of course, he thought, he wasn't a pervert. Sexual sadism wasn't his thing. No, he was a scientist of death. How much terror would cause the death on its own? How much pain could a normal human endure? With these questions and his 'experiments', he was unwittingly continuing the work of the scientists who had created him. He didn't recall those buried memories, but he'd been raised in the same laboratory where many such experiments informed the work that led to his artificially enhanced abilities.

Chapter Four

It took months to build Mackenzie's lab and recruit top-notch scientists to assist her. Especially since weather on Freydis was not conducive to construction. November and December typically saw the most rainfall of the year, and January and February were too cold to pour the foundations, so work on the building itself hadn't begun until spring.

Mackenzie tried to curb her impatience by conducting more research, investigating the equipment she would need for her facility, and starting the recruitment process for scientists to work for her. The latter was not a straightforward process. It was not as if she could place a few advertisements in the media or employ a recruitment agency to get the right candidates. Due to the top-secret nature of all A-Echelon work, she had to first identify candidates without them knowing about it. Then each candidate had to be background-checked and vetted by the CIA.

The candidates who passed through that process could then be approached but could not be told the details of for whom they would be working and the details of the project, other than using phrases such as "top-secret", "highly classified", et cetera. If the prospective worker had not been scared witless by then or refused to have anything to do with it, the next step was to get an appropriate security clearance. Only when all those things were in place was she able to tell them about the project and where they would be working. In the process, many candidates who initially seemed to be suitable were found not to be. Even among those who got through the wringer and obtained the required security clearance were some who had no desire to spend any time working on a project out in the wilderness of Quebec.

However, if that was not enough, there were more things to keep Mackenzie's plate full. Thanksgiving and Christmas were spent amid their growing community and her parents, Steven and Mary Anderson, and brother Ray, as well. It was her pleasure to entertain the company, while Bly planned and provided the feasts and planned the parties that made the dreary late-fall months and stormy winter days more bearable.

She reveled in the enjoyment of her children, too. They were growing so fast, both physically and mentally. Occasionally she and Carter took them out of school to go hiking or snowshoeing or to visit Keeva and her growing pups. Keeva had turned up in late October with them, Loki following to keep guard, and gently nudged the two young wolves toward the children. Since then, they'd played together often.

Beth showed signs of having the same sort of connection to the female pup that Mackenzie had with Keeva, as Mackenzie had hoped. Liam loved the pups, too, but his first loyalty was to his little Cavoodle, Jeha. Jeha took it upon herself to teach the pups how to behave around the children, and Mackenzie thought the little dog somehow knew that Liam would need a special relationship with a bigger creature as he grew older and more independent. Jeha was fiercely loyal to him, and to a lesser extent to Beth, but her tiny size meant there was little she could do to protect them. What was surprising was how tolerant Keeva was of the little dog's nips and corrections when the pups bit too hard in their play.

On occasion they also took the children with them when Carter had to visit the underwater archaeological site in the Alboran Sea. On those occasions, Carter would drop Mackenzie and the children off in one of the cities of Europe. He would visit the site for a few days, and then return to spend time with his family.

In the middle of February, an unexpected warm spell allowed the contractors to pour the foundation for the new lab. Mackenzie happily supervised until the weather turned cold again, and construction was frustratingly delayed. Carter suggested they take the children with them to Italy the following week, and everyone enthusiastically agreed.

So, it was March by the time construction got underway in good earnest. From then on, Mackenzie was involved in supervising every aspect of her new lab. By June, the building was finished, the interior furnished, and supplies laid in. The first party of the summer was a welcome for the new residents of the community – her assistants. They had all arrived on Freydis on a Saturday via the milk train, as they called the plane that visited Freydis twice a week, some-times more, to bring in supplies, and transport personnel between the US and Freydis. This arrangement between the Canadian and US governments assured that neither the milk train nor Carter's jet or EA's plane would have to clear customs on any side of the border.

On the first Monday after Independence Day, at eight a.m. local time, Mackenzie and her five assistants assembled for the kick-off meeting. She had explained their roles to each of them when she recruited them, but for the first time they were together and ready to understand the big picture.

"My research to date has been a survey of ancient texts to determine whether scientists in the distant past and even prehistory have solved one of the medical necessities of today before their technology was somehow lost. I have concluded that they have. When I hired you, I explained why you were all required to pass background checks and have each been granted top-secret clearance. You understand that we work strictly on a need-to-know basis. Apart from the information that I have already divulged to you before today, the next piece of secret information you need to know is that we will have access to the two libraries of the ancients that my husband has discovered. We refer to those as the Library of the Giants and the Alboran Codex. Both of those libraries were created by a race of giants who wandered the earth more than 70,000 years ago."

At this point she had to stop talking because of the collective gasping sound coming from her audience. She was sure she even heard a few mutters of "what the hell" spoken under a breath. She looked up from her notes and was met with the bewildered stares on their faces. It took her a split second to realize that none of her audience had the means or opportunity to have had the benefit of being part of those human history-altering discoveries which had been part of her life for so many years. She had to pause her briefing and divert into the history of Carter's discoveries. As could be expected, and as with anyone in the past who had to come to grips with Carter Devereux's discoveries, the reaction of her assistants ranged from outright rejection bordering on rebellion, to maybe contemplating resigning immediately. However, it all gradually turned into guarded skepticism, and when Mackenzie ended her explanation two hours later, had become I'll-stick-around-for-a-while-to-see-just-how-crazy-you-are.

After this unplanned but necessary departure, Mackenzie could get back to the original brief. "From the information we have extracted out of the parts of those libraries translated so far, we are convinced that we will find what we're looking for there. We have also, through the good offices of our agency, A-Echelon, negotiated a contract with DARPA, who will support us in our endeavor in any way they can. In exchange for their funding and support, they'll have the rights to become the first adopters of the respirocyte technology when we develop it. Please note my choice of words, "when" not "if". DARPA's chief purpose will be medical, and the first commercially-deliverable stores will be used to save the lives of our soldiers on the battlefields.

"While the libraries' existence is known publicly, some aspects of what they contain are closely tied to national security. We will be working with some of those aspects to complete our mission, and that is part of the reason you have received your security clearances and been required to sign the non-disclosures." At this point Mackenzie paused and looked around at everyone seated at the table. "Any questions?"

There were none, and she proceeded. "Okay, with that part out of the way let's jump straight into the details. "Our mission here is aimed at one thing, though we will take several paths to get there. It is my greatest hope that we can successfully produce an artificial blood cell, one that will medically extend the lives of millions of people suffering from diseases that could be eased if we could only deliver more oxygen to their bloodstreams.

"You are all aware of the theoretical work done by Robert Freitas in 1998. He proposed a nano-molecular device he called a respirocyte. The device would be made from a diamondoid fullerene, sometimes known as a 'buckyball', sub-microscopic in size, and yet capable of storing and transporting two-hundred and thirty-six times more oxygen than a natural red blood cell.

"At the time, his ideas were thought interesting but impractical — technology had not yet advanced to the point of creating the artificial intelligence, nor the mechanical function that would make such a device possible. My research indicates that not only have we approached that horizon, but by other means available to scientists in the distant past, it has already been done.

"As we develop ways of duplicating those discoveries and mass-manufacturing respirocytes, they will revolutionize medicine for the masses. You, ladies and gentlemen, will help me make that dream a reality."

The meeting in the cozy conference room broke up, and everyone took a tour of the rest of the building, took note of where each scientist's lab was located, and chattered excitedly with their new colleagues. Mackenzie considered it a great start as she visited each in his or her own lab later in the day.

She had a separate office off her lab, where she'd moved her extensive personal research library. A separate entrance to the office was for the others to enter when they needed to meet with her or consult her library, and the door was always open. Her molecular biology assistant, a PhD in her own right, shared her lab, while the data analyst, the veterinarian, the research clinician, and the nano-engineer each had their own. Liu would work in a cubicle set off from the rest of Mackenzie's office when she needed to be in the lab in person, but she would usually communicate from the translation building where she had her main office.

Mackenzie had already gathered research on ancient technologies, and there was more to study. But the most promising area of research would probably be found in the Library of the Giants, housed on secure servers only a few yards away in the translation building, or even in the Alboran Codex. Liu had found promising references there, leading to the DARPA deal. Now she was searching in the Library of the Giants for the knowledge those references had mentioned.

Mackenzie had established that in the intervening millenia, oxygen levels in the atmosphere had become much lower now than they'd been in the Giants' time, about 70,000 years ago. She hypothesized that the levels had fallen in small increments that had allowed the earth's animals, including humans, to adapt to them through evolution. It was the same kind of acclimatization that allowed modern mountain climbers to adapt over a few weeks to the lower levels high in the Andes or Himalayans, just in a longer time-frame.

From her prior research she had also learned that the higher oxygen level was one way to explain the evidence of gigantism in prehistoric humans. Scientists knew that the Earth's atmosphere had changed drastically over the millennia. She had found quite a few scientific studies showing that sometime in the distant past, Earth's atmosphere had contained about 30% oxygen compared to only 20% today. This had been determined when air analyzed from bubbles inside drops of amber showed a higher concentration of oxygen than in modern times.

Humans are limited in how tall we grow because of our skeletal structure, but high levels of oxygen in the atmosphere could provide a feasible explanation for gigantism. "Just look at the dinosaurs and how big they were," some scientists pointed out. "Granted, they were probably a lot slower than elephants because of the time it takes for neurons to fire, but we haven't seen creatures of such size for millions of years."

Mackenzie recalled a conversation, years ago, she had with James Rhodes discussing this very topic, when she said, "Based on what has been discovered at the City of Lights, I set out to find more supporting data about giant humans, animals, and plants. I was not disappointed. There are masses of evidence from all over the world. Houses and graves, fossil footprints, bones, artifacts, the Bible - all these tell the same story about the existence of Titanic humans, incredible lifespans, superiority, and nobility. But sadly, it seems we their descendants have all but forgotten them."

She pulled her laptop closer, searched for a file, and once again read the information provided by Dr. Carl Baugh of Glen Rose, Texas. He had constructed a large high-pressure oxygen chamber, also known as a hyperbaric biosphere. His purpose was to recreate the conditions of our original world. After concluding his experiments, he'd written:

> *We've been doing extensive research into the ancient atmosphere, the one that produced the fossil record. Our research indicates that essentially everything was larger in the past. For instance, the club mosses, which today reach sixteen to eighteen inches, often approach two hundred feet in the fossil record. The great dinosaurs, with their rela-*

tively small lung capacity, reached tremendous stature. Seismosaurus could reach his head almost seventy feet in the air. Something has to explain this anomaly in terms of today's atmosphere.

In today's atmosphere, we have fourteen point seven pounds of atmospheric pressure per inch at sea level. But to oxygenate the deep cell tissue of these great dinosaurs, we need much greater atmospheric pressure. Research has shown that when you approach two times today's atmospheric pressure, the entire blood plasma is saturated with oxygen.

Our research indicates there was about 27 pounds per square inch of atmospheric pressure in the past. That would beautifully solve a problem even paleontologists admit exists.

In addition, the oxygen supply in the fossil record has been found to be 30 percent oxygen compared to 20 percent today. Ancient air bubbles trapped in amber have been analyzed and revealed this heavier concentration of oxygen. If we had those conditions today, we could run two hundred miles without fatigue.

However, Mackenzie's hope was that the Giants especially had seen a need to develop a way to more efficiently use the diminishing oxygen levels and had at least made a start. In every other field of human knowledge, they'd been advanced beyond the current knowledge. Carter and his team were still working to discover what had destroyed their civilization and plunged the world into the ensuing thousands of years of human history leading to the present time. If they had worked on the oxygen level problem, and if the technology could be duplicated, it would save her team perhaps years, even decades, of research.

On her rounds, her colleagues had specific questions

regarding their own roles. The veterinarian wanted to know when animals might arrive, and what he should do until that time. Mackenzie assured him that several pairs of healthy rats would be delivered within the week. She hated the necessity of testing on helpless animals, but the potential for toxicity or immune reaction was too great to first test on humans.

"We'll be as kind to them as we possibly can, but let's not lose sight of the goal. Every day, thousands of people die who could be saved by this technology. I consider this an urgent mission, and our DARPA sponsors even more so."

"I wish DARPA weren't involved," answered her assistant. "How do we know they won't use the research to make super-soldiers?"

"The short answer is, we don't," Mackenzie said, a slight frown marring her expression. "If you have moral objections, I will understand, and now is the time to tell me. I can't afford to lose you halfway through."

"I'll be okay. I guess I'm just a passionate pacifist at heart, Dr. Devereux."

Mackenzie favored him with one of her brilliant, disarming smiles. "Please, it's Mackenzie. Please don't hesitate to talk with me any time. We are dedicated to relieving human suffering, but as you may know, I have a particular soft spot for animals as well."

"I've heard you have a mystical connection with a pack of wild wolves who live here on the ranch," he remarked. "That's fascinating. I'd love to meet them."

"We share something like ESP," Mackenzie answered. "Another time, I'll tell you all about it. And if Keeva and Loki have no objections, I'll be happy to introduce you. They do make their own choices about whom they trust."

"Fascinating."

The research clinician had a similar question about when her expertise would be called upon. "I understand animal trials will come first, and I agree. But I'm here already, so there must be a reason."

"Indeed, there is. In the first place, you need to be intimately familiar with our progress. But with whatever head start we can get from the libraries of the ancients, I hope to make that progress rapid. Meanwhile, between locating information in the libraries and implementing our experiments, I'd like you to also carefully study the information and see if you can relate it to modern humans. Not going down unfruitful research pathways is as important as going down the right ones."

"It will be my privilege, Dr. Devereux. I can't tell you how exciting this work promises to be." She smiled.

Again, Mackenzie requested to be called by her first name, and she winked when she said, "No need for you to tell me. I'm over the moon myself! My work was interrupted over a year ago, and I'm anxious to get back to it. Why don't you spend the next day or two cataloguing and arranging your lab supplies to your satisfaction? I'm sure we'll have some reading material for you by then. In fact, as soon as you're ready, I have something I turned up in a European library. It's quite a bit later than the material in the libraries of the ancients, but I found it interesting."

Mackenzie didn't name the source of the material she meant for a reason. She'd illegally copied an ancient text called the Sirralnnudam, which was later stolen. She'd been in deep trouble for her role in the disappearance, though she'd been cleared of the theft. It had all worked out, her copying thereof forgiven in the aftermath of the text's destruction. At least they had the copy, and if she hadn't made it the material would have been lost forever.

When she got back to her own lab, her assistant wasn't there. She went through to her office and found the assistant perusing her library, and Liu waiting for Mackenzie.

"What are we doing today, boss?" Liu asked, teasing Mackenzie by calling her 'boss'.

"Where did we leave off?"

"Gosh, it's been months. Why don't we start with the lab notes, and bring everyone back up to speed?"

"Sounds great. Do you know how to find them on this thing?" Mackenzie waved vaguely at the elaborate desktop setup.

"Maybe we'd better start by calling in your new IT specialist," Liu said, laughing. "I'm sure to get it wrong and erase everything."

Mackenzie made a horrified face. "I do hope you're kidding, but that's a good idea. However, I'll have to call Sam. The person you're referring to is more of a data specialist and mathematician than a hardware and network person."

The rest of the afternoon was spent in learning the ins and outs of the computers and network, understanding the multiply-redundant backup system, and finding the accumulated work Mackenzie had done on the project before she was interrupted.

To her surprise, she found files on her work while in captivity in Saudi Arabia. "I didn't know we had this! Thank goodness it wasn't lost!"

Liu smiled. She had been with Mackenzie when Carter and his team rescued them, along with Liam and the surprise baby girl, Beth. "We were all traumatized after our rescue, and then you were pulled into another of Carter's adventures. I guess it slipped my mind. I had a flash drive when I was captured, and when they searched me… Well, let's just say they weren't as thorough as they could have been. I copied our research notes every day, and when we left our, mmmm, 'guest quarters', I brought it with me."

Mackenzie had a feeling Liu had conspired with Carter to spring this surprise on her. She smiled happily and gave Liu a bear-hug. "I'm so glad you're sneaky, Liu. Thank you!"

"Ladies, can we focus here?" the assistant asked. "What are we talking about?"

Mackenzie and Liu looked at her and simultaneously burst into laughter. "I guess it isn't common knowledge," Mackenzie gasped after she stopped laughing. "Can you wait until tomorrow? I think I'd better have another staff meeting to bring everyone up to speed on what I've done already, along with where I've done it, and who I was with."

The next morning, after Mackenzie had checked with Irene whether she could divulge her time in captivity to her team, she assembled them again and filled them in on the progress she'd made in Saudi Arabia with Liu's help. However, she cautioned that some of the results had been obtained by inhumane testing of her work against her will and before she'd been satisfied with the safety thereof.

"We'll have to repeat everything, and this time go more cautiously. Science done under duress is not trustworthy."

She dismissed a sober group of teammates with the fear that they would consider her a victim. "Do you think they've lost respect for me?" she asked Liu.

"Not only do I not think that," Liu answered, "but I think their respect has doubled. As it should. You endured our captivity with grace and dignity, even in the darkest hours. What other woman would have made any progress on a scientific question while believing her husband had been killed, and that she, her young son, and an unborn child were at risk of the same fate?"

"You were there, too, Liu. You had as much courage or more. You helped keep me sane."

"That would not have been possible for me alone. Your Keeva and the telepathic connection you had with her did that."

"Well, both of you have my eternal gratitude, and Carter's," Mackenzie said. There was nothing more to be said that the hug they shared then didn't convey. Such experiences as they'd had together either forged unbreakable bonds or made intractable enemies. Mackenzie was certain that Liu would have given her life to keep the children safe. There was no deeper friendship than that.

Chapter Five

A week after Mackenzie's research team began their work, it was time for Carter to visit the Alboran dig again, or as he sometimes called it, the dredge. It was his droll way of acknowledging that the work was being done underwater.

Every month or so, a discovery would require his presence at the site. Frequently, Mackenzie accompanied him, or had done so before her research got back underway. She always enjoyed visiting with the pod of dolphins that had been so helpful in the discovery. Merrybeth and her pod took a continuing interest in the work, and they patrolled the waters around the operation regularly, though they also ranged throughout the Mediterranean. On this occasion, however, Mackenzie was too involved in supervising her team as they took up the research. She couldn't leave them so soon.

"I'll say hello to Merrybeth for you," Carter said as he kissed her and the children goodbye. "Be back in a couple of weeks."

Mackenzie sighed. She wished the dig was finished and

Carter could stay home with them for a longer time. It seemed they no sooner settled into a comfortable home routine, then off he went again. But she knew it was the nature of his work, and the fact that he'd made the commitment to A-Echelon meant that even when the Alboran dig was finished, if not before, there'd be another assignment.

A little while later, it was her turn to kiss the children and send them off to school for the day. Liam was advanced for his age. Other nine-year-olds would be in fourth grade. Thanks to his early home-schooling, he'd been reading at five, and though they tried to keep him with his age group now that there were other children around, he was reading at a level that few twelve-year-olds could boast. He'd also taught Beth to read, so at five she'd started first grade. Mackenzie was proud of them, but she also worried about their social development. Brilliant children often outstripped their age cohort in intellectual learning and were maladjusted socially as a result. She and Carter would do anything they could to prevent that.

Once Liam and Beth were out the door, Mackenzie changed into jeans and a favorite old soft T-shirt and made the short walk to the lab. In July, the weather on Freydis was near-perfect, with warm, sunny days and mild but cool nights. The half-mile walks to her lab always made her happy, and she was sure it would be no different in other seasons, but the scent of wildflowers perfuming the air, the gentle breeze, and the peaceful feel of the ranch lifted her spirits like nothing else could. Different from her love for Carter and the children, or her friendship with the people she and Carter had surrounded themselves with, it was a visceral joy she couldn't explain. She only knew it happened when she was immersed in nature.

In the distance, she spotted Keeva and Loki teaching the

pups, now half-grown, to hunt, and sent a thought of greeting to them. Keeva lifted her head and seemed to gaze at her for a moment. A bright, fierce longing to hunt for prey entered her mind and was gone in a second. Keeva was distracted by her task, and had no time to visit, even telepathically. Mackenzie laughed. She was not a hunter by any stretch of the imagination. And Keeva never understood it – she was always trying to engage Mackenzie in her efforts.

Merrybeth, the dolphin, didn't understand it either, though she was able to articulate her confusion. She and Mackenzie had a few philosophical land-human to sea-human deliberations about whether it was moral for Mackenzie to eat the 'prey' of others when she didn't want to hunt herself. It was a cultural difference they couldn't bridge, but it hadn't marred their friendship. They'd agreed that their species had different standards of morality, but that the universal love for their children made them more alike than different. Mackenzie thought Keeva would have agreed, had the wolf been inclined to self-introspection, and had she been able to communicate like the dolphin.

Mackenzie entered the lab with a smile, thinking about the distant friends that Carter would soon greet for her. It had been the surprise of a lifetime when they'd discovered that dolphins were more intelligent than anyone had theorized before – that they understood human speech, kept records of their history in their heads, and most surprisingly of all, that they and humans had once been able to understand each other's speech without the need of computer technology to act as translator.

She and Carter had also learned that the dolphins had long-distance communication with their species around the world, and that they had a sophisticated understanding of human life, as well as some of the same social instincts. *Land-human*, she mentally corrected herself. It was what the dolphins called *homo sapiens*, which itself turned out to be a rather narrow-minded description of human characteristics. The Latin phrase *homo sapiens* meant wise man and had been used for centuries to distinguish 'land-humans' from animals – that is, every species other than mankind.

But dolphins also referred to themselves in words that meant the same thing: wise, or intelligent, beings of their species. The translation devices she, Carter, and his exploration team now used to communicate in real time with the dolphins translated the word as 'human'. Admittedly, it had taken some getting used to. But now Mackenzie thought of Merrybeth just as she did other women, as a friend rather than like a beloved pet. Only with a different sense of fashion, she reflected, grinning.

"What's got you so chipper this early?" Liu asked as Mackenzie entered the building.

"Just thinking about Merrybeth, and how much I miss her. I wish she could visit here like other friends."

"Don't tell me you're now going to build a guest ocean," Liu teased.

"If only I could!"

"Have you ever thought about respirocytes with respect to dolphins?" Liu asked.

"What do you mean?"

"I mean, would there be any advantage to dolphins if we could develop respirocytes for them?"

"That's a great question, but I can't answer it. Next time I have a visit with Merrybeth, I'll ask her. But I think we'd better perfect them for humans — land-humans that is — first. That's what we're being sponsored to do."

"Oh, yes, our overlords, DARPA," Liu said, making a wry face.

"It's okay, Liu. I can't think of a better application than saving the life of a nineteen or twenty-year-old who would otherwise lose it on a battlefield halfway around the world from his home. Can you imagine? Barely older than Liam, and yet they volunteer to go and fight terrorism far from friends and family, to preserve our way of life."

"Mackenzie, they're twice Liam's age, at least. And I'm sure not all of them are so altruistic. Aren't there other reasons for joining the military?"

"Of course, there are. But they know before they do that the price is potentially their death or devastating injury. And they're just babies!"

"Now I've gone and spoiled your good mood," Liu mourned.

"No, just turned my thoughts in a more productive direction. Let's get to work. I can daydream about Merrybeth visiting another time." *And about Carter being at home, safe in my arms.*

"I just dropped by to let you know I've finished the translation of the last treatise you gave me," Liu said. "It was interesting. I guess this research has been ongoing throughout modern history."

"I know, which makes it more daunting. How am I to expect success, when the greatest minds in the modern-day past could not have it?"

Liu smiled. "Well, for one thing, you have all their work to build on. For another, you have confirmation that there was more oxygen in the atmosphere in ancient times, just as you theorized before Carter found the Giants."

"To be technical, Carter didn't find them…"

"I know. Okay, before he found their library. Anyway,

you know you're on the right track, and that the culmination of your research, assuming you're successful, will revolutionize medicine. The ability to inject oxygen directly and safely into a vein will save countless lives and provide a better quality of life to people whose respiratory function is compromised. Just think of the implications to MS and CF patients, stroke and heart attack victims, victims of auto accidents and oxygen deprivation – drowning! I could go on."

"Thank you for the lecture, Liu. I think I'm the one who told you about all that," Mackenzie said, laughing. "You're preaching to the choir."

"You're right, but as your biggest fan, save Carter and the kids, I can't help but get excited when I think about what a benefit it will be. Can you tell me what progress you've made since you opened the facility here?"

"Not much, I'm afraid. It's only been a week. But everyone is almost up to speed on what I'd done before, and they're getting there on the old research I've gathered. Thanks for getting that last thing done. The Hippocrates, wasn't it?"

"Yes. Smart old dude. Interesting how his theories have come back into vogue."

"Yes, it is! Well, I'd better get to work to earn my keep around here. Thanks again!"

Liu waved as she stepped past Mackenzie toward the door. "You bet."

Chapter Six

Ahab's preparations were almost complete. He'd written a grant request for funds to spend six months on Crete, searching for the definitive proof that a Labyrinth had ever physically existed. He'd cleverly disguised his real purpose for doing so. After sending the request unsuccessfully to several major universities in Europe and the United States, he'd been approved by a joint venture between Egypt and Libya.

The two countries hoped he'd find there was no archaeological reason for them not to explore for oil and gas in the Mediterranean Sea between Crete and their claimed offshore limits. The nearest distance between Crete and the mainland was less than 200 miles. Despite international law and agreements, the seabed between the island and its southern neighbors on the African continent had been a source of controversy throughout history. Libya could technically have claimed Crete as its own, and Egypt had almost as valid a claim, assuming both were based on the continental shelf theory giving countries dominion over up to 350 miles of continental shelf, versus the territorial sea sovereignty standard of twelve nautical miles.

Both countries could use new sources of natural resources, and they'd be willing to finance an expedition that might support their claims. Furthermore, both countries were willing to keep their involvement in the expedition secret, and neither was interested in any report other than whether the seabed gave evidence of ancient ruins below. International pressure would presumably hinder their drilling in the sea if ruins were found, but if not, and if they could keep the project secret until drilling platforms were complete, the *fait accompli* would make it difficult for any other country to mount an effective objection. Ahab didn't care one way or the other, so long as he got his funds.

By the time Mackenzie and her team were beginning their work on Freydis, Ahab had outfitted his one-man expedition and arrived on Crete posing as a wealthy sport fisherman on an extended trip of several months. His purposes didn't allow for a team, but he did charter a yacht for his sea adventures. He paid double the going rate to be allowed to captain it himself. He could not risk a crew getting wind of his extraordinary abilities to stay underwater for up to four hours at a time and sustain great physical exertion like a draft horse. In fact, he wouldn't have needed the yacht except for his desire to efficiently search a grid that would require its navigation system.

Ahab began by taking the boat out daily on a clockwise exploration of the seabed surrounding Crete. He thought of it as the continental shelf, though in truth, Crete was neither a continent, nor was there a shelf per se. The Mediterranean Sea was a remnant of a much larger ocean, dubbed the Tethys Ocean by geologists who studied the history of the earth's crust. Over millions of years, during which the Tethys Ocean had been cut off at the eastern end by tectonic drift of Africa toward Europe, the resulting body of water had dried up at least once, for a period of about 630,000 years, before being flooded again. This body of water was now called the Mediterranean Sea, and some believed it had completely or nearly desiccated several times during the roughly five and a half million years since it was formed.

News reports of the ancient civilization of giants in Northern Africa, northwest of Egypt, to be more precise, and more recently, an advanced civilization centered in an area that was now beneath the Alboran Sea, encouraged Ahab to believe there might lie buried or submerged around Crete the true structure that gave rise to the legend of the Labyrinth and the monster known as the Minotaur. In fact, he'd worked on the Alboran dig recently, hiding his natural abilities, to learn what he could about the civilization, for he thought it possible that it had been spread much wider. Crete was only about 1500 miles from the Alboran site, less if one traveled in a straight line rather than by sea.

Though the Ancient Greek myths and legends arose during the Greek Dark ages, beginning around the 12th century BC, Ahab believed they derived from collective memories of the remnants of civilizations that had been destroyed with no other evidence they'd ever existed. Perhaps even one of those recently discovered. As each extinction event left only a few individuals to adapt to new conditions and begin the process of growing a civilization over again, the memories became myths and legends. The stories survived to this day as curiosities believed by the ancients, now understood to be false, yet all too real in their origins.

Ahab was looking for a phenomenon so small that he could easily miss it if he didn't carefully plot his grid search. A karst spring surfacing off the Cretan shore would be too subtle to see in any kind of rough water. However, he'd seen pictures of just such a phenomenon located yards off-shore around Crete. Subtle ripples in an otherwise calm sea would indicate a spring draining its system, an underground area called a karst, into the ocean. Karst springs are usually the end of a cave system at the place where a river cave reaches the Earth's surface, or in this case, the sea. If he found one large enough, he'd be able to enter the caves at the spring, without the knowledge or permission of anyone on the island. And that was how he wanted it – secret – until he was ready to reveal the results to the world.

Ahab knew his appetites might not allow for an uninterrupted search. He'd satisfied his blood lust before beginning, but Crete was too small an area to risk indulging himself during his sojourn. If he must, he'd visit the mainland, but he was disciplined enough to forego the temptation for several months.

An organized killer, he would be almost impossible to stop unless he began to decompensate. But he was intelligent enough to have diagnosed himself and studied how to evade discovery by spreading his kills both geographically and in terms of elapsed time. Therefore, he felt he'd have at least eight or nine months to make a thorough exploration before being compelled to kill again.

However, as luck would have it, he found the first of the springs he was looking for only a week after he spent the first day searching the grid he'd laid out. Leaving the yacht on sea anchor, a generator running to forestall the curiosity of anyone boarding to check on the yacht's occupants, he fitted a full-face mask and dove smoothly into the water to follow the spring to its origin.

Disappointingly, the spring emerged from a rift in the bedrock that was too small for him to enter. He considered surfacing and bringing back explosives to enlarge the opening but decided it wouldn't be productive to start blowing up every drainage he located. Better to find what he was sure was here somewhere. If he was right about the Labyrinth being a real place, then there'd be an opening large enough to enter. In this belief, he was engaged in magical thinking, but didn't recognize it as such. His narcissism did not allow him to understand that just because he wanted something, didn't necessarily mean it was so.

However, he explored up and down the underwater slope for over an hour before giving up on the location and returning to the yacht.

A cursory examination of the interior relieved his anxiety about any unwanted visitor. After enjoying a meal that would have foundered an ordinary man his size, he moved to the next location on his grid.

Day after day, Ahab continued his search, at night returning to the villa he'd rented to continue his research into how to grow a small sample of DNA into a fully-realized, full-grown Minotaur. Ahab required little sleep, so the night hours afforded him plenty of time to do his research and develop his theories. Though he considered himself to be a patient man, he'd already decided that introducing the DNA into a human baby would take too long. A bull calf, which would reach maturity somewhere between 15 and 24 months, would be a better choice. However, there was the question of where he'd keep the monster out of sight until it was mature, so, he kept exploring the idea of a human subject.

He knew the experiments on himself began when he was about eight or nine years old. Would it be possible to change the DNA of a child that age? He didn't know, but the concept fit his other compulsion. Children were easier to kidnap than adults and were therefore his preferred prey. They were also easier to hide. So, he'd decided on his 'petri dish', and was now engaged in the study of gene splicing.

He'd prefer to do the work himself, but without a medical background, he knew he'd have to 'recruit' others to help. Whether that recruitment would be voluntary or involuntary he hadn't yet decided. Naturally, he'd prefer to keep all the glory and credit for the discovery for himself, so he leaned toward involuntary. But he'd need to also determine who was the best person to do the job, how that person could be kidnapped, where the entire experiment would take place. In short, there was more than enough work to do in the evenings.

The easiest would be if he found a living Minotaur. He dreamed about that on occasion. How would he capture it? How would he transport it and confine it? He was confident in his superior strength to men, but how strong was a Minotaur? Usually, he dismissed the idea as a childish fantasy. How would they have survived, hidden, for hundreds of millennia? On the other hand, maybe those Greek myths and legends held a kernel of truth. What if they'd only needed to survive for fourteen thousand years? Nowhere was there any mention of the life-span of a Minotaur. And if his theory was correct, there were probably a race of them, not just one. They might have somehow survived.

On the mornings after he'd gone to sleep thinking about finding a live, full-grown Minotaur, he'd wake up with an almost-irresistible hunger to indulge his secret. Every time that happened, he wrestled with the urge until he could convince anyone he met that he was just what he seemed – a wealthy young man on an extended fishing vacation. But every time it happened, the urge grew stronger. If he didn't find the caverns soon, he felt he may have to take a short trip off the island to satisfy it.

Chapter Seven

Thanks to the previous work Mackenzie had done and Liu's translations of the ancient texts, the research team, who'd dubbed themselves the Aquaman Project Team over Mackenzie's weak protests, was making rapid progress. The self-proclaimed nerds among them joked that the only powers the DC Comics superhero possessed that humans fitted with nano-robotic respirocytes wouldn't, was telepathy with sea creatures. As they also joked, who needed telepathy with sea creatures, when Mackenzie had the ability to talk directly with them?

Mackenzie had to laugh at the team's culture of humor. Medical research often made its servants too serious, but she was convinced that happiness and contentment produced better work. She was on board with whatever made them truly happy, so long as the work didn't suffer. Even if their team mascot *was* Aquaman, the weakest hero in DC's arsenal, as Liam informed her with disgust.

In her office, they'd mocked up models of a normal red blood cell and the theoretical respirocyte that Freitas had originally described. Created as a spherical fullerine, that is, a hollow molecule of carbon atoms resembling a soccer ball, the respirocyte, once they'd found a way to stabilize it, would deliver pure oxygen directly into the bloodstream. Earlier research had already led to environmentally-friendly uses for ordinary carbon nanotubes, such as making touch-screen devices, hydrogen fuel cells for alternative fuels, and even items requiring high-strength materials, like bullet-proof vests.

These ordinary carbon nanotubes used recycled plastics in their manufacture, freeing landfills of much of the plastic waste that would otherwise have taken up an inordinate amount of space. The multiple wins – cheaper manufacture of high-tech goods, generating money from a waste product, and use of a wide range of plastics that would have been hard to recycle by other means – made them highly popular.

However, it had quickly been learned that their use as a delivery mechanism for drugs required a higher quality of carbon source. Problems such as allergy and toxicity had to be overcome before they could safely be used to carry and release the quantities of oxygen that Mackenzie's vision required. And creating stable, buckyball-shaped nanotubes from the synthetic adamantine, or diamonoid, molecules preferred for their purity, was proving problematic.

At first, the nano-engineer had believed that with suffi-cient raw material, he could 'grow' his own fullerenes. But it was soon brought home to him that the complex geometry involved would require the expertise of a chemical engineer. He applied to Mackenzie for a colleague to share his lab, and the search for a new team member began.

As with every other new person on Freydis, the chemical engineer required a background check and security clearance, living arrangements, the addition of a salary, food and travel allowance to the project budget, and of course, her attention to recruitment. Mackenzie called another meeting of the staff.

"As you know, we're going to be adding a new team member as soon as possible," she began without preamble. "I'd like to make sure we have everyone we need, so that we don't have to go through the long process and painful interruption again soon. Does anyone need an assistant, someone with other expertise, or anything else?"

The nanoengineer spoke hesitantly. "Have you given any thought to the fact that once we succeed in doing this in a small batch, we're going to need something that will manufacture mass quantities?"

"I'm not sure I understand what you have in mind," Mackenzie said.

The engineer glanced at her research assistant and the doctor for support. The doctor spoke up. "We're looking beyond the initial research, Mackenzie. For practical use, or even for human testing when we're ready for that, we're going to need something like a generator to collect the large number of respirocytes needed to make a difference to a wounded soldier. Consider that they may be bleeding or burned extensively. We can't just inject a few respirocytes into someone who's bleeding and expect them to remain inside the body. The same goes for replacing hyperbaric oxygen therapy with respirocyte therapy for burn victims in the field. We'll need hundreds of thousands of respirocytes for the initial roll-out phase."

Mackenzie understood his comment but replied, "You have to keep in mind that our objective is not to commercially manufacture the respirocytes. We're only to develop the method to do so."

"Maybe not, but we're still going to need a generator to produce enough for the animal tests, as well as for the human testing phase. If you don't want to do another round of recruiting and budgeting, then perhaps a mechanical engineer would be a good addition to the team now. Maybe getting him or her familiar with the problem as your other engineers work on it will save time later, as well."

Put that way, she had to agree. "Agreed," she confirmed. "I'll get on that. Anything else? Anyone?"

After fielding requests for a few minor items of equipment and laughing at the veterinarian's joking request for a pet sloth, Mackenzie dismissed the meeting and returned to her office. She hadn't anticipated the administrative work load of running the team, and in a way, it was a burden. Her love was for the research, and having to put that aside to be an administrator, was galling. While she was head-hunting, she'd get an admin assistant in who could also serve as coordinator with DARPA's HR.

When Carter returned a month later, they'd had their first breakthrough. With the help of the chemical engineer she'd recruited, they'd made a few stable diamondoid fullerenes in the spherical shape she'd modeled on Freitas' theory. The lab rats had tolerated them well, and they now had a few who could stay underwater for up to an hour.

Work was far from complete, though. The fullerenes apparently did not break down as expected when they had released all their oxygen. And there was no practical way to replenish the oxygen supply inside them, or none they'd found. So, they had to inject more fullerenes, and eventually they built up in the bloodstream, causing toxicity issues.

They lost a couple of rats before they realized it, and Mackenzie mourned the waste of any life. She asked the veterinarian to be sure to note signs of distress in the rats and ordered the data specialist to keep track of the number of fullerenes injected and calculate their saturation by volume of blood for each rat. She didn't want the rats to suffer, but they needed to know at what level of blood saturation the fullerenes became toxic.

And then, just before the mechanical engineer finally arrived, it was Liu who discovered the real breakthrough.

Liu had been involved in the first translation efforts for the Library of the Giants, or the LG as they now called it for short. She now divided her time between Freydis and Washington in supervising the translation teams and working with the computer geeks who programmed the automated translation software. But she still enjoyed working on sections of the libraries that had challenged the other translators and defied the automation. Most often, it was in the medical section of the LG. She was still interested in the area where she'd helped Mackenzie in Saudi Arabia – translating ancient medical texts in support of the respirocyte research.

She called these projects her hobby, and though her husband, Dylan, complained that you can't have a hobby that's the same as your day job, she'd bring the printouts of the ancient text home and pore over them instead of reading or watching TV in the evenings. One night, she'd stayed up after he went to bed, working on a document whose title she'd translated as 'blood machine'. Those words got her excited. That was exactly what Mackenzie was looking for – an ancient "blood machine."

She'd started with the words that had become familiar, leaving gaps where she didn't immediately understand the proto-Semitic abjads of the Giant's language. What she had in front of her on that night looked much like a redacted document, except that instead of black marks on some words, there were spaces. Once she had the entire passage transferred to a handwritten English page, she began on the unfamiliar words, relying on context to some extent to fill them in. Without a background in medicine, it was slow going, but she'd learned a lot during her confinement with Mackenzie, and in the years afterward while helping her with translations. So she persisted, growing more determined as she recognized this could be very important to the respirocyte work.

Liu's concentration was unbroken when a sleepy Dylan quietly entered the room to check on her. Her silky black hair hid her face, but Dylan knew her tongue would be peeking out from between her closed lips as she worked. He watched her for a few minutes, and then quietly left again without interrupting her. She was so captivated she probably didn't even notice his presence. He would do that twice more before her shout woke him at around five the next morning. She had worked all night.

Alarmed, Dylan leaped out of bed, grabbed his pistol, and ran to protect his wife. But he found no threat, only a jubilant Liu, dancing around the table on which lay her work and pumping her fist in the air. His heart rate slowed when he saw she was okay.

"Liu, what in the world?" he asked, gaining her notice for the first time all night.

"Eureka!" she answered.

"Eureka?" he asked, bewildered.

"It's Greek for 'I've found it'," she explained, as if that answered his question. "Archimedes shouted that when he discovered how to measure volume based on displacement."

"Yeah, yeah, yeah. Believe it or not, I've been to school, but what's this Greek guy got to do with your work?"

"I've found Mackenzie's answer! This document," she said, picking up the printout and brandishing it like a weapon, "explains how to create a respirocyte generator!"

Dylan gave his head a vigorous shake. Either his wife had gone 'round the bend, or he was being particularly obtuse this morning. "Mackenzie? Respirocytes?"

Liu crossed the room to kiss him. "Sit down, honey. I'll make you some coffee."

"Okayyyyy… but…"

"Come, let me get some caffeine into your system first. Maybe that will get your brains working again," she said.

Still in a sleep-deprived daze, Dylan followed her to the kitchen and plonked down in a chair at the table.

While she bustled around the kitchen getting the coffee started and then started making their breakfasts – yogurt and granola for her, bacon, eggs, toast, and orange juice for him – she explained the significance of what she'd found.

"You know Mackenzie is working on how to make masses of stable respirocytes – the artificial red blood cells. She's explained that to you several times, Dylan."

"Yeah." Dylan had his hands around his first cup of coffee by the time she got back to his half-awake questions.

"Well, the Giants knew how to do it. And the work I did last night will give her a tremendous short-cut. It seems they're on the wrong track with the diamondoid atoms they're using to build the cells. Those will build up in the bloodstream and eventually kill the host. The Giants made them out of a biological substance that worked by replicating themselves in the lungs. It made their lungs able to absorb and use more oxygen."

"But I thought that Carter told us there used to be more oxygen in the air. Why would the Giants need respirocytes?"

"I think they were trying to compensate for the oxygen depletion. Remember, they were giants. When the oxygen levels started going down, less oxygen in the air meant they'd begin dying off from hypoxia. It must have taken centuries for their stature to adjust to it. Meanwhile, they had to keep themselves alive somehow."

"Makes sense. Are you going over to the lab this morning?" Dylan asked.

"I have to. I can't let Mackenzie and her team chase down the wrong path if this will help them sooner."

"Okay. Before you go, can I have a couple more eggs and another piece of toast?"

She knew he worked hard and trained hard, but how he kept his fighting-trim physique when he ate like he did, she'd give good money to know. It seemed he consumed five thousand calories per day, and never gained a pound. As she turned the burner on under the skillet again, she wondered if she could interest Mackenzie in a new study when she'd perfected the respirocytes.

Chapter Eight

It had been more than a month, and Ahab's quest was still unrewarded. As his frustration grew, so did his bloodlust. Knowing he was on the edge of decompensating, he made what he felt was the only rational decision. He took the yacht to the mainland and arranged to have it cleaned and stored for a few days while he went home to London.

Once home, his mask – the persona he showed to other people – felt a bit more secure. He spent the night in his own bed after unlocking the safe where he kept his souvenirs. Those were innocuous bits of keepsakes – a hair ribbon from his first kill, a shoelace from another. Though he was an equal-opportunity killer, taking adults when the urge struck, and it was an easy capture, all his souvenirs were from the children. He thought it would be best to grab a child this time. The thirst was quenched longer with a kid, for some reason. He wasn't introspective enough to have determined why. He'd just noticed it was so.

Ahab understood how the police investigated disappearances. They looked first to family and friends. A husband or wife for an adult; the parents, other relatives, or friends of the family for a child. So long as he was careful about witnesses and didn't hunt in his own backyard, so to speak, he would never fall under suspicion. For that reason, he never considered taking one of his colleagues at the university or one of their family members, not even one of their kids. Too close to home.

His most fertile hunting grounds were slums in South London, where the working poor were forced to leave children unattended or attended by older siblings that were still too young to have the responsibility. He kept to a strict schedule, though not a systematic one, so as not to create a pattern that authorities might discern. It had been more than eighteen months since he'd taken the last kid from a converted warehouse where the local council authorities provided emergency housing for the homeless on a night by night basis.

The setup was perfect. Temporary residents didn't know each other well and were too busy looking out for their own interests to look out for each other's. He'd allow himself one pass through the area, no more. Even in such an environment, he'd be noticed if he cruised it more than once. Any kid he could lure would do. Ahab had his preferences, but he never allowed them to dictate his victims. That was a way to be caught, to let the authorities know there was a serial predator working. Randomness was key to his continued freedom.

Before he went hunting, however, he checked in at the Uni. The atmosphere of the campus in summer had a different vibe from the other seasons. The students were a different demographic, often foreign, taking advantage of the short courses offered in summer. Inevitably, he found a few of his fellow academics proctoring an exam or poking about in the library. He made sure to let them know he'd be returning to Crete the next day, though he planned to stay several more. It was a precaution designed to give him a sort of alibi, though he didn't expect to need one.

Later that day, he drove to Hull, where he kept a cottage on the outskirts. It was here he meant to bring his next victim when he was done. The marshes at Sutton Park already held the remains of several previous victims, and he wanted to get a feel for the level of activity in the park before settling on it as the resting place of the next. To his dismay, he learned a festival had attracted crowds. It was the first disappointment he'd encounter on this trip, though not the last. On the four-hour drive back to London in the night, he searched his memory for a resting place closer to London, where his Middle Eastern looks wouldn't be remarkable.

He slammed his hand onto the steering wheel. It was the ethnic population of Hull that had brought him there in the first place. Now it seemed he may need to find another city, if the park was no longer a suitable hiding place for his kills.

Back in London and after sleeping late on the following day, he used an incognito window on his laptop to search for another suitable hiding place. The fruitless trip to Hull had set him back on what he'd intended as a three-day turn-around. He couldn't take a victim today without having a plan for disposal. Scouting for a suitable area would take the rest of the day. Of concern in his endeavor would be spotting the CCTV cameras ubiquitous in London, both for the snatch and for the disposal. His earlier expeditions had mapped many of them in his preferred hunting grounds, but there was always the possibility that others had been added. On the other hand, the constant need for maintenance usually meant that those in the poorest slums might easily be out of order, even though there was where the most crime took place.

Ahab considered acquiring a uniform in the style of the maintenance crews and making sure several in his intended area were on the fritz, but decided it would take too long. He'd simply rely on speed and disinterest, like he usually did. The lack of planning for the kidnapping cut both ways. Though he couldn't control every aspect of it, the random aspect was one of the best precautions he could have taken. There'd be no trail of surveillance to be caught on camera. He wasn't in the social sphere of the victim. And of course, he'd be using a stolen car for the snatch, and another for the disposal.

Since he couldn't use the Hull location for disposal, he went back to another idea he'd used in the past. It tickled his fancy to choose archaeological sites for the bodies. If he chose a charnel house or ossuary, the bones wouldn't be remarkable once the body had decomposed sufficiently. Some of the sites had been long abandoned, and discovery wasn't likely before the flesh had melted away.

This time, he chose a different site, though. It amused him to select the Roman Fort, a remnant of the Londinium archaeological site. Though the approach would be tricky, the requisite marshes nearby would be a good place. The smell wouldn't be enough to remark on before he was well out of the country. With his plans set, he went hunting that very night after all.

A week after Ahab had secreted the body in the marshes near the old, round, stone structure, a teenaged visitor from

America remarked on the odor while on a tour of the site. Adults on the tour seemed embarrassed, but one agreed, the stench was remarkably bad. More so than usual. Museum employees were dispatched to search for the source and traced it to near the remains of the fort gate.

Expecting the corpse of a large feral animal, perhaps a badger or otter, the employees were horrified to see a flash of color like no animal had ever displayed. They immediately called the local constabulary. Hours later, police dredged the decomposing remains of a child from among the reeds, and the city's media went ballistic. How could a child so young have gone missing, and no one knew in this internet-connected era? Who was this child? Why weren't there parents demanding to know the child's identity?

Reporters descended on police headquarters, and eventually discovered that an eight-year-old girl had been reported missing from a South London homeless shelter. The investigation stalled when no one came forward with information, and the CCTV camera closest to the shelter had been discovered to be inoperative. A minor bombing in the center of London had been the biggest story that week. The loss of a homeless child hadn't even blipped the radar.

As outrage grew, the police revealed dozens of unsolved disappearances and fielded questions about serial killers. In one interview, a spokesperson admitted that it could be possible, but the police didn't have the resources to investigate every crime where there was no evidence to be found. That was when the Mayor of London demanded MI5 get involved.

MI5, the equivalent of America's FBI, had plenty to do already. The sudden dumping of several dozen unsolved disappearances of children over the past ten years wasn't their priority. Nevertheless, they couldn't create the impression that they were not doing anything about it, and a team of data analysts was assigned to work on it immediately to forestall the more outspoken members of the press claiming that the poor were of no importance to police. The team quickly established a database of every bit of information the police did have.

Less than a week after the body of Ahab's latest victim was found, patterns he hadn't anticipated emerged in the data. Fortunately for Ahab, he hadn't been the first to stash a body in the waters surrounding the Roman Fort. MI5 had caused the site to be dredged, and two more turned up. After that, the press began to call the crimes the Archaeology Murders. Though the two older bodies weren't related, the fact they were adult bodies widened the data net, and soon a full investigation was gaining traction.

The last thing MI5 wanted was a panic over a serial killer or more scrutiny of their operations. Someone suggested that these bodies could be the work of one of those chaps – the Nabateans – who'd been in the news the previous year. One of the investigators had back-door knowledge of the Nabatean case through an old friend in MI6 and had seen the faint trace of something familiar on the clavicles of two of the Roman Fort victims.

The 'something' was a crow's feet symbol like the one on the leader's documents, which had been seized when authorities raided her Paris townhouse. Her decrees had been made electronically, of course, but Graziella Nabati, head of the Council that had come very near to taking over world financial institutions, had exhibited a bit of narcissism by also printing them, in calligraphy on vellum, and then sealing them with wax and a signet ring before filing them in her secret archives. The marks on the victims looked the same to him. The suggestion was enough to get the head of MI5 to request the help of MI6.

MI6, the American equivalent of the CIA, was not pleased. They were in the spy business, not murder, and almost never operated on home soil. But the fact that the idea that the Nabateans could be involved, preposterous as it might have been, came from a senior official at MI5, MI6 had no choice – they had to comply. It wasn't every day they got to meddle in domestic affairs. Perhaps it was an opening they should see as an advantage, their Chief told them.

By then, however, several weeks had passed. Ahab was back at his careful grid search off the coast of Crete and paid no attention to the news from London.

Chapter Nine

In London, a task force was formed to survey every archeological site and urban body of water in southeastern England. The agencies involved got much more than they bargained for. Over a hundred bodies in various stages of decomposition turned up, over twenty in archeological sites. Despite police assurances that it couldn't possibly be the work of one killer, England's notorious gossip rags whipped up the citizenry into a frenzy of demands for answers.

It didn't take long for news articles to appear listing Britain's worst serial killers, mentioning names such as Harold Shipman. Although convicted of fifteen murders, official reports later stated he had killed between 215 and 260 people between 1975 and 1998. Dennis Nilsen, former Army cook, and Civil servant apparently killed up to 15 people, Peter Sutcliffe who became known as the "Yorkshire Ripper" murdered at least 13 women, mainly prostitutes, over a period of five years. And of course, such a list would not be complete if it didn't mention Jack the Ripper. The most famous serial killer of all, 'Jack', who was never identified and brought to justice, terrorized the people of London between 1888 and 1891 and killed at least 11.

The work eventually settled into a painstaking analysis of the data to understand whether *any* of the bodies were the work of a serial killer, but focus on the bodies in the archaeological sites made analysts lean toward these being just that. MI6 wanted an archaeologist involved but stipulated it couldn't be anyone from the UK. All of those, they insisted, were suspects.

MI5 agreed. They put their heads together and decided on who they wanted, then called upon the Prime Minister to call in a favor. The PM would rather have dealt with ex-President Samuel Houston Grant, but Grant had finished his statutory two terms, and a new President was in the saddle, as Grant would have said. After a few pleasantries, he got down to business.

"I assume you were fully briefed on the recent threat our countries and indeed the world faced. I'm talking about what happened early last year, the Nabatean affair," he prompted.

"I'm aware of it, yes. What about it?"

"We have a situation here that may or may not be related, and I have had a request from our investigating agencies to borrow one of your top people. A man by the name of Carter Devereux. Do you know him?"

"Yes, of course. He discovered…"

"Yes, yes, the Library of the Giants and all that. This is something a bit different."

"Go on."

"Well, it seems we need an archaeologist, and none of ours will do. It's a bother, frankly. But if he isn't otherwise engaged, my people are asking for him specifically."

"Do you know why him?"

"That I don't. Need-to-know, of course. D'you want me to find out?"

"I don't think that will be necessary. I'll have him sent to you right away. Is there anything else America can do for you, Mr. Prime Minister?"

The PM indulged in a little internal pique at the suggestion that the President was the entirety of America, but he answered mildly. "Not at this time, Mr. President, thank you."

"It's done," he reported to his security advisors. "He said he'd have Devereux 'sent to us' right away. As if he were a package, mind you."

The others laughed with him.

Less than an hour later, Carter fielded a call from Irene O'Connell. He thought she was kidding when she told him what she wanted.

"I'm not a detective," he said.

"Doesn't matter. You've been specially requested by MI6. They said it could have something to do with the Nabateans, so you have to go."

"I thought we'd put those guys to rest once and for all," Carter grumbled.

"Apparently not. Get there."

Though he protested that murder investigations weren't in his background, Irene informed him they were now. Favors had been called in, and that's all she would say.

Carter knew it would be fruitless to argue any further. Instead, he called Mackenzie. "Mackie, they want me in London. Do you want to come?"

"I'd love to, darling, but I can't right now. Liu has

turned up something really exciting, and we're retooling. How long will you be there?"

"Until we solve it? I don't know, really. No one seems to know why me. The visit would be educational for the kids, though. Please consider it. And what do you mean by retooling?"

"I'll leave that for another time. You have a plane to catch, don't you? I think I can get the boss to give me a week off once we've dealt with this retooling issue," she wisecracked.

"Ask her pretty please and tell her I'll have a special thank you in mind if she does."

"Carter, behave." Her voice betrayed the smile on her face, though. He could hear it through the phone all the way from the Mediterranean.

"My plane's being called," he joked. Carter's plane was his own Dassault Falcon 7X, and he was the pilot as she knew very well. But she'd started the banter.

Flying the big jet with no passengers was an indulgence, but he could afford it, and it was much more convenient than commercial, which was why he'd bought it. "I'll call again when I'm settled in the hotel. I'll get a suite."

"Carter…"

"Got to go! Bye."

He considered he'd won a small victory by cutting off her protest that she might not make it to London. The more he thought about it, the more he wanted to share some of the sights of the city with the kids. Liam especially would enjoy them. Beth might be too young, but she was in a dinosaur-loving phase, and she'd be sure to enjoy the Crystal Palace, if nothing else.

A representative from MI6 met him at Heathrow and insisted on driving him to a hotel where they'd arranged for him to stay. One look at the old structure told him he'd be changing hotels when Mackie arrived, but for now he graciously accepted the accommodations.

"I probably don't have the appropriate wardrobe with me," he explained to his escort. "Can you direct me to somewhere I can rectify that?"

"Not to worry. You have a briefing in twenty minutes, and afterward I'll be pleased to go shopping with you."

"But…"

"We all understand you've been in the field, so to speak," the man interrupted. "Your, ah, attire will be perfectly acceptable under the circumstances."

Carter looked down at his Levi's, T-shirt, and Sperry's Topsiders and sighed. He was pretty sure they were not acceptable at a high-level meeting, but he had nothing else to change into. He hadn't expected to be called to London when he'd packed for the Alboran site. *Twenty minutes. They must be desperate.*

———————

Half an hour later, Carter learned that the investigation had so far stalled out as to suspects. The remains of the three victims from the London Fort had been dated many years apart. As the briefing progressed, he realized he was further out of his element than he'd even known. But at least he now knew why him. One of the skeletons did indeed display a symbol associated with the Nabateans, and he was the world's foremost expert on the criminals who'd been among the last survivors of the ancient group.

As the lead investigator explained, they either had an unusually experienced killer or more than one. The careless disposal of the latest victim, thought to be only a week dead when they'd found her, indicated the latter. However, an active killer or killers of this level of brutality was someone they wanted caught immediately, before another victim met with the same grisly fate. The fact the killer had been able to both snatch the victim and dispose of the body while leaving no clues indicated he was experienced. Investigators hadn't determined whether other victims left in archaeological sites were his work or not.

The briefing went on while Carter mused on the task ahead of him. Wounds on the body were ante mortem, the medical examiner had found. The victim must have undergone unimaginable pain. *The girl was only Liam's age*, Carter thought. His outrage at the crime threatened to undermine his usefulness. The only positive finding was that she had not been sexually assaulted. It was little comfort, however. Carter's fists alternately curled and uncurled, and he became aware of his strong desire to throttle the responsible party barehanded. Such a monster could not be called a man. Carter couldn't bring himself to believe a woman would be capable of it.

"What about other sites?" he asked. "I understand the archaeological aspect is why I was requested to assist. I still don't know how I can help, though. Have there been other bodies discovered?"

"We haven't completed the search," the lead investigator replied. "But yes, we've discovered unauthorized disturbances at Lesnes Abbey, the Greenwich Saxon Cemetery, and in several spots along the Parkland Walk."

"I'm not familiar with the latter," Carter confessed.

"I suppose it would be too modern for your interest. It was once the route of part of one of the London and North Eastern Railway's lines. Built in 1867 and finally closed for good in the 1970s. Very overgrown in places. Good hiding place for a body, frankly."

"I see. And I assume you've determined all these bodies are the work of one killer?"

"Not at all. However, there's loads of investigation to do. Identifying them comes first, of course. Then cross-checking everything."

"And what did you envision I'd be able to help with?" Carter said again. He couldn't see any role for himself in the investigation. He waited to hear their ideas.

"Some of the remains are skeletal. We'd hoped you could tell us what's recent and what isn't. At least, for those that have been found in archaeological sites. And we don't know, but we hope it's possible something in the way the bodies have been concealed will help link them."

Two questions clashed for attention in Carter's mind. "Wait – you've found some that aren't in archaeological sites?"

"We've got unidentified remains from several cases, yes, and some appear to be related by the amount of damage to the bodies."

"I see. And regarding those found at archaeological sites – aren't you doing carbon dating?"

"Yes, but that takes time. We were hoping you could tell us visually."

Carter thought for a moment. "I may be able to. But not with the accuracy of carbon dating. However, any help I can give, I'm happy to. This bas… this killer must be stopped."

"Agreed sir. This bastard must be stopped. And preferably given his own treatment, though I suppose due process must be given precedence. I'll have to refer any other questions to the investigator who raised the possibility of the

Nabatean involvement. I'm sure that's why he requested you specifically. I'll have an answer for you tomorrow."

Carter grinned ferociously. These were his kind of people after all, despite his impression of their proper and formal Britishness, as he called their demeanor in his mind.

True to his word, Carter's escort chauffeured him to Oxford street, and then guided him to Marks and Spencer, where he purchased several pairs of casual long pants and shirts suitable for outdoor activities, and one good suit, a couple of ties, and some dress shirts. He'd have to buy an extra suitcase to get home, he supposed, but at least he wouldn't appear in another meeting wearing a T-shirt, jeans, and boat shoes.

With that thought came a grim smile. What difference did his apparel make, when a killer who was willing to brutalize children walked the streets of London?

Chapter Ten

Liu's discovery in the Library of the Giants was momentous. The Sirralnnudam had it wrong or had left something out. Mackenzie kindly refused to think that Liu could have mistranslated it. The bottom line was that it wasn't the respirocytes themselves that were created with the diamondoid material, but instead composed the nanobots that manufactured the super-cells.

Liu had burst into Mackenzie's office on the morning of her discovery, looking as if she'd been up all night. As Mackenzie learned moments later, she had been. But even though she looked like a bad night's sleep, she was wide awake and, as Dylan described it, bouncing off the walls.

"Has she been like this all morning?" Mackenzie asked him.

"Off and on. She woke me up about three hours ago shouting about some Greek dude who discovered something while taking a bath and was so excited he jumped out of the bath and ran naked through his house shouting Eureka! Eureka!"

Mackenzie couldn't help but giggle at Dylan's description of Archimedes' momentous discovery that the volume of water displaced in the bathtub was equal to the volume of the part of his body he had submerged.

Dylan was unfazed by Mackenzie's snickering and continued. "She calmed down long enough to make my breakfast, but I've had a hard time holding her back from running straight to your house. I'm just grateful she wasn't in the bath when she made this discovery, otherwise she would have been naked now."

By now, tears of laughter were running down Mackenzie's face.

Liu kept trying to interrupt. "Mackenzie... Listen... Hey!" Dylan had his hand around her upper arm, preventing her from jumping up and down. When he stopped talking, she took her chance. "Mackenzie, you're doing it wrong!"

Mackenzie managed to stop laughing and made her sit down and draw a deep breath. "Now, slowly... what do you mean 'I'm doing it wrong'?

Liu took another breath. Mackenzie held hers. Dylan let go of her arm and stopped talking.

"I found the plans for the respirocyte generator in the Library of the Giants," Liu said.

"What?!" Mackenzie shouted. "You're kidding! You're not kidding... Liu, if you're kidding, I'm going to kill you."

Liu jumped up and hugged Mackenzie, then both women started jumping up and down, laughing, and screaming. Dylan stood there with a stunned expression.

"Have you two gone nuts?" he asked.

The office door burst open, and Mackenzie's assistant ran into the room to see what the commotion was about. Not far behind her, the others ran in, all talking at once.

Dylan brought the chaos to an end with a voice that sounded like the crack of a whip. "Everyone shut *up!*"

Silence descended like a conductor had signaled the orchestra to stop playing. Dylan, still using his command voice, said, "Let's go to the conference room and sort this out. Move out!"

Once in the conference room, Mackenzie had recovered her composure. "Please sit down, everyone. Liu has an important announcement, and then we'll discuss it."

Liu remained standing as the others took their seats.

"Cut to the chase, Liu," Dylan ordered.

"Okay. Long story short, I've found plans for the respirocyte generator in the Library of the Giants. You're on the wrong track."

The room erupted in chaos again until Dylan yelled, "Hey!" Then, when the scientists had quieted, Mackenzie signaled Liu to go on.

"I'm not technical," she explained, "but I've been helping Mackenzie with her research for a long time. I know you've been working to create cells to hold and release larger quantities of oxygen. And I know you've been using adamantine as the building blocks."

The nano-engineer and the chemical engineer slowly nodded in agreement.

"The plans I've found use a different approach. They use the same material, but instead of forcing it into a fullerene shape, it's used as the raw material for a self-constructing nanobot, whose job it is to assemble super-sized hemoglobin molecules for a self-renewing source of respirocytes." Liu was out of breath when she stopped.

Mackenzie's wasn't the only jaw that dropped. It was such an elegant model. Using the body's own components to manufacture an unlimited supply of respirocytes, all of which could absorb and carry more oxygen to wherever it was needed in the body – such a simple concept. Why hadn't they thought of it before?

Mackenzie knew why. She had been led astray by Frietas' theory and the apparent confirmation in the Sirralnnudam translation.

"This will solve the toxicity problem," she said, almost to herself.

"It sure will! We only need to figure out how many of the nanobots to inject, and how long we can expect them to work," her assistant agreed.

Excited conversation broke out among the scientists, rising to the level of a crowded room before Mackenzie quieted them using her own version of Dylan's command voice.

"Liu, was there anything else?"

"Yes. And I have the translation with me if you want to read it for yourself. I've also emailed it to you."

"I haven't…"

"I know. I got here before you opened your email. Anyway, the nanobots are affixed in the lungs somehow. That's where they do their thing."

"Their 'thing' being manufacturing the respirocytes?"

"Yes."

"Once more, you've proven how invaluable you are to us, Liu. How can we ever repay you?"

Liu looked at Dylan, a question in her eyes. He shrugged. She blushed and turned to Mackenzie. "Well, seeing that we're dealing with Eureka moments… I'm going to need maternity leave…"

Another round of whooping and congratulations went up, and Mackenzie got up to hug Liu, then Dylan. "We'll make it happen. That's awesome, Liu! And Dylan, of course." She smiled. Just days ago, she'd been speculating about this, and she was so happy it was happening already. "The kids are going to be thrilled. But Carter's going to be unhappy he wasn't here to hear the news out of your mouth."

Dylan spoke, a note of grimness in his voice. "By the time he gets back, she'll be showing. It was time to break the news. You can tell him if you want, Mackenzie."

"No, that's your news. You'll just have to tell him on video call. I know he'll be happy for you."

They stood awkwardly for a moment, and then Mackenzie said, "Liu, you'd better go and get some sleep. All-nighters aren't good for babies. We have some planning and discussing to do here. Could I get that copy of the translation?"

"Of course." Liu handed over the flash drive and leaned against Dylan. "You know, I *am* tired. Let's go home, Dylan."

As soon as they'd left, Mackenzie opened the discussion. "Okay, what do we need to do now?"

"I need a way to flush the foreign bodies from my rats," said the vet.

"I need to figure out how to keep the nanobots in the lungs where they belong," said the clinician.

"I think we all know what the three of us need to do," said the nano-engineer, sweeping his hand around to include his chemical and mechanical colleagues.

"And I need to devise a new database and a program to automate the data collection," said the data specialist.

"Then let's get to work."

It had been eight a.m. on the dot when Liu flew through the door. It seemed both a long time ago and only a few minutes since then, but Mackenzie noted it had been not quite an hour. Her administrative assistant was due in any minute. She'd have her print out copies of Liu's translation for everyone, and then she'd get on a voice call with her husband, if he was available. Even if she couldn't share Dylan and Liu's personal news, she could tell him about the breakthrough.

Chapter Eleven

The day Ahab found the correct karst spring was almost an anticlimax in a way. He'd previously located several that were large enough to enter, but none had led far before petering out in cracks too small to navigate. He had to believe that the geology hadn't changed enough to cut off his entry to the underground cave system he believed was the site of the ancient Labyrinth. But when he found the right one, he knew it immediately.

Ahab had learned through rumbles in the worldwide archaeology community that Carter Devereux had made other discoveries as important as the now-famous libraries of the ancients. There were rumors about the discovery of the super-intelligence of dolphins and, although hard to believe, that Devereux had found a way to talk to them. He'd been skeptical at first, but then he'd reconsidered. If he was willing to believe in a half-man, half-bull, mythical beast, then surely talking dolphins weren't much of a leap.

The remaining vestiges of his skepticism died the moment he saw a dolphin swimming back and forth in front of a large opening upstream of the karst spring he'd followed from the surface. It almost appeared as though the animal was a sentry.

Ahab considered what he knew of dolphins. They'd long been known to be intelligent, that much he knew – it was just the notion they had a society and a language that he'd found hard to believe. They also appeared to be friendly to humans. He had read and heard the stories about them saving and helping humans. Ahab's psychological makeup however, didn't understand altruistic behavior, so he found it hard to swallow that such a notion may be attributed to animals.

In any case, he didn't think they were dangerous. His first attempt to enter the underwater opening made him rethink that conclusion, though. The dolphin met him before he'd swum within yards of the opening and rebuffed all his attempts to get around it. Based on the rumor that Devereux and his wife had found a way to converse with them, he tried signing to it.

He pointed to the opening and then to himself, and pushed the water in front of him sideways, indicating the dolphin should move aside. The dolphin chittered back at him, and when he failed to respond, wagged its entire body from side to side, as if it was shaking its head to say, "No"!

Fascinating, but I must be wrong, he thought. It couldn't have understood me. Nor would it have used a human gesture to communicate, surely.

He tried it a different way to test his theory. He pulled a dive knife from its holster on his hip and brandished it.

This time, the dolphin didn't bother with utterances. It simply wagged 'no' again, and refused to let him pass, but stayed well out of the reach of his knife. There was no mistaking it now. The dolphin was actually guarding that opening. Perhaps it was a female with young. Information about dolphin behavior, aside from rescuing distressed swimmers, was missing from Ahab's body of knowledge, but it appeared he wasn't going to get to explore that opening today.

He resolved to retreat, look up dolphin behavior, and come back. With a spear-gun if necessary. No animal was going to thwart his purpose. Not if he had anything to say about it.

The next day, armed with everything he could gather from the internet on dolphins, he returned. He left his stun-gun on board the yacht for his first attempt. Instead, he took a bucket of fish to lure the dolphin away, if it was still there. He'd learned there were sharks near Crete, though he'd seen none in his extensive explorations. According to something he'd seen after Googling the question, there were forty-seven different species of shark that called the Mediterranean home, at least fifteen of which could be dangerous to humans. So, he didn't particularly want to kill the dolphin if he could help it. Blood in the water could attract even the shyest of sharks, but since sharks prey on dolphins, he especially didn't want dolphin blood in the water.

His scientific curiosity had turned up several facts that weren't germane to his problem, one of which was the method to determine if the dolphin was male or female. He couldn't find anything online about communication with the beasts, but he didn't intend to reason with this one. If he couldn't lure it away, he'd try stunning it somehow.

Ahab had little hope of engaging in combat with a dolphin and winning, even with his uncommon strength. He estimated the dolphin was at least ten feet long, and according to the National Geographic website weighed perhaps as much as 1100 pounds. His memory of its appearance was that it was amused at his efforts, but he learned that was because its mouth, like all bottlenose dolphins, curved up at the ends naturally, so it seemed to be smiling. But now he knew better and would not be fooled by its friendly face.

His main advantage would be the fact he could hold his breath longer. Thanks to the respirocytes in his body, he could outlast the dolphin underwater as it would be forced to surface every ten to fifteen minutes. Perhaps he could dart past it when it did that. The most frustrating thing about that was if he'd known it yesterday, he would already know whether this was the cave system he was looking for or not.

His guess was that there was a good reason the dolphin was standing sentry, for he could think of no other description for its behavior. There had to be something inside that the dolphin didn't want him to discover. If it wasn't guarding its young, then did he dare believe that it knew of the beasts that had once lived in the caves? Was it protecting him from perceived danger?

Ahab prepared for his dive by hanging the bucket of fish over the side of the yacht, where he could reach it once he was in the water. Then he climbed over the side and dropped easily into the water. This time, he'd donned a face mask, so he could try to talk to the dolphin, and swim fins to enhance his natural speed in the water. To be sure he could get past the dolphin once he'd lured it from its post, he'd also rented a Scubajet – a propulsion device that looked like a miniature torpedo, capable of operating underwater for up to six hours of battery life. It wouldn't outrun the dolphin if it decided to race him to the entrance, but it would give him a chance at gaining the inside while the dolphin was distracted.

It wasn't in his nature to notice the breathtaking blue of the water, the magic of the sun sparkling off the ripples made by a slight breeze, or the blue sky above dotted with fluffy white clouds. He did notice the brisk temperature of the water, about seventy-two degrees Fahrenheit. But his body soon became accustomed to it as usual, and he started swimming on the surface after securing the bucket over one of the hand throttles on the Sea-Bob.

At first, he didn't see the dolphin where it had stopped him the day before. Rather than drop the bucket, he decided to swim with it to the opening, and drag it inside with him in case he needed it on the way back to the yacht. But before he was halfway to the entrance from where he'd anchored the yacht, a swiftly-moving shape startled him, and he flinched back just in time to avoid being hit by the dolphin.

"Hey!" The sound of his protest seemed to catch the dolphin's attention, and it came back for a more leisurely pass at him. He forced a smile and asked, "Want some fish?"

The dolphin 'stood' on its tail, revealing the two mammary slits that proclaimed her a female, and 'nodded' her assent to the treat, while emitting some whistles and squeaks. Ahab swam to the side, dangling the bucket enticingly. The dolphin followed. She took a quick trip to the surface for a breath, and Ahab noticed she seemed to trust him more today than yesterday. Within seconds, she was back, and he was confident she'd follow him far to the side, where he'd leave the bucket and hope he could beat her to the underwater opening that was his target.

He swam swiftly, traveling parallel to the shelf of the

land that dropped off perhaps a hundred yards to his left as he led the dolphin away from the opening. When he'd gone an estimated mile, he dropped the bucket and watched as the dolphin tracked its descent, then returned to the surface for another breath.

He'd learned that dolphins swim at about seven or eight miles an hour. That would give him maybe six minutes to travel the mile back to the opening, unless his ruse didn't work. While the dolphin was on the surface, Ahab turned and swam at his top speed, surpassing the sprinting speed of the world record holder. He reckoned he couldn't outrace the dolphin, but he might beat her back to the opening if the fish distracted her for even a few minutes.

Unfortunately for him, Ahab had not read far enough. The dolphin was waiting for him when he reached the area near the opening. If he'd investigated further, he'd have discovered that when they're in a hurry for some reason, dolphins could swim up to four times faster than their usual speed. Ahab stopped in surprise to see her there. Then he wondered if it was the same dolphin at all. But, as if she'd read his mind, she wagged back and forth in yesterday's 'no' gesture. Ahab almost forgot himself and gasped at the implication.

Frustrated, he returned to the surface for his stun gun. Patented as a device to protect oneself from sharks, the stun gun was good for one shot before being serviced, because the tip of the electrical conducting spear had to be insulated from the water until used. It was bulky and unwieldy, but it should stun the dolphin long enough for him to pass.

He returned to confront her.

As soon as she saw him, though, the dolphin took the initiative away from him. Before he could aim the device, she charged him and hit him hard enough to make him drop it. Then she wagged 'no' again and swam in a circle to face him. Ahab was beginning to hate this dolphin. If it hadn't been for the possibility of attracting sharks, he would have used his dive knife to give her the same treatment he liked to give his human victims, only much faster. A few swipes of his knife would flay her. But he couldn't risk it.

He left the area without achieving his mission again that day, but as he motored away in the yacht, he vowed that the next day would be different.

Chapter Twelve

Carmen watched the land-human swim away and climb into his boat. Yesterday, he hadn't seemed dangerous. Today, when he offered her fish, he hadn't seemed dangerous. But when she returned for the fish, he was gone, and she raced back to her post, afraid she'd made a mistake by leaving her guard post.

The land-human had gone away when she told him no, but he came back with something bad. Carmen had never seen one of those things, but when he pointed it at her, she knew she must attack first. It went against her nature to attack any human, so she didn't hit him as hard as she could have. She didn't want to kill him.

Hitting him in the side made him drop the bad thing, and if he swam for it, she would stop him again. She didn't understand why he could stay below the water's surface longer than she could. He didn't have the round things her mother called tanks on his back. She knew that's what land-humans used to stay underwater a long time.

She was so busy trying to do her job and keep him away

from the bad place that she didn't think to contact Mother with these events, until the boat moved away from her post. Then she sent the images stored in her memory.

Mother, what is this? Seven hundred miles away, leading the pod to the Alboran site to visit with Carter, Merrybeth stopped suddenly as the image of an object that looked like the weapons land-humans used long ago to hunt whales entered her mind, along with her daughter's question. It was long and straight, and one end had a sharp point. Dolphins had no need of tools, but they'd had centuries of observation of the land-humans to know about them, to know about weapons, and to know that what the land-humans called weapons were just specialized tools with which to kill.

It looks like a weapon. Where did you see it? Merrybeth's alarm came across the miles.

A land-human pointed it at me, she answered. *But I hit him, and he dropped it. Then he went away.* She was proud of herself for recognizing the danger. But Mother was even more alarmed.

We're coming, child, she signaled. *Be very careful if he returns.*

He was here twice already. I will be careful.

Merrybeth thought quickly. At their top speed, she and those with her would take nearly an entire sun and dark to reach the area.

She heard no more from her daughter after that, and she urged the pod to swim faster, even though it hurt. Soon only she and her best friends, those whose young played with hers, and who she confided in and trusted to support her when her leadership was challenged, were swimming together. One friend had stayed back to lead the stragglers, while she and three other females sliced through the water. She sent an urgent message to two of her sons to meet her.

Merrybeth's heart turned over when they reached the entrance to the cave. Never since the beginning of their watch had the mouth of the cave been left unguarded. She felt it was her fault. She'd wanted to begin to groom her daughter for leadership. Maybe Carmen had been too young.

She kept on sending messages to Carmen, but there was no reply. The other dolphins in her pod fine-combed the area for miles around, while all of them kept on sending ansible messages to Carmen.

Hours later Merrybeth was mourning her daughter and worried about the secret they guarded. She knew there was only one way to get help now.

Sunhead.

Sunhead would help, she knew. But her pod was exhausted – at least the ones who'd kept up with her were. And the others would be confused and maybe angry if she reversed their direction again.

There was only one choice. Leaving her trusted friends to guard the site and watch for her daughter, she turned again and started for the Alboran dig. There she could talk to land-humans and let Sunhead know she needed help.

Chapter Thirteen

The veterinarian was nervous, she could tell. He was really too tender-hearted for this work, but Mackenzie liked him. So did Keeva, who had approved this new friend by letting him meet her pups. The Tala crew liked him, too. He regularly gave the wolves under training at Tala checkups.

The implantation surgery of the new respirocyte generators for the rats was about to begin when Mackenzie's administrative assistant came into the observation room to tell her there was an urgent message from the Alboran dig site.

Carter? she thought, a surge of adrenaline spiking. Then she recalled he wasn't at the site. He was still in London. *What could it be? That's not my bailiwick.*

There was no choice but to follow her assistant back to her office and take the call. She slipped away without letting the vet know. He was nervous enough without knowing he was working alone.

A moment later, she sat down in front of the computer,

where the anxious face of the dig supervisor awaited her. "Hi. What can I do for you?" she asked.

"It's that dolphin, Mrs. Devereux," he said, his English accented. He was a local, recruited from Spain to oversee the work when Carter wasn't present. Mackenzie didn't bother to correct him about her title.

"Which dolphin, Sandro?"

"You call her Merrybeth, I think. She is here, and very upset. The translator can't keep up with her. Do you think you can calm her?"

"All I can do is try. How will this work?"

"We have a link to the monitor at the pier," he said. "I'll patch you through."

No more than a couple of seconds later, Mackenzie's monitor showed the beautiful Mediterranean in the background, a sliver of the pier in the foreground, and Merrybeth, standing out of the water on her tail and whistling constantly. Even through the camera, Mackenzie could tell she was indeed agitated.

"Merrybeth," she said clearly. "It's Makenzie. Sunhead. I'm here."

Merrybeth stopped whistling and swam toward the pier. Mackenzie could tell the moment she spotted the monitor, which she assumed showed Merrybeth her own visage.

"What is it, my friend?" Like an echo, she heard the translation device whistle and squeak. The dolphin looked directly into the monitor.

"My daughter," she whistled, using Carmen's signature to specify which offspring. "She is missing, and we need your help."

"Tell me more," Mackenzie urged. Her heart hurt for her friend, but she didn't have enough information to help, yet. "How long has it been since you saw her? Where was she then?"

Merrybeth dipped below the water for a moment, and then was back. "Three suns ago, she showed me a bad man with a weapon. She said he pointed it at her. When we got to the place where she was, she was gone."

"Oh, no, Merrybeth. I understand. I'll see what I can do. Where was she?"

Merrybeth dipped again. Mackenzie thought it was strange. She'd never done that before when they were conversing. Maybe it was because she was upset. She waited, a bit longer this time, before the dolphin surfaced.

"I'm sorry, Mackenzie. I needed to find out if anyone knew what you call the place. I don't know how to tell you where it is, but I can lead someone there. It will take almost two suns to get there."

Two days! "Merrybeth, is it toward where the sun rises, or where it sets?"

"Toward where it rises."

Mackenzie did a swift calculation. Assuming the dolphin was swimming at top speed, it could be anywhere from nine-hundred to fifteen-hundred miles to the east of the Alboran. She pulled up a map on her second monitor. Somewhere between Sicily and Crete.

"Merrybeth, do you know the place where the sea is the narrowest in that direction?" It was frustrating, not being able to tell the dolphin the name of the place.

"Yes."

"Start toward there. I will ask the people where you are to follow you in a boat, and to stay in touch with me. I'll send a message when I find some help for you."

"Thank you, Sunhead."

Merrybeth waited until the land-humans got into the boat and brought it near her. She couldn't swim as fast on the surface, but they had a solution. She allowed them to fit her with a waterproof GPS tracker, and as soon as it was in place, she started back toward the bad place.

Sunhead would help, but Merrybeth was worried. She hadn't told Sunhead everything. Would they still be friends after Sunhead and her mate knew the truth?

The whole time she swam eastward, she thought about the secret her kind had carried for so many suns they had lost count. Could she trust any land-human, even Sunhead, to guard it? She thought she could trust Sunhead, but what about the others. Merrybeth knew Sunhead was many suns away, and would not be able to help in person. Besides, she could not go inside the bad place. It was too far, and her 'tanks' would not give her enough air. Not even dolphins could go inside.

That's what terrified her about her daughter. Had the bad man taken her there? Was she dead?

Sadness overwhelmed Merrybeth, and she surfaced early to whistle her grief. The land-humans in the boat shouted in response. They didn't have the translation device with them, so they didn't know her sound meant sad.

They called back to her, "We're here."

She had to take whatever comfort she could that they were following her. How strange, after so many suns, when her kind rescued land-humans whenever they could, while bad land-humans caught her kind in nets sometimes, that it was land-humans who now must help her. She only hoped they could.

At Freydis, Mackenzie paced. Her call to Carter had

gone unanswered. That was unusual. He usually at least answered long enough to tell her he was busy. More often, he could take a break to talk with her for a few minutes. Now she had two things to worry about.

Rationally, she knew if Carter were in trouble, she'd have heard before now. Most likely he was just involved in something important, or maybe even out of signal range. She considered calling the satphone instead, but told herself it could wait. It would take Merrybeth two days to get to the spot where her daughter had disappeared. There was plenty of time to send someone to help if Carter couldn't go himself.

More likely, she thought sadly, time for the young one had already run out. If a man had pointed a 'weapon' at her, something bad must have already happened, especially since it had taken Merrybeth two days to get word to her.

Helpless to do anything more for the crisis, she decided that they must make a push to have translation devices placed within a few hours of any spot on earth. She'd have to calculate how many that would be – thousands, no doubt. The more she thought about it, the more excited she became. It would serve so many great uses!

With that thought, she remembered the surgery going on in the veterinary lab, and went to check on the progress.

Chapter Fourteen

Two days later, Mackenzie still hadn't heard from Carter and she was beginning to seriously worry. She'd called Irene and asked for information, only to be told that Carter was fine, just busy. But not hearing from him in forty-eight hours was uncharacteristic.

Moreover, she'd had word from the security people from the Alboran site that they'd reached a spot just a few miles off Crete, and Merrybeth was swimming in circles. They assumed this was where she wanted to lead them. What now?

Mackenzie felt helpless. They hadn't taken the translation device, because it was needed at the dig. Without it, she could talk to Merrybeth, but Merrybeth couldn't talk to her. It was infuriating, frustrating, and it was causing her quite a bit of anxiety.

Then, Carter called, and her world settled back into its normal rotation around the sun. "Carter! Where have you been? I've been worried sick!"

"I'm sorry, Mackie. We found evidence that at least

some of these murders had to have been the work of an archaeologist. I've been underground for the past couple of days, doing what I could to identify the bastard from the way he worked. Seems strange that a guy who's willing to cut up people like nothing more than a chicken or something would then use proper site technique when he hides the bodies, but there you are."

Mackenzie was barely listening. "Honey, we have to help Merrybeth. Her daughter's gone missing."

"What? When?"

"Four days ago." She rapidly gave him what she knew, including her frustration that she couldn't talk to her friend. "I'm so afraid her daughter has been killed."

"Mackie, I'm sorry. Listen, I think I can get away, now. I'll fly to the site and pick up the translation device, then fly to Crete. But you know you're probably right, don't you? It's probably too late for – which daughter?"

"Carmen. She's the youngest, barely an adult, more like an eighteen-year-old in our terms. Merrybeth is devastated."

"I'll be in touch. Let me see if they can spare me for a couple of days."

Carter left as soon as he cleared it with the lead investigator. They wanted him back, but had nothing he could help with for now. He'd done what he could to narrow down the killer's work, but all he'd been able to tell them was that the work looked like the technique that a certain professor at the University College of London taught. Until they'd narrowed down the hundreds of students he'd taught, there wasn't much more Carter could do. In fact, he wasn't sure what more he could do even then.

As he'd promised, Carter flew to the Alboran site to borrow the translation device. Mackie had told him her idea to place the devices all over the world, and he liked the idea. They could have saved him hours and the environment a flight's worth of pollution if there'd been one on Crete.

He landed at the nearest airport to the location his security team had given, near Chania. Chartering a boat to take him to the exact location took an hour, but he was with the team just before sunset. He hailed Merrybeth, who rose to the surface immediately.

She started whistling as soon as she recognized him, and because he'd anticipated she would, the device was ready. But what she was saying came out garbled.

"Slow down, Merrybeth. You're going too fast for the device."

"Thank you for coming, Carter. I'm so happy you can understand me."

"You're welcome, Merrybeth. Is there any word on your daughter?"

"We can't understand him, but I think we've seen the man who threatened her. He tries to communicate, but we can't understand what he's saying."

"Is he speaking the same language I am?" Carter asked. He'd never thought to ask if the dolphins could understand other human – land-human – speech, or only English, and why English? He struggled to focus. It had been a long day.

"Yes, I think so. He's wearing something over his face, and the sounds don't sound the same underwater."

"Can you lead him to the surface? Maybe I can talk to him."

"I'll try."

Merrybeth disappeared, and night had fallen by the time she came back. "He would not follow me."

"I'm sorry, Merrybeth. What else did he do?"

"He swam back to his boat. Carter, he can stay underwater longer than we can."

"He's wearing scuba gear, right? The mask, and tanks?"

"Just the mask, no tanks. We didn't know land-humans could breathe water like fish." She used the word for food.

"We can't. Merrybeth, I need to go to shore and talk to Mackenzie. I'm sorry, but we can't do anything more until the sun comes up. Will you be okay?"

"I will be okay, Carter. I don't know if my daughter will."

"I understand. We'll be back as soon as it's light enough to see."

The next morning, when they found Merrybeth at the same coordinates, Carter was surprised to see something in her mouth. On closer inspection, it was a sealed plastic bag, with a piece of paper inside. She swam close to the boat and let him take it from her.

"The bad man was here," she said. "He gave me this. I think I'm supposed to give it to you."

Carter opened the bag and started to pull the note out. At the last second, he remembered some of the things he'd learned while working with MI5 and MI6. He pulled on a pair of neoprene gloves that went with his dive kit, and gingerly pulled the note out of the bag.

I saw you talking with this dolphin yesterday, it read. I have a dolphin who would not let me pass when I wanted to explore an underwater cave. She is safe for now, but I couldn't get into the cave. If this one will lead me to a place where I can get in, I'll release the other one.

"What the hell?" Carter said out loud. "This doesn't make any sense. A dolphin guarding a cave? He *kidnapped* her? Who the hell is this guy?" His question went unanswered, of course.

"Merrybeth, this says that the man has another dolphin. Is anyone else missing, or is he talking about your daughter?"

"No one else is missing, Carter. I'm sure he means my daughter. He will let her go?"

"He wants you to lead him to a place where he can enter some kind of underwater cave. He couldn't get in where your daughter wouldn't let him pass. What's that about?"

Instead of answering, she disappeared from the surface and didn't return. *What the… maybe she's gone to find him and lead him where he wants to go*, Carter thought.

While he waited for her return to tell him her daughter was safe, Carter decided to call Mackie and update her on the strange goings-on. She answered after only one ring.

"Carter! Oh, I'm so glad you called! I've been so worried!"

"Hi, babe. Listen, this is really strange. When I got out here this morning, Merrybeth brought me a note sealed in a plastic bag. Believe it or not, it was a ransom note! The guy saw me talking to her last night, though come to think of it, I didn't see him, so… Well, anyway, he wants Merrybeth to lead him to a place where he can get into an underwater cave. Seemed to think Carmen was guarding the entrance? Says he has her and will release her when Merrybeth does what he wants."

"So, is she going to do it? Why would Carmen be guarding a cave?"

"You got me there. I have no idea. And I guess she's doing it right now. As soon as I told her what the guy wanted, she disappeared under the water. Didn't say anything, just submerged. She hasn't come back."

"That's odd. She's usually very polite. She did something like that when I was talking to her at the site. Before she answered me a couple of times, she dipped under the water. I assumed she was hot and needed to cool off. The sun must be brutal on the water this time of year."

"Hmmm."

"You'll stay until she reports in? I want to know for sure that Carmen is safe."

"Yes, dear. I want to know what this whole thing is about. I'll stay until I can ask Merrybeth what's going on."

Chapter Fifteen

Carter didn't have long to wait. Merrybeth was back within fifteen minutes after he ended the call with Mackie.

"Carter, I must tell you something." She didn't wait for an answer before dipping underwater and then coming back up immediately.

Here it is, he thought.

"Go ahead, Merrybeth. What do you have to tell me?"

"We have knowledge we must not tell land-humans."

"A secret?"

"Secret. That is a good word. Yes, we have a secret. But I must tell you now, before my daughter is killed." She dipped under again.

Carter wondered if the dipping behavior indicated nervousness or something worse. Were dolphins capable of lying? He wasn't an animal behaviorist, but he knew primates, especially chimps, were. Before he'd read that, he would have said only humans could lie. *Land-humans, that is*, he thought wryly. He hadn't quite made the leap that Mackie had. He still thought of the dolphins as highly intelligent animals unless he made a conscious effort to include them as another race of *homo sapiens*.

Merrybeth returned. If Carter hadn't known better, he'd have thought she was acting as if she were ashamed.

"Forgive me, Carter. This is very hard for me. We have kept our...secret... for countless suns. There is something very bad in this cave. Very bad for land-humans. Many, many, many suns ago, one of our kind lost his best land-human friend to this bad-thing. We have guarded the cave since then, to keep land-humans safe."

Carter listened with growing disbelief. What could possibly be in there, and after so many years? He despaired of getting an accurate idea of how long she was talking about, or a reasonable description of *what* she was talking about. The dolphins' vocabulary, though rich in words for their undersea life, lacked variety for the world above.

They knew things like boat, and they were quick studies. You could show them an object, name it, and because of their ansible communication, dolphins around the world would suddenly have the word in their vocabularies. But if they couldn't see a thing from their watery homes, they didn't know what it was.

"Merrybeth, can you tell me what this bad thing is? Is it a weapon?" He was thinking of the ancient nuclear weapons the dolphins had helped him locate.

"No. It is a living thing."

"A man? A land-human?"

"It looks like a man, but the head is wrong. We do not know of land-humans who tear apart and eat other land-humans."

Merrybeth broke off and swam in a quick circle. "It is a land-shark!" she whistled, leaping from the water.

Carter's mind went to a clip he'd seen of a comedy TV

show, and the opening notes of an old movie. He swallowed the bubble of laughter the word evoked. Merrybeth's excitement wasn't about humor – the circumstances were too serious. She was happy to be able to describe what he could only imagine as a monster. But he seriously doubted it was a human with the head of a sh…

"Wait! This is Crete!" he shouted. He quickly drew an image of a human with the head of a bull on the whiteboard they had for this sort of communication issue with the dolphins. "Merrybeth, does it look like this?"

She swam closer and eyed the drawing, twisting from side to side like they did when shown a mirror. "Yes, something like that, Carter. More hair, and darker. Longer pointed things, and they curve."

Carter made the adjustments to the beast's horns and hair. "Like this?"

"Yes. Very much like that."

Carter turned the whiteboard, so he could examine what he'd drawn. It couldn't be true. That was just a myth!

"Merrybeth, how long has it been since your kind saw this thing?"

"Many, many, many, many, many…"

"Okay, I get the picture. So, maybe it died?"

"It did, or it didn't, Carter. But what about its offspring? We cannot let our land-human friends be eaten by these land-sharks."

"Uh, Merrybeth, I think what it's called is a Minotaur. And if what you say is true, then I need to tell my leaders about it. But what about Carmen? Will you lead the bad man to the cave? If the Minotaur eats him, then all your problems are solved."

"What if the bad man releases the Minotaur instead?"

Carter was grateful the translation device had made the

adjustment. He was sure Merrybeth had said land-shark again, and he wasn't certain he could hold it together if he kept hearing that. The music from that shark movie was still underlining his thoughts, too. His mind raced like an out-of-control railway engine. This was a matter for A-Echelon. But the moment they became involved, he'd be ordered to find any evidence that the story Merrybeth told was true. And her daughter's life would not take precedence over that order.

He owed Merrybeth an answer.

"Let us worry about that, Merrybeth. Lead him there so he'll release Carmen."

Merrybeth wagged her body in the dolphin equivalent of no. "I will deceive him, Carter, while you and Sunhead form a plan. We trust you."

Carter's heart sank. He'd be letting Mackenzie down as well as Merrybeth if he didn't figure out who this guy was and what he wanted with the Minotaur.

"Be careful, Merrybeth. We don't want to lose you or your daughter. I'll be back as soon as I can."

Merrybeth turned on her side, one flipper in the air. She must have learned that from some of the 'trained' dolphins. She was waving him goodbye.

He ordered the boat back to shore. For this, he'd need a secure line. And a private place to talk. Anyone who heard what he had to say would call the funny-farm squad on him, and he'd be locked up as delusional.

An hour later, he reached Irene O'Connell. "Irene, are you sitting down?"

"What is it, Carter? I'm busy. How's London, by the way?"

"I'm not in London. I'm on Crete. You're not going to believe this.

Chapter Sixteen

Ahab wasn't particularly pleased that Carter Devereux had shown up, but it did give him the opportunity to talk to the dolphin. He'd been worried she would give away his presence under Devereux's boat, but when he realized she was the mother, he understood. She was distracted. Maybe she didn't even see or hear him, hidden among some ancient submerged shoreline debris. This whole area must once have been above the water line.

The new information gave him an idea. He'd never thought of enjoying his peculiar entertainment with an animal. He needed to see the terror, the effects of pain, the progression from fear of death to its final acceptance. Hearing the conversation between Devereux and the dolphin, though, gave him a better understanding of the dolphin's intelligence. They, the mother and the daughter, would understand death. He was curious to learn if they feared it like humans feared it.

Land-humans, he thought. *What an odd way to refer to mankind. Or did she mean something else?* And how clever of the dolphin to describe the Minotaur as a land-shark. Ahab had no knowledge of American popular culture, and wouldn't have known so old a reference if he had.

Granted, Devereux's involvement meant that Ahab's target was now known. He'd have to get rid of Devereux somehow, before he revealed his own involvement. Devereux was smart – he'd put it together.

But before any of this could come to pass, he had to first find the Minotaur. And the dolphin's part of the conversation had given him renewed hope that he'd find one or more still living in the cave. The rising of the sea or subsidence of the land, or both, must have cut off entry, allowing the species to survive in the Labyrinth all this time. He wasn't sure how, or how many there could be by now, but he was more excited than ever to find out.

For the first time, he began to hope that he could have both his fantasies – the fame of the discovery that it hadn't all been a myth, that the Minotaur literally existed, as well as being able to secretly own and control one in some remote location.

He'd heard Merrybeth's intention to stall him, though. He couldn't allow that to happen. He didn't know who Devereux meant by his 'leaders', but he couldn't let anything interfere with his research. Now that he knew those squeaks and whistles were truly language, he'd turn up the heat a bit on the mother.

What he needed wasn't among his equipment. The dolphin female was stashed in a place where no one would find her, and he'd kept her sedated, so he could handle her. He'd be sure she was out for another few hours while he went to the mainland for underwater recording equipment, and then he'd let her wake up.

Not only would he have a way to ensure the mother's

prompt cooperation, but it would be the beginning of his death experiments on dolphins.

As he drove to Heraklion from his base at Chania, Ahab tried to think of what he could record the young dolphin enduring to force the mother to give up the secrets she and her ancestors had guarded. It wasn't as if the dolphins had many appendages to give up, like the fingers and toes he'd cut off one at a time if he were dealing with a human parent. And what was this business about 'land-humans'? What did that mean? Was he to believe that half-human, half-fish people, like mermaids, were real, too? That maybe a race of sea-humans existed? That the dolphins may be the go-betweens between people and creatures long thought to be mythical?

He rejected that notion as too ridiculous. The Minotaurs would be enough to cement his fame among archaeologists. If he then began looking for mermaids, he'd be laughed out of his college. He returned to the problem at hand. He could shock the young dolphin, of course. The stun gun could be set to various levels of current. He'd begin with that, just enough to make her plead for mercy at first.

If that wasn't enough, he could keep her underwater. How long could she go without surfacing for air? He'd have to experiment. It wouldn't do to accidentally kill her before the mother had led him to the Minotaurs' habitat.

Did the dolphins even know whether the Minotaurs were still alive?

The entertainment of thinking of ways to torture a dolphin made the two-hour trip seem short. Ahab found his way to a camera store and used cash to purchase underwater recording equipment, thinking to disguise his intent. In truth, the store employees would think nothing of a tourist purchasing such equipment. The diving off Crete was world-famous.

What the clerk noticed was the furtive manner of his customer.

Chapter Seventeen

Carmen woke up in a dark place. As she regained consciousness, she could feel cool water on her underside, but her back and dorsal fin felt dry. The realization brought her fully awake with a surge of fear. Where was she? Was she beached?

Once she was fully awake, she realized she had some buoyancy. However, she couldn't dive. She was in shallow water, just enough to keep her afloat but not allow her to submerge. It was then she became grateful for the darkness. If she'd slept for long in a place like this in sunlight, she would be near death.

But where was she? The question returned with urgency when she realized that she also couldn't swim to deeper water. Something like a net surrounded her and was under her. Fear surged again. Had she been caught by a fisherman? She'd heard stories of young dolphins being caught in giant nets along with tuna. But there didn't seem to be anyone else here. Not even a tuna.

Gradually, as her eyes adjusted, she became aware that

it wasn't completely dark. Something that gave off light was above her. At first, she thought it was stars, and she worried that soon the sun would rise, and she'd be in trouble if she couldn't dive. Then she noticed there were far too many of the little points of light. The night sky was bright with stars, but not as bright as this. Now that her eyes had adjusted, she could see very clearly. She was in a cave.

Memory flooded back. The bad land-human had struck her with his weapon! It had hurt. Carmen thrashed around wildly, looking for the bad land-human. He'd come from behind her before, and after he hit her, she'd gone to sleep. Carmen was confused. She wasn't supposed to go to sleep in a fight. And she'd never gone to sleep so deeply that she didn't remember continuing to swim.

What had he done to her? Where had he taken her?

Carmen had a funny feeling in her head. It was like she couldn't hear anymore. Wait! She couldn't! She couldn't hear other dolphins, or the sounds of fish swimming nearby. That made her realize she was hungry. Without knowing it, she sent a distress call by ansible. To dolphins near and far, it would sound like 'hunger, fear, lost'. However, her signal was so weak that it reached only a killer whale that was hungry itself. And even her giant cousin could not pinpoint the location of the signal. It went in search of easier prey.

Carmen didn't like the feeling in her head. She didn't understand why she couldn't hear anyone, and it scared her. Before she completely shook it off, she saw a shadowy figure blot out the points of light above her.

"So, you're awake," the land-human said. Carmen could understand land-human language, a little. She didn't have the experience her mother did, so there were many words she could not understand, but she understood those.

"Help me," she returned, in Dolphinese. "I need food. I need to dive. I need to find my mother."

"It's no good squeaking at me," the land-human said. "I don't have a translation device, so I can't understand you. I don't care what you have to say anyway. I need to talk to your mother, too." He made a noise that hurt her ears, and then said, "We're going to have a little fun, Miss Dolphin."

Carmen understood the words, but not the meaning. She didn't understand the cruel laughter that Ahab had injected into his speech. But her hopes lifted when he said 'fun'. Like most dolphins, *except the old ones*, she thought, she loved to have fun. Fun with land-humans was some of the best kind.

"Could I have some food first?" she asked. "If you'll help me get out of this net, I'll get my own."

"There you go squeaking again. Told you I can't understand you."

Then he did something, and a small sun suddenly shone in her eyes. "That hurts," she said. "Please make it stop."

It didn't stop. Carmen had closed her eyes, but when she heard him moving, she opened them again. He had stepped into the light, and her fear surged as she recognized the bad land-human. She began to thrash in the net again.

"Oh, you know who I am now, do you? Tell me. Do you know the way to where the Minotaurs live? If you'll show me, I won't have to hurt you anymore. Although, that won't be any fun for me. Frankly, I'd rather hurt you."

Carmen struggled to understand what he meant. Hurting her was fun? Maybe she didn't understand fun, or maybe he didn't. She didn't know the word Minotaur, but it gave her an ugly feeling. Did he mean the monsters that ate land-humans? Maybe she *should* show him. While they ate him, she could get away.

A feeling she didn't recognize made every cell of her body tingle. Her mother could have told her it was shame, but she'd had no reason to describe shame to Carmen. Dolphins had little use for the concept. Only when they could help each other, or a land-human, and chose not to. That didn't happen often. Hurting a land-human was unthinkable. After all, they were an intelligent species, like dolphins. And they were just now beginning to regain the full range of their intelligence and realize they weren't alone.

Her mother had hope that she could train them not to accidentally catch dolphins in their nets, for example. But Carmen thought this land-human was not as intelligent as others she'd met. He couldn't understand her, and he was angry all the time. Perhaps he was angry because he was not as smart as other humans, even other land-humans. There were dolphins like that. Not as smart as most of their kind. In fact, those were the ones who got caught in nets.

Carmen's thoughts had wandered, but she watched the land-human even while she was thinking of other things. And then, she heard her mother!

Carmen, where are you?

Mother! I'm in a cave. The bad land-human is here. He can't understand me. I'm hungry, Mother.

What cave?

I don't know. He brought me here while I was asleep, I think. I'm in a net, and I can't get out to hunt. I can't get under the water, either. He has a little sun, and he asked me if I know where the Minotaur is. And he wants to talk to you. Mother, what's a Minotaur?

A picture of the monster that ate land-humans entered her mind.

That's what I thought, she answered. *I will lead him there. The Minotaur will eat him.*

No, my daughter. You must not do that. Keep talking to me. We will find you and help you get away. Sunhead's mate is here helping us. Be brave.

Carmen continued to describe her whereabouts and what the land-human was doing until he showed her his weapon.

Mother! He's going to strike me with his weapon again!

Daughter, it may hurt, but he will not kill you. He wants me to lead him, and you know I cannot. If he lets the monsters loose, it will harm many land-humans. But we're searching for you.

The land-human spoke to her. "This will tickle. I don't want it to be too much for you, yet. Put on a good act for your mother. Say cheese."

Carmen didn't know what cheese was and couldn't have said it if she had. Nor did she understand the word tickle. When the weapon touched her, her whole body felt hot and then cold, and she convulsed. *Mother, it hurts!*

We're coming, my child. Keep talking. We'll find you.

Ahab was a bit disappointed in the result of his first video. He'd expected the dolphin to make a sound when the stun gun hit her. Whatever the dolphin equivalent of a scream was. Instead, she'd just had a short seizure. She seemed none the worse for wear, but he didn't know enough about dolphins to risk stunning her again so soon.

The game would not be as much fun if she died too soon. And he'd stand the risk of losing the mother, as well. No, he had to keep this one alive until the mother showed up. He'd set up some live feed equipment near the entrance to the cave where he'd found the young one patrolling. If she didn't come soon, he'd have to go and find her. She was probably still hanging out near Devereux's boat.

He'd prefer not to go near there again. Too much risk of exposure, and Devereux knew him. He'd have to kill Devereux if they met face to face. Better to avoid that. Killing was for sport, but killing Devereux felt like a bigger risk than Ahab wanted to take.

———

Merrybeth surfaced near Carter's boat a few minutes after she'd sent her last message to Carmen. No one was on deck, but Merrybeth knew they were inside the land-human caves on top of the boat. She hailed them by leaping and splashing while whistling Carter's individual identification whistle over and over. She was rewarded by seeing him running out of the door and to the side rail immediately.

"What is it, Merrybeth?" he called.

The device broadcast her answer in land-human. "I have heard from Carmen! The bad land-human has her. He is hurting her. He wants her or me to lead him to the land-shark thing."

"Merrybeth, maybe you should."

"No, Carter. If I do what he wants, he will kill Carmen anyway, and the monster will be loose among you. We must find them and stop him."

"Can you locate her?"

"I can, if she can continue to send communications. But we must hurry!"

"We'll follow you."

Chapter Eighteen

"Mackenzie, I need to show you something." Her veterinarian seemed grave.

"Is it urgent? I'm in the middle of something," she replied, already thinking how she could rearrange the rest of her day if what he had to show her was bad news.

"No, not urgent. But important."

"I'll be there in half an hour." Mackenzie had turned most of the administrative work over to her admin assistant and was happy she'd thought of it. It was important work, but not her forte and not exciting to her. However, some things still needed her attention. Today it was her signature on several food orders to be delivered on the next milk run from the States, and authorizations on supplies for her lab. At least she didn't have to worry about all of them being necessary and within budget. Her admin assistant was a jewel and completely trustworthy.

"I'll be back as soon as I can, Mom," she told her.

Mary smiled. "That's all I need you for today, dear. I'll be at our cabin if you want me to do anything else."

"Thanks, Mom. And thanks for applying for this position. I don't know if I could have trusted anyone else, at least not so quickly."

"I'm happy to do it. I was a little bored, now that both of the children are in school and I didn't have their company all day."

"What about Dad?" Mackenzie teased. She knew that her parents were still deeply in love but could get on each other's nerves if they were together twenty-four/seven. Besides, her dad was documenting everything Ahote and Bly could tell him about life in their tribe when they were children. He was often away from the cabin all day. Mackenzie suspected he and Ahote were getting in more fishing than documentation.

Mary grinned. "Your dad is good company, but I'm a career woman. And I'm not ready to be put out to pasture."

"I can't imagine you ever being ready for that, Mom," Mackenzie answered. "I'd love to chat more, but I'm needed in the vet lab. See you tomorrow?"

"Of course."

Mackenzie waved as she left her office and walked purposefully down the hall. She walked into the lab with five minutes to spare on her half-hour promise.

Ten minutes later, she had a lot to think about. She would need to call an all-staff meeting for early the next day to discuss the ethical situation their progress on the respirocytes had put them in.

———

"Thank you all for coming. Help yourselves to breakfast – it may be a long day."

Mackenzie had called the meeting for an hour before

normal starting time in the lab. While the work didn't lend itself to a strict schedule, and her scientists were free to set their own hours, most of them made a practice of showing up in the lab at eight a.m., as did she. Today, however, they had grave matters to discuss, and she anticipated a long debate about what her vet had discovered.

When everyone had settled at the conference table with their choice of the food she'd asked Bly to prepare on short notice, Mackenzie gave a short introduction to the issue, and then had the vet take over.

"I'll make a long story short. When I chose the rat I would use for the first surgical insertion of the respirocyte nanobots, I selected the oldest in the lab. There were several reasons for that. One, if the surgery didn't go well, I would not have unnecessarily shortened the lifespan of the animal. Two, I expected to see the results of the respirocytes in renewed health of the animal."

The data specialist raised his hand. "Why would you choose an animal in poor health. Wouldn't that compromise the surgical procedure?"

"Oh, he wasn't in poor health. Just nearing the end of his lifespan. The rats we use for this kind of work have an average life span of two to three years. The rat I selected is two and a half years old, but he is healthy for his age. He's never been subjected to induced disease like other experimental subjects. Nevertheless, tests I ran for comparison's sake showed him to be slower than other rats his size at running a maze, for example. You could consider him the equivalent of a healthy sixty-year-old human with no age-related disease. Does that answer your question?"

The clinician spoke up. "So, you expected that the addition of respirocytes might increase his speed at running that maze?"

"Among other things, yes. If I may?" The vet used a remote to turn on the large flat-screen wall monitor. A video of a rat outpacing another rat on a divided run appeared. "The rat on the right, well ahead of his younger counterpart, is our respirocyte subject. I'd like you to see what the results of the surgery appear to be."

As the group watched, the video the vet had spliced from several experiments showed the respirocyte subject outrunning the others, running longer on a wheel, and perhaps most surprisingly, solving various mazes more quickly.

Mackenzie spoke first after the video was finished. "For the sake of everyone who isn't familiar with the exercises you put them through, will you please interpret the results for us?"

"Glad to. In a word, the rat has not just experienced renewed health. He's been rejuvenated in the literal sense of the word, and that's not all. He is faster than rats in their prime on all physical tests. He has more endurance, and this is the kicker – he's smarter. You saw that in the maze runs. Each time I had him run the maze alongside a control rat, I changed the configuration of the maze.

"Normally, I can accurately predict the time it takes them to learn the maze perfectly, and then time the perfect run. This rat, whom I've renamed Methuselah, not only runs it faster once he's learned it, but he learns it faster. I can only conclude that the respirocytes have somehow increased his IQ."

Smiles broke out around the table, indicating to Mackenzie that most of her team hadn't spotted the ethical issue yet. "Go on," she said. "You're doing great. Now tell us the rest of the story."

The vet took a deep breath. "There have been consequences I never would have expected," he announced.

The smiles disappeared at the tone of his voice. Everyone listened raptly as he described how rats are normally very social, not only with their own kind, but with humans. "Experiments have shown that rats can read pain and body language of other rats, and exhibit empathy. They have also been discovered to share limited resources, even when food deprived." He paused, and sighed. "This is how Methuselah now acts…"

The next video showed the enhanced rat hoarding food and fending off the others, even though there was plenty of food for all. He pushed others off the wheels that they used for entertainment, and when his cage was placed next to those of receptive females, he spent most of his time working on the release mechanism for his cage.

The vet explained. "I should mention that Mackenzie asked me to limit the rats' reproduction. She was right to do so. A pair of rats left to breed unchecked can produce as many as 2000 descendants in a year. We would have had a huge problem. I keep the males and females in separate rooms to lower the males' stress levels, but when Methuselah started exhibiting signs of higher intelligence, I devised this experiment to see if he could learn to escape his cage." He paused, silent.

After a long fifteen seconds, the clinician couldn't wait any more. "Well? Could he?"

"He escaped in five minutes the first time. I had a padlock on the female's cage. The next time, Methuselah was out of his cage in one minute, and he went straight to the drawer where I kept the padlock key and tried to open it."

"Are you serious?" shouted several of the others.

"Dead serious. The third time, it took him less than thirty seconds, and he ignored the drawer. Instead, he tried to dismantle the female's cage by lifting the bars where they snap to the bottom. I stopped him after he unsnapped the first corner."

Mackenzie spoke up. "I think the point is that if respirocytes are responsible for this behavior, we have an ethical dilemma on our hands. I'd like some debate."

The veterinarian spoke up first. "I'm concerned. Methuselah seems to be developing some anti-social tendencies. In a human being, this could result in criminal behavior."

"But do we know whether he already had these tendencies before he got the respirocytes? Maybe he just wasn't able to physically do what he wanted to do?" This came from Mackenzie's research assistant.

"Yes. How would respirocytes change personality?" asked the nano-engineer. "Do we need a rat-whisperer now? A psychologist for rats?"

The veterinarian glared at him.

"Let's settle down a little bit," said Mackenzie. "There's no need for sarcasm. Frankly, I'm more concerned about the rejuvenation. Do you have any idea," she asked, addressing the vet, "how long this rat might live now?"

"It's just a guess, of course," he answered. "But he's exhibiting behavior more normal for a one-year-old rat. Extrapolating, I'd say we may have doubled his normal life span. At least increased it by 30%"

The clinician calculated quickly. "Average life expectancy for an American of either gender is about 80 years. Double that, and you've got some 160-year-olds running around. But are they healthy?"

"Furthermore, what does that do to their relationships if

only they have been treated?" Mackenzie asked. "How many of you would choose to outlive your families, your future children, by fifty years or more? I know I wouldn't. Not in the normal course of life. A parent should not have to bury a child."

The clinician started to speak, but Mackenzie held up her hand. "I know, that does happen, and more than we would wish. But ask any of those parents, the normal ones, if they'd trade places with their child in a heartbeat. I would."

"Can the effects be reversed, or attenuated?" This came from the chemical engineer.

"Good question. Should we try to reverse Methuselah's surgery and see what happens?"

The veterinarian clearly didn't want to perform surgery on the same rat again so soon, but it was the only way they'd be able to observe the effects. Would the rat age rapidly and go back to his normal condition? Or would he enjoy increased vigor even though the respirocytes would eventually leave his body without being renewed? And in either case, would he return to his former behavior, or continue to act aggressively?

Only time would tell.

Chapter Nineteen

In London, the investigation into the Archaeology Murders continued. Almost all leads other than the approach Carter had suggested – locating and eliminating the archaeology students from suspicion – had dried up. However, there were scores of archaeology students to question. To make the job easier, the investigators began with the previous ten years' students, since that seemed to be the age limit of the murders they'd related by the burial technique in the remains they'd found in archaeological sites.

That still left an extraordinary amount of the kind of work most investigators found tedious. They had names and approximate ages of the students, many of them now well-respected members of their profession. But they still had to track down where they were located now, interview them, have background checks done, and get alibis for the day of the most recent of the murders, that of the child found near the Roman Fort.

Because it had now been some weeks since that murder,

many couldn't provide an alibi, so crossing them off the list was slow going.

The professor who'd taught the technique they were targeting was devastated that one of his students could have desecrated an archaeological site, much less committed murder. Investigators worked with him to try to narrow their search further by getting him to talk about his students' personalities, but he was little help.

It began to appear as if they'd never catch the murderer until he committed another. There was little doubt that he would. Forensic anthropologists had found evidence clearly linking at least ten of the deaths, with another dozen or so considered highly probable.

The only good news was that with three of the victims identified as having come from the same area of London as the most recent, people were looking out for each other more in the slums, and work had begun on repairing or replacing the neglected CCTV cameras.

Aside from the ongoing work of eliminating the archaeology students who weren't responsible, MI6 was working overtime to connect any archaeology student to the Nabatean conspiracy. The only thread they had to go on was the link between the Nabateans and archaeology. It was a thin one, indeed, but also the reason they'd asked for the loan of Carter Devereux for the investigation. Now that Devereux had left the area, they were making no progress at all, and they weren't happy about it. Some of the team had even begun to blame Devereux for their lack of progress.

Eventually, a call went to Irene O'Connell to request her to force Devereux back to London. Irene didn't appreciate the approach.

"Tell me exactly why you think Carter can be of any

help. He's not a detective by any stretch of the imagination. Catching murderers is not his job."

"But these murders may be linked to the Nabateans. Some of them are old enough."

"Pardon my Americanism, but that's BS," she replied. "Carter told me there was no evidence whatsoever for that link other than the carvings on the bones of just two of the older victims. I think you're grasping at straws."

"If straws are all we have to grasp, then grasp them we will," the investigator on the other end of the call said hotly. "The evidence is that archaeology is involved."

"No, an archaeologist may be involved, but that's not even a straw," she answered. "I'm sorry, but Devereux is involved in something important to him right now. I won't order him back to London. Call me if you find anything else to convince you the Nabateans are involved, but we cleaned out that lot last year. We have no reason to believe they're still active."

After ending the call, Irene looked around her office for something to throw but found nothing that wouldn't make her regret the action. Sometimes her job was too frustrating for words. But there was no way in hell she was going to admit to anyone, much less MI6, that Carter was looking for the Minotaur. Just in case she was missing something, though, she called him.

"How's it going?" she asked when she had him on the line.

"Not well, I'm afraid. Merrybeth is torn between rescuing her daughter and betraying a trust the dolphins have been keeping for thousands of years."

"How many thousands?"

"Hard to say. The stories of the Minotaur that we know today originated in the century before the Christian era. But the story is likely much older. Most of these myths were passed down by word of mouth before being written down. The palace where the Labyrinth was supposed to have been was built around 1800 BC."

"So, three or four thousand years, give or take?"

"At least."

"The dolphins don't really believe this thing existed, do they?"

"They seem to. Apparently, they have a story of their own, of one of their kind witnessing it tearing the head off a teenaged girl."

"Do dolphins have mythology?"

"I guess that remains to be seen."

"Carter, are *you* taking this seriously?"

"There are more things in heaven and Earth, Horatio, than are dreamt of in your philosophy," he quoted.

"What the hell are you talking about?"

"Shakespeare said it, but I've lived it, Irene. Who could have believed there were actually giants in the earth?"

"Good point. Well, I called to tell you MI6 wants you back in London. I put them off for now, but we may get pressure."

"I can't leave here without resolving this issue, Irene, pressure or no pressure."

"What do you want me to tell them if they call again?"

"Tell them if I have to, I'll resign from A-Echelon before I'll break loose from here. But I could use your support here. We may need a submarine, or something I haven't even thought of yet."

"You're kidding."

"Not kidding. Isn't this perfect for our mission? Investigating ancient weapons?"

"What weapon?"

"Why, the Minotaur, of course. Can you imagine an army of these things? That would freak out an enemy, for sure."

"You send me a picture of a live one, and I'll do whatever you need. And don't you dare even think about resigning!"

"I need to go, Irene. Looks like we're getting ready to follow Merrybeth."

Chapter Twenty

Merrybeth led the way to a spot near where she and Carter had met the day before. She wanted to show him the place they'd guarded so many years, but she told him there was no longer a way into the cave system from that place. It had been, as she put it, many, many, many suns since they'd checked the entrance. If they'd known the monster couldn't escape from there, they would not have been guarding it. But they'd stayed far enough away that they couldn't see it, yet close enough to prevent approach.

Carter prepared to dive with SCUBA equipment, so he could follow her to the spot. While the boat could have come closer, he had no authority to approach inside Cretan waters. As a tourist, he could have, but if A-Echelon became involved, he'd need to be circumspect about respecting sovereign territory.

Before they left, Merrybeth gave him a description of what they'd see. "The water is much deeper now than it was when we started guarding, Carter. This entrance was once partly above the water, and then there was a long part below water that opened into the cave system. We could not go farther than the first cave, because the river that made the caves came out a small crack in the rock. But we know there were other caves beyond the first one. Land-humans we befriended told us."

Carter tried to calculate how long ago that must have been. The giants lived about 70,000 years ago. They understood dolphin speech as well as the dolphins now understood his. Had the sea grown deeper since then? Or had the land sunk? Probably both, he realized. He was no geologist, but the strata he'd dug through on some of his sites made it clear the earth had undergone many changes, even in so short a relative time.

"Merrybeth, were the land-humans larger than we are now?"

"I think so. Not as large as those you call the giants, but larger than you, Carter."

Carter was tall, maybe a bit taller than average, at over six feet. He knew that the men who'd worn ancient armor were much smaller. So, humans – land-humans – had undergone radical shrinkage, most likely due to poor nutrition as well as in response to oxygen levels diminishing. Now they were experiencing a rapid growth spurt as a species.

He settled on an arbitrary estimate that the dolphins had guarded this cave entrance for perhaps half the interval between the giant's times and now. Maybe 30,000 years. When he thought about how long that was in dolphin generations, it amazed him that they could remember. Land-humans, he thought, could barely remember yesterday if it wasn't written down. Whenever he got new insight into dolphin intelligence, he became more convinced that they were actually more intelligent than his own kind in many ways.

He slipped over the side after his crew checked his SCUBA gear and grasped Merrybeth's dorsal fin as they'd agreed. Having her tow him would conserve his air supply, and they'd make better time as well, even though she would surface for air every few minutes. When they got near the place, he'd swim on his own, to allow her to conserve her own air. It would be a long dive for her.

They swam as fast as they could without ripping Carter's hand off Merrybeth's fin. Even so, Carter's tank was less than half full when they reached the spot where Merrybeth indicated they'd need to separate. Carter let go of her fin and nodded. Merrybeth surfaced for a minute, and then swam past him at a near-vertical angle. Carter followed, seeing immediately that they were following a slope of land.

At about 15 meters in depth, Merrybeth entered an opening and disappeared. Carter followed, trusting they wouldn't be underwater more than seven or eight minutes, as Merrybeth would need air by then. At ten minutes, with no end to the tunnel they were traveling in sight, he began to worry about Merrybeth. At twelve minutes, he started worrying about getting back himself.

But a minute later, the close confines of the tunnel opened out, and Merrybeth swam upwards. As he followed, finally breaking out of the water into a low-ceilinged cave, Carter checked his watch. Merrybeth had held her breath for an astonishing fifteen minutes. They were still at about fifteen meters below his starting point, so the tunnel must have taken a downward turn. He pulled the mouthpiece away to breathe the air in the cave and found it fresh enough.

His demand valve would only deliver gas from his tank while he was inhaling, so he was saving the rest for the trip back. Merrybeth bobbed up and down to signal him to follow her, and he did, but swimming on the surface. He considered climbing out, but when he made to do so, she stopped him, the translator screaming at him that it wasn't safe. Instead, he swam, finding it awkward to do it with the tank on his back while staying at the surface.

But they didn't have far to go. The dim light from the bioluminescent organisms in the cave hadn't shown him just how close the far wall was. He estimated they'd gone less than ten yards when they ran into another rift in the rock, this one too narrow to pass through.

"Does it widen underwater?" he asked aloud. Merrybeth whistled 'no', a word he recognized even without the translator.

"Okay. Is this the cave where your ancestor saw the Minotaur?"

This time Merrybeth answered, "Yes."

"And there is no other entrance?" Carter realized his mistake immediately. Merrybeth would know of no other entrance if it was approached from the land. If the cave entrance was now further under sea level than it had been, then it was possible other entrances were buried under land strata as well. He'd have to get out of the water and explore the cave to find out. But Merrybeth was violently opposed to that plan, as he'd already discovered.

"You don't believe your daughter is here?" he ventured.

Again, she whistled 'no'. She was being briefer than usual, but when Carter asked her to explain why he shouldn't get out and explore, she didn't answer.

"Then let's go back to the boat. I have some questions."

The dolphin took off so quickly that Carter was rushed to jam the mouthpiece back in. He had no time to check his pressure, but even if he didn't have quite enough gas, he still had to go out through the tunnel. He just hoped if he ran out of air, he could hold his breath long enough to get to the surface.

The trip back to the boat took longer than the trip out, mostly because Carter had run out of air in his tank before they got all the way back, so the last six miles were done at the surface. This time it was Merrybeth's need to dive and cool off that slowed them. But Carter was still grateful for the tow. He didn't think he had it in him to swim six miles on the surface with an awkward tank on his back.

The experience brought home to him the problems they'd face when they located Carmen. There was no way he'd make the 12-mile swim to land again. It was time to officially involve A-Echelon. He didn't envy Irene her task of convincing the Greek government that a dolphin had told him her daughter was being held hostage until they revealed the hiding place of a mythical creature that the dolphins believed was real.

Chapter Twenty-One

"How did he do?" Mackenzie dropped in at the vet lab to check on Methuselah later on the day of the ethics debate.

"He survived the surgery. I won't really know more for a few days."

Mackenzie had only known her assistants for a few weeks, but she could read that the veterinarian still wasn't happy at being required to reverse the surgery. "Can we talk? Is it okay to leave him for a while? I'd like to get some air," she explained.

He nodded brusquely. "All right."

Mackenzie led the way outside. From previous rambles, she knew he could keep up with her outdoor stride, long steps taken quickly. It covered ground, and soon led them to a wooded area where Mackenzie liked to walk and think. She hoped it would calm his nerves as well.

"You understand why we had to put Methuselah through that, don't you?"

"Yes. Doesn't mean I have to like it."

Gently, she probed further. "Is this work too much for you? Do you want to leave?"

"No, Mackenzie. I'm sorry. I understand that it's important, and that my animals will potentially suffer." He lifted his hands in a gesture of defeat. "I've been fired for this before, you know. I'll do my duty, whether or not I like it."

She put her hand on his arm, stopping under a tree whose spreading limbs lent a dappled shade to its shelter. "I admire your heart for the animals. I won't fire you, but I can't have your attitude spreading discontent among the others. Can you find a way to temper its expression?"

He smiled. "That's the loveliest reprimand I've ever received. I'll do my best, Mackenzie."

"That's all I ask. Now, do you have any idea why the respirocyte generator would have created a change in Methuselah's personality?"

"Honestly? I've wracked my brain, and I can't. Unless…"

"Unless?" she prompted.

"The damn things are so tiny. What if one of the three we implanted migrated out of his lungs and into his brain?"

Mackenzie considered the idea. "I don't know if it's possible, but if it did, how would you see it working in the way it did?"

"I'd have to consult with the others. I don't know whether excess oxygen in the brain could result in a personality change, or not. But maybe that's the reason for the IQ change. And maybe *that* is the reason for the personality change."

"You think being smarter also makes him a bully?" Mackenzie smiled. The notion seemed preposterous.

"I've known geniuses who were antisocial and felt themselves superior to others."

Mackenzie's smile died. She remembered a few of those herself. The mother-son team who'd led the Nabatean conspiracy were certainly geniuses, and certifiable sociopaths. "That would complicate our research considerably. Can you devise some IQ tests for the other rats, so we'll have a baseline when we give them the respirocytes?"

"No need. There have been plenty of tests for lab rat intelligence. The most famous one, devised at Tokai University in Tokyo, had to do with the breeding of super-intelligent rats with which to test the effects of chemicals used in agriculture. Whether they would adversely affect intelligence in humans."

"Fascinating."

"Indeed. They spent thirty years breeding a line of genius rats."

"Are you thinking of asking them whether those rats were antisocial?"

"Oh, no. I was just thinking about the intelligence tests they gave them. Rats vary wildly in intelligence, you know."

"No, I didn't know."

"Well, they do. Listen, can we go back? You've got me curious now."

"In a moment. Your idea about the respirocyte generators is also intriguing. Did you examine the capsule you took out of Methuselah to determine if all three generators were still in it?"

"No. But I didn't dispose of it. We can do that now."

"Get the engineers involved. We need to know."

Before Methuselah was fitted with the nanobots, the group had determined together that the lungs were the best place for the respirocyte generators to be inserted, and the article in the Library of the Giants had seemed to corroborate the conclusion. The article had not indicated how to keep them there, however. The trio of engineers had been pressed to further miniaturize the devices, as the giants' lungs were so much larger than today's humans that making them on the same scale would create a device a modern human would be able to feel and involuntarily try to clear by coughing.

The miniaturization, however, presented another problem. How to affix the devices to stay put. The answer had been to encapsulate them in an impossibly fine mesh, which could be inserted inside an individual alveolus. One 'capsule', which looked nothing like the infinitely larger medial capsules one would think of when hearing the word, could hold three of the 500 nanometer-sized respirocyte generators. This number was calculated to be a little less than half what a human would be able to carry without feeling it, based on the average alveolus size of a mature rat being approximately half that of a human.

The surgery to insert the capsule was relatively simple. They had determined that, since the rat would not be able to feel the capsule, no involuntary expulsion would occur. The veterinarian had merely to insert a superfine needle with the capsule in the nozzle using an image-guided microscope. Due to the small size of the subject, only one surgeon could do the work, but the others observed. When Mackenzie questioned them one by one, no one could recall seeing anything that might have ruptured the capsule mesh to allow the generators to escape. But examination under the scanning electron microscope would give them the definitive answer.

As soon as the nano-engineer had done the examination, he reported to Mackenzie. "I think we can say the problem is solved. There was a tear in the mesh. You'd have to ask a pulmonary expert to tell you how it migrated from there, and where it might have gone."

"I'm glad to know you were able to confirm the mechanism, but our problem is by no means solved. Now we have two problems. One – does a respirocyte generator in the brain, if that's where it went, cause antisocial behavior, and if so, how. And two – how do we prevent this outcome when we begin to test on human subjects."

A talk with her clinician, her research assistant, and the veterinarian convinced her there were in fact three problems. The only way to know if the missing generator was in Methuselah's brain was to euthanize him, section his brain painstakingly, and search with the electron microscope. The veterinarian was devastated.

Mackenzie told him to take the rest of the day off to find his balance in her favorite area of the vast, wooded ranch. As he hiked away from the lab building, she noticed Keeva keeping pace with him. She pictured him finding peace with the necessity and sent the mental image to her wolf friend.

The team had already made remarkable progress in the short time they'd worked together, thanks to Liu's discovery but also to the team's dedication. They were beginning to form friendships among themselves, and the nano-engineer had sincerely apologized for his sarcasm in the ethics meeting. Mackenzie was proud of them, and of her choices. She had formed a highly effective research team, and when the respirocyte research was successfully concluded, there'd be other questions to take up for the betterment of human health.

Chapter Twenty-Two

Irene stared at the video link in frustration. "Carter, I don't know what to tell you. I can't very well go to the Navy with this request. They'd laugh me out of office. No, I'd be dragged out of this office by men in white coats. You can't seriously ask me to borrow a one-man sub to go searching for a Minotaur."

"Irene, if I had time to have one built, I'd do it and pay for it myself. Do you not remember how much we owe the dolphins? Time is running out for Merrybeth's daughter, and we need your help. A-Echelon's help."

"So, after I go to the Navy with this outrageous request, I'm also supposed to ask the State department to get Greece to allow a Navy submarine to go poking around in their sovereign waters. Is that what you're telling me?"

"Yep."

She threw up her hands. "All right, Carter. You've been right so far, and you've made important discoveries. But this is on you. When I go after these things, everyone involved will know that it's you who's asking. *Everyone*, and that will probably include the President. I doubt the Secretary of State will act on the request without his approval."

"That's fine. Then they can take me to the funny farm if it doesn't pan out. You and Mackie can visit me there, but at least I won't be going on more wild-goose chases."

Irene had to concede that she deserved that. Sending him to London had been so much a long shot that they could have missed the side of a barn with it. But he had identified the dig pattern they were calling their best lead.

"Very funny. Okay, I'm on it. Stay available."

Irene ended the call and studied her desk for a while. If she approached the Navy first, she didn't have a chance. And there was no way SecState would listen either. She was going to have to go right to the top. That meant calling on the Big Man, Bill Griffin.

Even though A-Echelon operated as an independent security agency, they were nominally under the aegis of the CIA, and Bill had survived the change in Presidential staff. Not only that, but because of his personal friendship with former President Sam Grant, he also had the ear of Grant's successor and protégé, President Ron Matthews. If she could persuade Bill to back her request, they could take it directly to the President, and then anyone else's objections would be moot.

This was not a conversation to have over the phone, not even over video chat. Late in the day as it was, she sent a courier to invite Bill and his wife to her home for dinner that evening. Her next call was to a friend who owned a Washington, DC catering service that was in high demand. She called in a favor – Mrs. Griffin was known to enjoy gourmet food. *Carter, I hope you appreciate the sacrifices I make for you.*

Griffin wasn't head of the CIA because of his political

acumen. He was one of the smartest people Irene knew, besides the Devereuxs, of course. Minutes after the courier left her office, Bill called her. "What's this all about, Irene?"

"Why, dinner, Sir," she answered.

"Don't be disingenuous. No one invites a couple to dinner just hours before the occasion. You want something. What is it?"

"Sir, I'd like the opportunity to tell you over dinner, not over the phone. Please. It's already ordered, and I can't eat it all myself."

"Very well. See you at six." He ended the call.

Irene called her friend back. "Change of plans. I need it by six, not seven. Yes, I know. I'm sorry. My guest insisted."

At six precisely, Irene opened her door to the Griffins. Bill shook her hand, and Mrs. Griffin greeted her coolly. "So fortunate we didn't already have plans."

Irene was chastened, but Bill was her main concern. Mrs. Griffin was just there to avoid the appearance of impropriety. Even though Bill was twenty years her senior, he was still a handsome and charming man.

"Yes, fortunate indeed," she answered.

Bill eyed her curiously throughout the three-course meal, but because Mrs. Griffin could not know the subject of the meeting, Irene patiently played hostess and waited until Mrs. Griffin excused herself 'to powder her nose'. This was her chance.

"Bill, I have a request from Carter Devereux that I can't swing on my own. It's going to need the President's sign-off, and I need you to back me."

"What is it?"

"Believe it or not, he's on the trail of a Minotaur."

Griffin had heard some unlikely information over the years of his acquaintance with Carter Devereux. Irene counted on the hope that nothing could surprise him now. She was not wrong.

"Only Devereux. How credible is this, and why is it a threat to our national security?"

And there was the rub. Irene could not think of a threat to national security from a single mythical monster. She fell back on the only argument she had. "I can't explain it, but Carter believes it is. It also has to do with a personal crisis with the dolphin who was instrumental in helping find the Alboran Codex. Her daughter has been, for lack of a better term, kidnapped."

Bill sighed. "It's not much to go on, but I'll vouch for Carter's reputation with the President. You're on your own to tell him what it's about, though. After this moment, the word Minotaur will never pass my lips again. How urgent is this?"

"Tonight," she answered.

Bill sighed. "Of course, it is."

"What was that, dear?" his wife asked as she came back into the room.

"Nothing, my dear," he said.

Irene saw Mrs. Griffin's lips press together. Evidently, she was used to her husband telling her things were nothing.

Two hours later, Bill Griffin and Irene O'Connell were ushered into the Oval Office, where President Matthews waited for them. To Irene's surprise, he had a mischievous grin. He stuck out his hand and shook hers vigorously. "Welcome, Director O'Connell. I've heard much about you and your agency. So pleased to meet you, at last."

Irene was taken aback by his charm. Maybe this

wouldn't be so hard after all. Ten minutes later, the President's affable demeanor had disappeared in favor of frank disbelief.

"You want me to direct the Secretary of State to do what?"

"Mr. President, I'm aware this is highly unusual. Let me just say that I have complete confidence in Dr. Devereux's judgment. If he says he needs a Navy sub and permission from the Greek government to take it into their sovereign waters, then I'm certain he has a good reason, no matter how bizarre it sounds." Griffin spoke firmly and confidently, and Irene was doubly glad she'd asked him to accompany her to the meeting with the President.

"Bill, Sam Grant has told me the same about you. I have to confess, this is the craziest thing I hope I ever have to deal with in my presidency, but if you think it's necessary, you've got it."

"Not only necessary, Mr. President," Irene replied, "but urgent. Can we prevail upon you to make this happen tonight?"

Now it was the President's turn to sigh. "If you think…"

"I do," she interrupted. This entire process was taking too long. It had been hours since Carter told her the young dolphin was running out of time.

Chapter Twenty-Three

Carmen had no way to understand how long she'd been in this place. She had to see the sun to count how many suns. She thought it was a long time. She was very hungry. The bad land-human gave her fish sometimes, but it was never enough. She was tired, and her skin felt bad, too.

She hadn't heard her mother in a long time, either. Maybe the others had forgotten her. She sent messages now and then, because her mother had told her to keep talking, but she couldn't find the energy to do it all the time. Mostly, she slept.

Sometimes, she thought she'd even welcome the company of the bad land-human. She was glad to see him when he brought fish, but then he would strike her with his weapon and make that unpleasant sound before he'd give them to her.

At first, she'd been afraid of the pain, and then afraid he would kill her. Now she thought if she knew how to die, she would just do it. This was not a life.

Ahab's state of mind was long stretches of boredom mixed with frustration and punctuated by flashes of rage. He couldn't sustain any emotion for long, however. He was driven by his goals and the urge to have fun. Fun for him meant pain for the dolphin.

He was trying to train her to hate eating. Logically, he knew his best chance at finding the Minotaurs was to keep his hostage alive as bait for the mother dolphin. But his experiments around pain and death led him to act against that interest by starving the dolphin he had in captivity.

How much pain would she endure before she turned away from the food he brought her? How little could he feed her and keep her alive? These questions were fun for him to contemplate. At the same time, he hoped she lasted long enough for the mother to give in and lead him to his prize.

The underground grotto in which he'd stashed his hostage could be reached only by swimming an underground river, the same one that issued through a crack in the rock in the original cave the dolphin had been guarding. It took him only an hour or so of exploration in that cave to find his way through several passages and find the river again. From the back side of the formation that blocked it, he could see that an ancient rockfall split the cave system and dammed the river, allowing only a relative trickle through the crevices in the rockfall. On the other side of it, water under pressure spurted out the crack and formed the karst spring he'd used to find it.

He'd explored confidently, knowing he could physically best any man he encountered, and assuming he could overcome a Minotaur if he found one. He not only had superior size and quickness to any man he'd ever met, but he also had his stun-gun, and the weapon would surely stop a charging bull-man.

Once he'd found the river, following it to its underground source led him to a spot where it bubbled out of bedrock and ran in two directions. The second one led out to the ocean again. Once he'd gained the sea, he looked back at a steep cliff, and noticed hikers on a trail leading down to the water. He climbed out of the water and picked up the trail, nodding casually to the hikers as he passed them. The trail led past a Catholic monastery, which oriented him to where he was on the island. By his reckoning, he'd swum twelve miles from his starting point – more when he considered the turns the river had taken in finding its way through the rock that was Crete's underpinning.

Along the way, he'd seen several places where the water pooled deep enough to keep the dolphin. It had been a chore, towing her around the peninsula and into the second entrance, but the reward was they were miles from either entrance, and the second one was not guarded by dolphins. This he took to mean they didn't know of it.

Ahab didn't know or care that the dolphin he'd captured, of the bottlenose species, would not do well in the fresh water of the underground river for very long. While she could survive, she was growing weaker, not only because he didn't feed her enough, but because she had less buoyancy in fresh water than in salt. The need to stay afloat exhausted her, and her skin wasn't adapted to fresh water. Though neither he nor his captive knew it, her skin would start to slough within the next few days.

What Ahab did know was that if his hostage died before he had accomplished his mission, he would need another, or a different strategy, to get the mother to cooperate. It had been more than a week since he'd taken the hostage, and two days since he'd eavesdropped on the mother communicating with Devereux. It was past time to find out what they were up to.

Ahab took his leased yacht to a spot near the place he'd first found the dolphin. He dove into the water, acutely aware that Devereux could recognize him if he saw him. He swam straight to the entrance of the tunnel leading to the underground cave, and lurked there, hoping the mother dolphin or Devereux would turn up. Surprisingly, they turned up together, Devereux clinging to the dolphin's fin, and entered the tunnel.

Devereux had SCUBA equipment, naturally. He'd never have been able to make the swim otherwise. His boat must be beyond the horizon. Maybe he wasn't here on a sanctioned mission and had to stay beyond the twelve-mile limit.

Ahab found a place to hide and stayed outside the tunnel. There was no reason to risk being spotted inside the narrow waterway. They'd emerge eventually, and he'd follow at a discreet distance.

When they did emerge, the dolphin and Devereux stayed close to the surface. Ahab considered swimming up behind Devereux and snatching him away from the dolphin, holding him underwater until the gas in his tanks ran out. But he and the dolphin seemed close. It was possible she'd attack, and Ahab didn't think he could control both.

Instead, he followed as he'd planned. As Devereux rested at the rail and conversed with the dolphin, he learned that he'd soon have more company than he'd bargained for.

Devereux planned to involve the US Navy, and something called AE.

Now Ahab would have to turn up the pressure. Unconsciously, his lips formed an evil grin. *It wasn't looking good for the young dolphin*, he thought.

The conversation on the boat had ended, but the dolphin was still waiting off the side. Ahab's attention wandered, and he was startled when she appeared before him with something in her mouth. He grinned when he realized they'd used his trick of putting a note in a plastic bag. He read it through the plastic.

"*Proof of life*," it read.

At first, he was puzzled. Then he realized they wanted to know if the young one was alive. This meant the mother was going to try to trap him by agreeing to lead him where he wanted to go, if he proved her daughter was alive. He could do that.

He started toward his yacht, where he had video equipment for the eventual proof he'd found the Minotaur. It wouldn't take much ingenuity to protect it from the water while he got to the young one. He could film her, and if he was right, he could tell her to say something in their language to convince her mother she was all right. He nodded at the dolphin and swam away.

Proof of life, coming right up.

After he'd swum away, Merrybeth returned to Devereux's boat. "I gave him the note," she said.

"So, he *was* there," Carter observed.

"I told you he was. I felt him behind us."

Carter didn't pretend to know how she could have felt

someone swimming behind them, but he didn't argue. She'd been right. They'd wait here until he returned with something to prove her daughter was alive, or until she heard from Carmen herself again. Then he had an idea.

"Merrybeth, can you tell how far away an ansible message comes from?" He'd expressed himself inelegantly, but he was thinking on his feet, with no time for elegance.

"I know where the messenger swims, yes," she answered. "Nearby."

Quickly, Carter tried to explain the concept of triangulation to her. Finding he lacked the words, he grabbed the whiteboard again and drew it out.

Merrybeth caught on quickly when she saw the picture. She sent a broadcast of the image to every dolphin in the area, and even picked up a faint echo from the Navy's trained dolphin, Joanna, all the way from California.

We need to find my daughter, she signaled. *Anyone who hears her talking to me, please signal me your location.*

She heard several signals of assent, and then the ansible network went silent. Everyone was listening intently for Carmen.

Chapter Twenty-Four

July had become August, and with it, the annual leave for the Executive Advantage team on Freydis. They'd learned that the most efficient way of handling vacations was to leave a skeleton crew at Tala to provide the security for the Freydis operation and everyone else go at once.

During the first three weeks of August, there was no school as most of the children would be traveling with their parents. Those whose dads or moms were left to guard the ranch usually went on trips with the other parent. Liam understood that his dad was on an important assignment, and his mom was just getting her research going and couldn't leave Freydis right now. But he had a plan.

"Grandma, do you think you and Grandpa could take us on a trip?" he asked her on the afternoon school let out for the summer vacation.

"That's a good idea! Let me see if your mom can spare me at the lab, and if your grandpa is at a stopping place with his history of the Hopi," she said.

"Grandpa's been fishing all summer," Liam confided. "I

think he's at a stopping place. But I won't say anything to Beth about it."

Grandma laughed. "You're probably right, but I'll ask anyway. And it's a good idea not to say anything to Beth, in case it doesn't work out. Did you have a vacation spot picked out?"

"Yes," Liam answered. "I'd like to go to Greece. I want to be an archaeologist like my dad, and there are a lot of cool sites there."

"This wouldn't have anything to do with him being near there right now, would it?"

"Of course, it would! We haven't seen Dad in like, forever," Liam said, his pseudo-adult demeanor disappearing. A tear formed in his eye, and he dashed it away angrily. "He's never here."

"Sweetheart, that's not exactly true, but I understand you miss him. Let's see what your mom says."

Mackenzie wasn't entirely thrilled with the idea. Her children overseas without her? She regretted not being able to take them herself, and for that matter, she missed Carter herself. But Liam had wisely enlisted Dylan's help, as well.

"I'll go with them, if you can spare Liu. We'll make it a vacation, and I'll be there to protect them. I won't let them distract Carter, either, I promise. But he's so close, he could spend a little time with them without compromising the mission, I think."

Dylan and Mackenzie both knew what Carter was doing, and their up-to-the-minute knowledge of the search for Carmen gave them the understanding that it was all up to the ansible triangulation or the perp cooperating with the proof-of-life demand. The ball was in the other court.

"How will we get the jet back here?" Mackenzie asked.

"I'll have one of the EA pilots go and fetch it, if Carter doesn't mind."

"Okay. I hate to disappoint Liam. He's such a good kid. Let's see if Carter has any objections. But go ahead and start making arrangements."

Mackenzie didn't want to distract Carter, either, but he called most afternoons. He'd be getting ready to go to bed if there was nothing going on, and it was almost that time. She decided to wait for his call.

She'd no more than made the decision than the comms unit on her desk indicated a video call coming in.

"Hi, honey. Any news?"

Carter shook his head. "I'm afraid the outlook is pretty grim, but we did get a message to the kidnapper that we wanted proof of life. Merrybeth said he nodded."

"You're thinking he meant he'd get it for you?"

"I hope so. It's always dicey, being sure that our species understand each other. Merrybeth was encouraged. I hope it isn't false hope on her part."

"A mother would never give up hope," Mackenzie said sadly. "And I can't imagine how painful it would be to not know. Almost worse than knowing your child had died, I think."

"I don't know. When you and Liam were missing, I thought you were dead, and it was agony."

"I love you, Carter."

"Me too," he said. "And I'm bushed. Going to cut it short tonight. Tomorrow may be a long day."

"Wait. I have something to ask you." Mackenzie wasn't sure this was the time but holding Liam off until tomorrow afternoon wasn't a pleasant thought, either. Quickly, she floated the idea past Carter.

He looked thoughtful for a moment. "Dylan said he'd sacrifice his vacation to come with them?"

"Not exactly. He said they'd all be on vacation, but he'd be there to protect them."

"And you can't break away to come with them?" he said hopefully.

"I'm sorry, I really can't. Lots going on with the research, and we're making rapid progress. I have to be here."

"Well, it will be good to see them, at least. I guess it's okay. Who's going to fly the plane?"

"I don't know. Dylan said he'd handle that part."

"I'll see them in Athens sometime in the next couple of days, then. Is Athens the plan?" he asked as an afterthought.

"Yes. Carter, Liam said he wants to be an archaeologist, like you! Aren't you proud?"

"Man, I love that kid. It feels good to be his hero."

"You're mine, too, you know."

"Of course," he said, winking. He ended the call before she could think of something witty to say back. Smiling, she called her mom.

"It's a go, Mom. Is Dad on board?"

"He's as excited as Liam is. You know him. If it's about science or history, he's all for it."

Mackenzie knew. Her parents had been teachers before they retired. Although her dad's subject was science, his interests were broad. She suspected her mother was just as excited. She loved to travel and had been ecstatic on their Italian holiday. That seemed so long ago. A dark period in their lives had come in between. She wished she could go to Greece with them.

Chapter Twenty-Five

As it turned out, Navy officials were happy to help. Their dolphin research program had been given years of progress by the Devereuxs' discoveries. Their relations with the dolphins were better than ever. They'd agreed to stop any experiments with dolphin-placed explosives, and they had sincerely apologized for any mishaps that injured dolphins in previous experiments.

Hearing that the daughter of one of their most valuable friends had been kidnapped made them as angry as it did Carter and Mackenzie. Irene thought that if she'd known they would have this attitude, she wouldn't have bothered the President. But protocol had been observed, so it was all good.

The Greek government wasn't quite so easy, but some gentle diplomatic persuasion brought them around. On the day that Dylan, Liu, the Andersons, and the Devereux children departed for their Athens holiday, word came through to Irene that the Navy had been given permission for a one-man sub to enter Cretan waters and help in the search for Carmen.

It was on its way from a Navy ship that was standing by just outside the twelve-mile limit when Merrybeth surfaced beside Carter's boat, with another plastic bag in her mouth. This one held a flash drive.

Carter was careful to back up his laptop's hard drive and disconnect the device from the internet before he put the flash drive in a port and brought up the video. The light was bright on a dolphin that looked sick to him but dim at the edges. He couldn't make anything out to help determine where the dolphin might be held, but assumed it was underground in a cave with water. She wouldn't be alive after all this time out of water.

He heard the captor tell the dolphin to speak to her mother, followed by a storm of whistles and squeaks. Carmen sounded distressed, but Carter recognized the captor's mistake. Surely, he couldn't understand Dolphinese. Carmen could be giving them her location. He connected the translation device and played the video again, cognizant that Merrybeth was waiting anxiously to hear what the flash drive held.

"Merrybeth, this shows Carmen alive, and the bad guy told her to talk to you. I'm going to translate what she said, so I can understand it too. And then I'll broadcast the original audio to you. Were you hearing any of this on ansible?"

"I don't know, Carter. I heard some things, but I couldn't make out much of it. Play the message."

Carter did as she asked, hearing the translation as he replayed the video.

"Mother, help me! He hurts me, and then he gives me just a few fish. I'm so hungry! My skin hurts. Come and get me, please!"

Frustrated, Carter asked, "If she said where she is, I didn't get it."

"She did not say. I don't think she knows. Carter, are the pictures good? Can you see her skin?"

"Sort of. The camera isn't close to her." He looked more closely, stopping the video to examine Carmen's skin. "It looks…rough," he said.

"She hasn't got much time. She's in land-water. It makes our skin fall off," Merrybeth said. Carter knew he was interpreting the rapid whistles through his own understanding of emotion, but he thought she was beginning to panic.

He struggled to understand what she meant by land-water. What Merrybeth had said about their skin sounded gruesome. He felt time was running out for Carmen. Then he figured it out. "Land-water. No salt?" he asked.

"Yes. No salt. Like in the cave."

Carter said, "Then I know where she might be. He's holding her somewhere underground, probably under this land nearby. The water underneath the land is what we call fresh water, no salt."

"Yes, that's it! But where?"

"Keep trying to triangulate her if you hear her. I'll contact the Navy. We need to find a way into that underground river that comes out of the crack in the cave you showed me." Something nudged Carter's brain, and he continued. "I meant to ask you. Why didn't you want me to climb out of the water when we were in there?"

"The Minotaurs. I did not want you to be eaten, Carter."

"You're telling me you believe the Minotaur is still alive, after all these centuries?"

"What is a century, Carter?"

"Thirty-six thousand, five hundred suns," he answered,

assuming the large number would be meaningless to the dolphin."

"Its descendants may be. Dolphins are still alive after many, many, many suns."

Carter couldn't argue with that. He also couldn't figure out how they could explore the cave system without taking the risk. He'd better consult with some Greek geologists, if he could find any that knew Crete's underground intimately, as well as any of his colleagues that specialized in the Classical sites. He knew many had searched for the Labyrinth, and claims were made for different sites. If this was one of them, surely someone would have explored it before.

"Merrybeth, a Navy submarine is coming, but I need to get to shore and talk with some people. Will you stay here and guide the sub to the tunnel entrance?"

"Yes, Carter. I will guide it. But will it fit inside the tunnel?"

"Maybe, maybe not. All we can do is try. But maybe there is another way into the same cave system. That's what I'm going to ask my colleagues. I'll be back as soon as I can."

Carter could have called, of course. He could also have done some online research. And in fact, he did both while his crew took the boat to the nearest harbor. But to talk with someone about a mythical creature being not only real, but alive after so many centuries... That required face-to-face. And he had to keep reminding himself that he wasn't searching for *a* Minotaur. He was searching for a race of them.

He also needed to consult with his wife about how such a thing could come to be. He knew it was possible to cross-breed the same species but didn't think it was possible to breed across genera, or families. He wasn't sure about the hierarchy of rank in biology. Put simply, he didn't think cattle and people could breed, despite the Biblical injunction against it. Then he wondered whether that injunction was because of the Minotaur. In any case, he didn't want to think about it. He wanted his wife to tell him if there was even the slightest possibility it could be true.

The kidnapping wasn't about Minotaurs on their side of the coin. It was about a madman who had Merrybeth's daughter for whatever twisted reason his insanity had concocted. Carter doubted anything he learned would convince the man his quest was futile, but he might be able to convince Merrybeth that he'd be perfectly safe exploring the cave system.

As they approached the harbor, Carter's last call before the boat docked was to Mackenzie.

"Hi, honey. Have you heard from the kids yet?"

"What? Oh – no. When are they due in?"

"I emailed their itinerary. You're distracted – what is it?"

"Can humans and cattle cross-breed?" he blurted.

"Carter, that's disgusting. No."

"Is there any possibility, no matter how off the wall, that a Minotaur could ever have existed."

"Well… It is off the wall. But gene splicing could possibly create some awful travesty of a *thing* that might have characteristics of both. Why?"

"Because Merrybeth has a racial memory of something that looks like the Minotaur myth. She's convinced they're real, and she doesn't want me to go into the caves where I think her daughter's being held. She's certain I'll be eaten."

"But cattle aren't carnivorous," Mackenzie objected.

"Never mind that. Humans are. If on the million-to-one chance some ancient civilization had the technology to do such a thing, and more than one was created, would they breed true?"

"I doubt it."

"So, in your educated opinion, even if there had been many in some distant past nightmare, there wouldn't be any now?"

"Carter, what are you asking me?"

"I'm asking if you can convince Merrybeth that I'll be perfectly safe if I go looking in that cave system for the underground river that will lead to her daughter."

"Don't ask me that. There are plenty of reasons you may not be safe that would have nothing to do with a Minotaur, or a whole herd of them. If you go exploring, you take someone experienced with you, do you hear me, Carter Devereux? Preferably someone with a military background. I know! Dylan's with the family. Take him."

"He needs to protect the kids and your parents."

"Who's in more danger, a spelunker without a buddy, or tourists in Athens? Besides, didn't you tell me the Navy is coming to help? As soon as you find the river, send him back to Athens and let them explore the river. Please, Carter. I'll feel better if Dylan is with you. But if not Dylan, at least take *someone* with you."

"You win. I'll talk to Dylan as soon as they land. I love you. And I'll call you as soon as I can."

Chapter Twenty-Six

On the way, Dylan had checked in with the local office of the Department of Antiquities to learn who had exploration permits on Crete this summer. He knew one by reputation, was personally acquainted with another, though he didn't get along with that one. A third was unknown to him. There was difficulty associated with approaching any of them, but he ranked them in order of the most likely to be of help and left the one he didn't get along with for last. That guy had openly ridiculed Carter's work. Telling him they were trying to find a guy who thought Minotaurs were real, with the help of a dolphin who agreed, would just add fuel to that fire. Carter didn't need the aggravation.

Though he knew one of them by reputation, Carter wasn't sure the knowledge was reciprocal. But at least that guy was reputable. He didn't know the other one, and he could have been just as knowledgeable, but Carter would start with the one he knew of.

Crete wasn't a small island. But he knew from his earlier inquiries where the dig was located. It would be too far to drive, so he chartered a helicopter. Arriving in such a dramatic fashion might impress the guy – who knew? It was the speed Carter was after.

He cautioned the pilot to land well away from the dig itself. He didn't want to start off on the wrong foot by blowing debris into the field of study. Consequently, he had a half-mile walk to the dig, and a greeting party waiting for him there.

"Dr. Connery, it's good to meet you," Carter said, his hand extended.

"What a surprise, Dr. Devereux! Please, call me Alan."

"I'm Carter. I'm surprised to find you know me by sight."

"Well, you have been in the news, Carter. To what do I owe this surprise visit?"

Connery's crew had gathered around them, and Carter wanted as few ears for this as possible. "Could we meet in private?" he asked.

"Of course! We can go to my tent-slash-field-office. Can I offer you some refreshment?"

"Perhaps some water."

Carter thought it was going well, so far. Whether it would continue that way would depend on how articulate he was, and how open-minded Alan Connery was.

Once they were settled in camp chairs inside the spacious tent that Connery used for his headquarters as well as for sleeping, Carter grasped the cold water bottle and held it to his forehead. "It's a hot one, isn't it?"

"Indeed. But I assume you didn't helicopter here for small talk. What can I do for you, Carter? Is this to do with some of your, mmmm, unorthodox research?"

"It is, actually. I'm glad you understand. That will save some time. I suppose you know that my wife and I have made some extraordinary discoveries about dolphins, yes?"

"I'd read that. But I'm afraid I don't know much about it."

"To make a long story short, we've discovered how to communicate with them, and that they are as intelligent as we are in many ways. They helped tremendously with the discovery of the second ancient library I found. Now they need a favor from us."

"How interesting! But again, how can I help?"

"I need to know how much exploration of the Labyrinth has been done in subterranean cave systems. Whether by you, or any you know of."

Connery sat back in his chair. "The Labyrinth! Well, there are opposing theories of where it was located, and both sites have been thoroughly studied. But that's fairly modern, compared to your usual studies. And what could it possibly have to do with dolphins?"

And here it is, Carter thought. *I'm going to have to tell him the whole story to get any help.* "Before I begin to explain that, let me preface it by saying I'm keeping an open mind, all right? It would help if you did, as well."

"Intriguing! Go on."

"The long and short of it is, one of our most valuable dolphin assets has a missing daughter. I'm sure this will be difficult for you to believe, but they have the same feeling for their offspring as we do. They also keep what we would call oral history, and they communicate not only with vocalization, but with mental images they can broadcast across thousands of miles."

"Fascinating! If it were anyone but you telling me these things, I wouldn't believe it."

"I'm grateful. And I'm afraid I'm about to tax your trust

in my veracity. We have reason to believe the younger dolphin has been kidnapped, as it were, by a man who is looking for evidence that the Minotaur of legend was real. Not only real, but also only one of many. An entire race of the things. Furthermore, the dolphins have a memory of just that."

"What? You're kidding!"

"I'm not. I'm on the fence about the dolphin's story, but it really doesn't matter. The fact is, this person believes it, and he's holding the daughter to force the mother to show him where they are. And she's determined he must be stopped, for the good of mankind. Land-humans, they call us," he added, softening his words with a smile.

"Well, since you put it that way, I understand why you're willing to help. What do you need from me?"

"I gather you haven't done any of this exploration yourself. Failing your personal knowledge, I need names of anyone who has, or might have."

Connery's face fell. "I'm so sorry. I haven't done any underground exploration, nor do I know of anyone who has. I hate to tell you you've made this trip for nothing, though. Would it help if I asked around? I'm sure you have better things to do than hunt down an obscure exploration effort."

"I'd be grateful if you could."

"Glad to. Give me your number and your email address. I'll be in touch when I learn anything."

Carter visited the archaeologist he didn't know, with the same results. He decided to forego the ridicule he'd face if he went to his nemesis. By the time he got back to the boat, Dylan and the others would have landed in Athens. He'd take the helicopter there, spend a little time with the kids and his in-laws, and then fly back with Dylan to start their exploration fresh in the morning.

He emailed Alan Connery, telling him of his plans and thanking him for his hospitality.

Carter's heart cracked a little when he had to leave the children with no more than a hug and half an hour's visit later that evening. Liam begged him to stay and show them an ongoing dig, but he was old enough to understand that Merrybeth needed him more. Beth cried, though. He made a vow to her that he would spend more time at home after this.

When he and Dylan got back, they immediately took the boat to his usual rendezvous spot with Merrybeth. There was no reason to stay twelve miles offshore, now that he had permission from the Greek government to do whatever it took to rescue Carmen, but this was where Merrybeth expected him until they made other arrangements.

When he got there, Merrybeth was waiting. She told him the sub had been there, and they'd gone to the tunnel entrance, but the sub was too large to enter. "It wouldn't have made it through the narrowest part anyway," she reported. "What did you learn?"

"Nothing, I'm afraid. Except that Mackenzie doesn't think the Minotaurs could have bred true, so there's little danger I'll meet one in the caves. Do you remember Dylan? He's here with me, and tomorrow we'll get out of the water inside the cave and see if we can find the rest of the river, and where the bad guy is holding Carmen. Then we'll figure out how to get her out. He got her in, somehow, so

I'm thinking there's another entrance somewhere. We'll just follow the river until we find it."

Merrybeth dove, and she didn't surface for almost five minutes. Carter didn't know what to make of it. When she returned, she brought two other dolphins with her.

"You are a good friend, Carter. You are putting yourself and your land-human friend, Dylan, in danger for us. These are Carmen's older brothers. They will search the edges of the underwater land for other openings and try to find you inside the land. They can help if you find Carmen."

"That's good, Merrybeth. We must rest before we go in. We'll start as soon as tomorrow's sun rises."

With the dolphin brothers exploring the shoreline, the sub standing by to navigate up the river if they could find a way in, and Dylan to assist him, Carter hoped they had enough time to find Carmen before she succumbed to illness from being kept in fresh water. But he also felt it was worth a try to acquiesce to the kidnapper's demands.

"Merrybeth, won't you consider leading this bad man into the cave system? Perhaps Dylan and I could capture him there, and force him to tell us where Carmen is?"

"He has already been there, Carter. He knows the Minotaur is not there. If I knew of another place to lead him, I would."

"All right. Keep it in mind in case your sons find another entrance. Are you keeping track of where he goes after he contacts us?"

"We have tried. He is fast, though."

"What do you mean?"

"He can swim faster than we can. He loses us."

Carter thought about it. "How is that possible? No human, I mean land-human, could swim faster than you can. Does he have something to help him?"

"He has a thing like a boat, but it pulls him underwater. He has the things you call flippers on his feet, but he doesn't use tanks. Not even in the tunnel, where he couldn't take his boat thing."

Now Carter was doubly confused. He needed to talk to Mackie again, right away. What would give a man the ability to swim through an underwater tunnel that took a dolphin fifteen minutes to swim through, without a SCUBA tank?

Chapter Twenty-Seven

Ahab watched from nearby the next morning, when Devereux's boat moved from its usual location to within a quarter-mile of the tunnel entrance. He observed Devereux and another man tumble into the water with SCUBA equipment, and assumed they were headed for the cave.

It wouldn't matter. He'd sealed the opening that led to the rest of the cave system, so they wouldn't be able to find the pool where the underground river had backed up against the crack that let only a small trickle through. The only other way in was in the small bay at the edge of the park, miles from this part of the shoreline.

Instead of waiting for them, he decided he'd try to find out who the other man was. Ahab wasn't worried about the sub. It wouldn't fit in either entrance to the river, even if they found the other one. Apparently, the dolphins didn't know about it either, and in any case, the river led through some tunnels that were completely filled with water. He'd had to get creative to get the young female through them without drowning her.

Ahab swam to his yacht and motored to shore. He had some investigation to do.

Before he'd left London, he'd made a point of learning who would be on Crete during the summer break. Now he had use for that information. His first visit was to Alan Connery, a prominent Crete scholar. To get to the dig, he took a commuter train to the nearest town and then rented an SUV. He arrived at noon and was warmly welcomed. As an alumnus of Connery's college, Ahab was acquainted with the man, though he'd never worked with him.

After touring Connery's dig, Ahab went with him to his tent, where Connery offered him a cold soda, assuming he was Muslim. Ahab didn't correct the assumption. Connery asked him about his studies.

"Oh, I'm not here for a dig, much as I'd like to be. I'm just enjoying some sport fishing," Ahab said.

"Surely, you're taking in some of the ancient sites, though?" Connery asked. "I'm sorry, I don't know your particular interest. What do you study when you aren't on holiday?"

"Oh, yes. I have explored Crete many times. My thesis was a comparison of the various sites claimed to be that of the ancient Labyrinth."

"How interesting! I entertained a man the other day who was looking for experts on the Labyrinth. You should get in touch. His name is Carter Devereux. Do you know of his work?"

"Yes. In fact, I worked with him on the Alboran site when it was first discovered. I'll give him whatever help I can. Do you know how to reach him?"

Connery gave Ahab the email address, told him he thought Devereux had gone to Athens, and then excused himself to get back to work. Ahab thanked him for his hospitality.

He had no need of visiting the others now. He wasn't certain what use he'd make of Devereux's contact information, but having it would come in useful somehow. He was sure of it. But why had he gone to Athens? Ahab suspected it was to pick up the man he'd been with earlier.

Ahab's next task was to discover what Devereux had meant by 'his leaders'. He'd heard the phrase as Devereux conversed with the dolphin mother about the Minotaur. It didn't make sense. Ahab had learned Devereux was quite wealthy, but it sounded as if he worked for someone else. Why would he do that? Using the same methods by which he'd learned of the wealth, Ahab found clues, but no specifics.

From what he could tell, there must be a group that sent Devereux on his explorations. He turned up some speculation on conspiracy theory blogs that both Devereux and his wife worked for a shadowy government agency. Little by little, he pieced together the clues until he had a good idea who the other man was who'd been with Devereux. Now he only needed to know where he'd come from, but he suspected it was Athens.

There weren't many places to charter a helicopter on Crete, so it didn't take long to find the one who'd taken Devereux to Athens and brought him and another man back. Ahab told the charter operator he may want to make the same trip soon and went to his rented villa to think about it.

What would he find in Athens? And in so populous a place, how would he find it? The most obvious answer was airline records. Ahab knew the airlines wouldn't give him any information, but their reservation system could be hacked. The only problem was, he didn't know how to do it. He'd read the way to find hackers was on the Dark Web, and a little more research told him how to get in. He had plenty of grant money, so he took the plunge.

Only a few hours later, he had the information he needed. The name Devereux turned up – not on an airline database, but in airport records of private jets landing. The hacker had gone a step further to learn what ground transportation had met the jet, and where the passengers had been taken. From there, he'd learned the names of the passengers. An older couple, a young couple, and two children named Liam and Beth Devereux.

Ahab was neither a religious man, nor a superstitious one. But if he had been, he'd have assumed the Devereux children had been handed to him in some cosmic plan. They were the perfect leverage to get Carter Devereux off his back and allow him to deal with the dolphins without interference.

Foregoing the helicopter because he couldn't risk the questions when he brought two sedated children back with him, he decided to take the yacht to Athens instead. It would be about a two-day turnaround, assuming he could snatch the kids easily. More if not. Before he left, he decided he had to feed his captive dolphin, so she wouldn't starve before he got back to his task.

Liam was too excited to walk sedately by his grandparents as they approached the Parthenon. He'd been afraid they wouldn't be able to go out and see the ruins until Dylan got back, but his grandparents had persuaded his mom that they could watch over Beth and him. He didn't know why they needed Dylan, anyway. It had been more than a year since they'd been in any danger, and Dad had taken care of all the bad guys.

"Liam, don't get too far ahead," Grandpa called.

"I won't!" he called over his shoulder. "Beth, come on!"

His little sister was dragging her heels. She was more interested in all the people around them, and the many languages they were speaking. Recently, Bly had been teaching her a few words of Hopi, and had been teaching Liam, too, but he didn't hear anyone speaking that. He turned and went back to her, taking her hand.

She was talking to a man who was smiling at her, but Liam thought the smile looked fake.

"Come on, Beth."

She resisted him. "Are you a Hopi?" she asked the man.

Liam saw the man had brown skin, like Bly and Ahote, but he didn't look like a Hopi. He started to tell Beth to leave the man alone, but suddenly the man bent down and picked Beth up. That wasn't okay. He kicked at the man, but suddenly he was in the air, under the man's arm, and they were moving fast through the crowd.

"Grandma! Grandpa!" he cried. He couldn't see them anywhere. And he was sleepy. Beth looked like she was already asleep...

Mary was sobbing into the phone. "It happened so fast! The children were a few yards ahead of us, and your dad had just warned Liam not to get too far ahead. We lost sight of them in the crowd for less than half a minute, Mackenzie. Thirty seconds! Tom thought he heard Liam call to us, but..."

She pictured Mackenzie on the other end of the call, trying to remain calm, and nearly broke down. It was all her fault. *She* had told Mackenzie they could be trusted with the kids. *She* had persuaded her to let them take the kids to Athens in the first place.

"Yes. Your dad is talking to them now. A few people reported seeing a man carrying two children and moving fast, but the children weren't struggling. Liam would struggle, wouldn't he? Can you reach Carter? I think we need him and Dylan more than the dolphins do."

Chapter Twenty-Eight

Mackenzie was in mental and emotional agony. If she hadn't persuaded Carter to take Dylan, this never would have happened. If she hadn't let them talk her into going, her parents and kids would never have been in Athens in the first place. She tried to compose herself so she could call Carter and get him headed to Athens, but each time she started to dial the phone, a fresh round of sobs overwhelmed her. Her babies!

Twenty minutes after she'd received the call from her mother, she was still fighting to gain control over her emotions, when Keeva arrived, her youngest offspring trailing her. She took her cell phone and went out to the deck, where she could be close to the wolves when she called Carter. Keeva came closer and leaned against her leg. The pups settled down next to her, but the little female whined until Keeva nosed her and she quieted.

A few minutes later, Mackenzie felt strong enough to call Carter. For this, she had to face him, so she made it a video call. When he answered, she could see he was on the boat. "Carter, thank Heaven I caught you before your dive," she began.

It broke her heart to watch his face change as she relayed the devastating news. "I'm so sorry, Carter. This is all my fault."

"No," he said strongly. "It isn't. It's no one's fault but the bastard who took them, and I'll make him pay if it's the last thing I do."

"How are you going to leave Merrybeth, with her daughter missing, too?" Mackenzie asked.

Thousands of miles away, Carter had a flash of insight. "It's related," he said. "It has to be. Mackie, do you trust me?"

"With my life," she said. "With our children's lives."

"I'm going to send Dylan back to Athens to help find Liam and Beth. I'm going to continue to look for Carmen. I have a strong feeling that if we find either our kids or Merrybeth's daughter, we'll have the key to find the other."

"But Carter, shouldn't you go after our kids and leave Dylan to search for Carmen?"

"With all my heart, I want to. But here's the thing. I'm emotionally involved with our kids' case. The police won't let me near it, and for good reason. I'd just get in the way. Dylan is the better choice. On top of that, I'm a better diver and spelunker than Dylan. More experience. I'll find someone here to help me, I promise, but I'm the better choice for here."

Carter's logic felt hollow to him. He was maintaining tight control over his emotions, though. Panic and rage would do his children no good. He remembered when he'd thought Mackenzie and Liam were dead, and he remem-

169

bered who'd had them. If his efforts had left any of the Nabateans at large, this was all *his* fault.

"Mackie, I need to get things lined up. Let me call you back."

"All right. But I'm coming over there."

"Please, wait until I have some time to think and plan. Stay there until I say, okay?"

"Carter…"

"Please, Mackie. I can't worry about you, too. Get hold of Sean and tell him we need his team. And stay put for now."

"All right. Let me know what else I can do."

It didn't feel right to Mackenzie not to be with her family at a time like this. But Carter was right. Running to them without a plan in place wasn't the right thing to do. She'd do as he asked. With Keeva and the pups pacing her, she got into the electric cart and headed for Tala. A call would have been faster, but she needed a hug.

Sean greeted her as she entered the gate at Tala. He'd been on the phone with Dylan, who told him Carter was calling Mackenzie. After ending that call, he'd called Irene, whose phone was busy. Then he'd studied his network for the best team to send to Athens. Before he got the first call made, he'd been alerted by the electronic motion sensors that someone was on the way. With almost everyone else gone, he'd personally gone to greet the visitor. He was surprised it had taken her so long to get there.

Mackenzie stumbled off the cart, and fell into his arms, sobbing again.

"Mackenzie, will you be all right?"

"The children," she gasped. Keeva, only a pace behind her, came and leaned into her leg again. Mackenzie reached down and grasped the wolf's thick fur to ground herself and took a deep breath. She stepped back a pace and stood up straight. "I'm sorry, Sean. Let me start again."

With that, she related the news, and that Carter had asked for a team to join Dylan in Athens.

"I know, Mackenzie. Dylan called. Everyone's gone, except for the skeleton crew guarding Freydis. But I'm already on it. I'll be sending out an emergency call and have the others rendezvous in Athens. I'm trying to reach Irene, too. Carter needs some backup with him."

"I'd appreciate it if you sent someone who's experienced in SCUBA diving and spelunking to him. At least one," she answered. "Thank you."

Sean reached for her and pulled her in for a brotherly hug. "I'm your man for Crete. Ex-SEAL, remember? We'll get them all back, Mackenzie. You can count on us."

Mackenzie felt better, but a knot of terror still resided in her stomach. "I know you will. I just hope it's before they're hurt... or – "

Sean interrupted. "Don't go there. I'll have a team in Athens before the end of the day."

Mackenzie nodded, touched Sean's arm in thanks, and then climbed back on the cart and headed for home, the wolves following. Keeva's presence in her mind had kept her sane during what had previously been the darkest days of her life. She could only hope it would be the same this time. The children needed her to remain strong for them.

Sean finally got through to Irene. She told him she'd heard first from Dylan, and then from Carter. She'd called Bill Griffin, who went straight to the President and convinced him to clear the way for their combined operation with the Greek authorities. She expected cooperation – it seemed POTUS had immediately made a call to his Greek counterpart while Bill was still in the Oval Office. The man had not been able to get a word in edgewise for a solid five minutes and had only stammered a nervous agreement to cooperate when POTUS got through enumerating the consequences to Greece if the Devereux children had one hair on their heads harmed.

"I wish I'd been there," Irene told Sean. "Bill told me that the Chief of Staff called the Secretary of State when he first told POTUS what he wanted. And *he* almost had a heart attack when he walked in just in time to hear POTUS saying 'I want it very clear that MY people are in charge of this investigation. Your police, military, and secret services will report to them. And we will leave no stone unturned. Is that clear, Mr. President?' Then, after he'd hung up, SecState said, 'Mr. President, you can't speak to the head of a sovereign nation that way.' And POTUS told him, 'I'm the damn President of the most powerful nation on earth, and no damn *sovereign nation* is going to stand by and let our kids be kidnapped. Greece is part of NATO, and the allied forces saved their sorry asses during World War II. What's more, the USA and the UK were the ones who managed to keep Greece out of the Soviet Union when Europe was divided after the war. So, I damned well expect them to cooperate. Dismissed.' Sam Grant would be so proud of him!"

Sean shook his head in admiration. "We're going to be able to work with him. I'm just happy that's out of the way and I didn't have to do it." He chuckled grimly, the first time he'd seen any modicum of humor in anything since he'd heard from Dylan that morning. He'd have taken a different approach, but the President's worked just fine for him. "Who are you sending with me, Irene?"

"You're going where, to Athens? Or Crete?"

"Crete. Carter needs my SEAL experience with him. We could use a couple of agents to watch our backs, handle things onshore, and set up standing comms links with Dylan's crew in Athens. I'm sending everyone we can spare to him."

"My best comms people are with the FBI. I'll send one to Athens and another to Crete, with you. I'll have the rest ready when you get here. How are you getting here?"

"The milk run came in this morning. I've detained the plane here, since Carter's jet is in Athens. I'll be boarding as soon as I've made a few other calls. What's our transport?"

"Air Force One is standing by. The President insisted. And I'm sending a faster military plane that your landing strip can handle, to pick you up."

"Roger that. Give me an hour."

"They'll be there when you're ready."

Sean called on his own network of operatives. Not everyone in Executive Advantage was lodged at Tala, of course, and assets belonging to allies were available throughout the world. Every one of them was dedicated and ready to drop everything at a moment's notice to answer the call. The Devereuxs were among the most valuable assets A-Echelon and the United States had. No expense was too much to retrieve their kids for them.

Within hours, operatives began to gather in Athens, and Irene O'Connell, horrified at the news the children were at risk, had smoothed the way for them to assist the Greek police. A massive effort to locate anyone who'd been on the Acropolis on the morning of the kidnapping was under way. Executive Advantage operatives would assist in the interviews and accompany police to run down any leads.

Meanwhile, Sean was on his way to Crete.

———

Mackenzie called her mother back. "Sean's team is there or on the way. Dylan will be there as soon as he can to lead them. Do you and Dad want to come home and wait with me?" She had accepted Carter's argument that she could do no good on site and needed to stay at home where she would be safe to wait for the kids to be rescued and sent to her.

"No, dear. We're the ones who lost them. We will bring them home to you," her mother said stoutly.

"Mom, it isn't your fault. I felt the same way, but Carter told me it's no one's fault but the kidnapper's. You and Dad should come home."

"I just can't… can't leave them here," her mom answered, sobbing. "They'll be so scared. I have to be here."

She didn't say she thought Mackenzie should be, too, but Mackenzie heard the message loud and clear anyway. "Then I'll be there as soon as I can, too. I'll just have to make Carter understand."

Before she started to make travel arrangements, she decided to wait for Carter's next call. Meanwhile, she needed to inform her research people what was going on. She headed on foot to the lab. Keeva was still with her, and still trailing Keeva was the little female, still whining.

Mackenzie stopped in her tracks. "Keeva, does your little girl know where my little girl is?"

Keeva just looked at her with wise wolf eyes and leaned on her leg again. Mackenzie chose to take it as a sign. She squatted on her heels and held her arms out. To her surprise, the young wolf came to her and allowed itself to be hugged. Mackenzie hoped and prayed that Beth could feel it.

She got up and hurried to the lab, feeling confident her children were alive, somehow. She'd come to trust the connection with Keeva, and she felt that the little female would be in even more distress if her connection with Beth were cut off. She interpreted the whining as the young wolf knowing Beth was in danger, but she was convinced it would be howling if Beth were... *gone*.

Once inside the lab, Mackenzie sent the first person she saw to gather the others and meet her in the conference room. With as much dignity as she could muster, she explained what was going on and that she'd be leaving as soon as possible to join her parents in Athens to wait for news. Then she asked for a status report.

One by one, the scientists reported that there was nothing likely to need her attention for the next few days. The veterinarian reported that Methuselah was still showing signs of increased vigor and antisocial behavior, even though two of the three respirocyte generators had been removed. He still had no way of knowing where the other one had migrated after escaping the mesh.

"You know that we're eventually going to have to find out, don't you?" she asked him gently.

He hung his head. "I know."

There was nothing more to say. With the best wishes of her team ringing in her ears, Mackenzie returned home to wait for Carter's call.

Chapter Twenty-Nine

When Ahab had captured Carmen, he'd had the luxury of time, or so he thought. He'd kept her in the cave she was guarding at first, after luring her into the tunnel and then stunning her. He'd expected to kill her, and that was all right with him, because he assumed she was guarding it because it contained something valuable or dangerous. His imagination didn't deviate from his fixation. Since, to him, the Minotaur was both valuable and dangerous, his logic dictated that the Minotaur must be in the cave.

It was a bitter disappointment when he didn't find one there.

He'd returned to the tunnel and pulled her into the cave, meaning to pantomime his demands, since she clearly understood his hand gestures and mimicked human responses. But nothing he could do or say to her in the cave produced the response he wanted.

On the day he'd overheard Carter Devereux's conversation with the mother, he'd known that though she wasn't valuable to him as a guide, her value as a hostage was immense. Hearing that the mother dolphin and Devereux would enter the cave the next day, he had stunned the dolphin again to control her, and pulled her out through the tunnel.

With the young one tethered in a net beside the yacht, he'd done some research to see if he could get her through the other river entrance, even though some of the completely flooded areas would tax her ability to control her breathing for the time required. In the early morning hours of the next day, he left her tethered to his yacht and swam to shore.

A stroll through the back streets and alleys of the town netted him a meeting with an unsavory character who, for a price and with a wait of a couple of hours, got him what he needed to sedate the dolphin. When he returned to the yacht, he injected her with a dose of ketamine that he assumed would put both sides of her brain to sleep. Then he fashioned a makeshift oxygen supply and fastened it over the dolphin's blowhole.

Towing her through the underground river was more difficult than he'd thought it would be. In spots, the passage was so narrow that he was afraid the mask would come off her, and without her help in propelling herself, it took him longer than it had when he was alone. But he'd managed.

Now, he was forced to do the same with the Devereux children. He didn't particularly care if both survived the trip through the river, so long as one did. However, since he couldn't guess which one was most likely to survive it, he prepared them both.

They were so much smaller than he that he thought they would make it through the tight spots with SCUBA tanks. However, they wouldn't be able to swim fast enough to avoid running out of air. He'd have to tow them, like he did the dolphin. This time, he'd use the Sea-Bob, but in some places he'd have to shut off its motor and push it ahead of him to fit through the narrow spots. And he'd give them some of the ketamine to sedate them and slow their respiration. Presumably, at least the smaller one, the little girl, would have enough air in the tanks to make it.

Liam woke to utter darkness. Wherever he was, it smelled like the caves on Freydis. It took him a while to remember what had happened, and when he did, the memory jerked him all the way to full consciousness with a jolt of fear. Where was Beth?

He tried calling her at first. His throat was sore, and his mouth was dry, though he could feel dampness in the air. He widened his eyes to be sure they were open. Though there was no light at all, he was certain they were. "Beth," he called again.

No answer.

Liam tried moving his arms, and to his relief, they were not tied. With that experiment successful, he moved his legs. Then he sat up. He was free, but he couldn't see his hand in front of his face. The sound of moving water nearby made him cautious. He rolled to his hands and knees and crawled toward where he thought it was coming from, slowly, so as not to fall into whatever the water was.

Before he reached the water, his hand landed on something that wasn't rock or dirt. He felt back and forth. "Beth?"

A small moan startled him, but realization he'd probably found his sister was close on the heels of his fright. He felt for her face and began patting her.

"Beth, wake up."

Just before he'd begun to despair of waking her, she stirred. A few moments later, he felt when she came awake, because she recoiled and gave a little scream.

"Beth, it's me. Liam," he added, in case she didn't recognize his voice.

"Liam! You scared me," she said in a voice he recognized as indignant. "Turn on the light!"

"Beth, listen. Do you remember the man that picked you up?"

"What man?"

"We were on the Acropolis, remember? And you stopped to talk to a stranger." He didn't even try to keep it from sounding like an accusation. They both knew better than to talk to strangers, but she had, and this is what happened.

"I..." Beth's voice faltered. "He asked me where my daddy was," she explained.

"He grabbed you, and when I tried to stop him, he grabbed me, too," Liam pointed out.

"I'm sorry, Liam. I won't do it again. Can we go home now?"

Her voice went up at the end of her sentence, and Liam knew that meant she was about to cry. Then he heard her sniffle. Liam sometimes thought his little sister was annoying, and he was mad at her for getting them into this situation. But he was the big brother. It was up to him to comfort her and to figure out what to do. He pulled her to a sitting position and put his arms around her.

"Don't worry, Beth. Dad will find us. And I'll protect you until he does."

Beth's little arms went around his neck. "Liam, I'm scared."

"I know. Stay right here. I have to try to find the entrance to this cave."

"How do you know it's a cave?"

"It smells like a cave. And if you'll listen quietly, you can hear the water running. I'll bet it's an underground river. Ahote told me about those."

The children were both quiet for a minute. Then Beth said, in a very small voice, "Be careful Liam. Don't fall in the river."

"I won't."

Liam had to pull his sister's hands away when he started crawling around again. She'd grabbed his shirt and wouldn't let go. But she hadn't grabbed him again after he reassured her he'd be right back.

He was beginning to imagine he could see in the darkness. There was a faint glow in the cave, he thought. He even imagined it glinting off the water a few feet away. He sat back on his heels again and rubbed his eyes. There was something dark in the water.

"I don't believe in monsters," he said stoutly.

"I do," echoed Beth.

"Shh."

Liam looked up and realized it wasn't his imagination. The cave was glowing, an eerie green like in illustrations in some books he'd read. He didn't care where the glow came from, he was just grateful he could see, even a little bit. But he still didn't want to risk getting to his feet and stumbling over something or misjudging the edge of the water. He crawled toward the dark shape.

The shape was draped with a net, and it was in the water. He put his hand out tentatively, ready to snatch it back if the shape moved. When he touched it, the shape suddenly thrashed inside the net, and he withdrew his hand quickly. The shape started making noises.

He'd heard those noises before. Was it…?

Beth spoke. "Is that a dolphin, Liam? Tell it to send a message to Mom."

Carmen was weak with hunger and trying to escape the net. It had been a long time since she'd felt strong enough to try to signal her mother, and she didn't know if the signal could reach anyone from this dark place.

And then she'd heard land-human speech. It sounded different, much higher pitched than the land-humans' voices she'd heard before. She didn't understand some of the words, and she struggled to think why. When the small hand touched her, she'd recoiled instinctively, but when she'd recovered from the fright, she knew what was happening.

These were land-human children in this place with her. She began to tell them to run away, that there was a bad land-human here with them. But they couldn't understand her, of course. So, she used the last of her energy to send as strong a signal as she could.

Chapter Thirty

Dylan was the first to arrive on the scene in Athens. He went straight to the hotel where Liu waited along with Carter's in-laws. Assuring them he was on the job, he then went to arrange lodging for the operatives Sean was sending, along with a larger room where they could meet.

As soon as they arrived, Dylan laid out the mission. "Okay, listen up! This is an Executive Advantage mission. You all understand that you report to me, correct?"

Nods and murmurs of assent all around assured him he didn't need to further establish his authority. He'd worked with a few of these guys before, including some SAS operators he'd greeted by name when they arrived. If there was any question, they'd let the others know he was, modestly, a good leader. His annual evals usually said 'excellent'. He would involve them in decisions, but ultimately the buck stopped with him.

He gave them a brief overview of the circumstances. Then, "Okay. Our first task is to find the children and secure them. Once they are safe, I'll assign who will stay

The Labyrinth of Minos

here to guard them and their grandparents, and the rest of you will be with me to track down the bastard that took them. We have the full cooperation of the Athens police."

"Do we have arrest authority?" an MI5 agent asked.

"We do. However, we are also authorized to use deadly force if necessary to save the kids. That is not the outcome we want. I'm sure you're all aware we want to question the perp and find out why he took the kids. But keep your side-arms ready."

"This is not a kidnapping for ransom?"

"We don't know, yet, but no ransom demand has been communicated."

"I don't mean to criticize, mate," another began. "But how'd he get by you?"

"Unfortunately, I wasn't here. I was called away on another kidnapping." He didn't add that it was a dolphin who'd been kidnapped. That was need-to-know.

"Related?"

Dylan thought for a minute, then slowly said, "Don't see how it could be, but I'll check it out. Everyone clear on their assignments?"

The MI5 agent who'd spoken answered crisply. "Take point on questioning wits. The Athens police will give us a list. Get a description and circulate to all European law-enforcement agencies. Issue a BOLO. Get the kids back, nail the bastard."

"That sums it up. I'll be right behind you, as soon as I've checked out the possible link." He dismissed the team and immediately called Carter.

Carter was at the small airport where he'd taken off in the helicopter to pick up Dylan two days before. While waiting for Sean's arrival, he was playing the blame-game with himself for taking Dylan away from the kids, pacing the small lobby like a caged animal. As much as he told himself he wasn't at fault, he couldn't make as convincing an argument to himself as he'd made to Mackie. The what-ifs were killing him.

Barely suppressing the urge to put his fist through the nearest solid argument, he almost didn't hear his phone. When he answered, Dylan spoke without a greeting.

"Carter, one of the team members here has offered a theory. Is there any way this kidnapping could be related to the dolphin's?"

"Maybe. I don't see how, yet. I mean, I don't even know how anyone could know those kids are mine, much less that my kids would be in Athens without a bodyguard. But he's right. I do think they are." Carter didn't realize he'd wounded his friend until he'd waited for a few seconds without an answer. "Aw, hell, Dylan, don't blame yourself. I'm the one who pulled you away."

"I know, but I shouldn't have let you," Dylan answered.

"Hey, stop. Blaming ourselves isn't getting the kids back. So, if there's any merit in the theory, how would it have worked?" Carter asked, too distraught to think for himself.

"You got a ransom demand from the guy who has the dolphin, am I right?" Dylan asked.

"Of sorts. He wants Merrybeth to show him where the Minotaur supposedly is."

"How does he even know that Merrybeth would know? And how did he know to send you the note?"

Carter stopped pacing. "I don't…"

"He'd have to have heard you two talking, right? You were broadcasting the translation device, not using a headset?"

"Yeah."

"So, he knows you can talk to the dolphins, and he knows you're helping her. How would he know?"

The answer flashed for Carter like a bolt of lightning. "He was there. He heard us."

"What else could he have heard?"

"Damn, Dylan, I don't know, but I left a trail a blind man could follow."

"What do you mean?"

"I chartered that helicopter from a local, and I didn't caution him not to tell anyone where I went, or anything. I'll bet he heard us talking about the kids, on the way back. If the bad actor who has Carmen questioned him…"

"I think you'd better find out. When's Sean due?"

"Any minute."

"Okay, well, I'm going to give the police this information. Don't know how it will help, but let's keep each other posted. If it's the same guy, he's likely to get you the ransom demand instead of anyone here. Your in-laws are practically sitting on the phone, by the way."

"I pray this is what it is. The worst thing possible would be a random sick-o." Carter was doing his best not to think of the remains of the child in London, without success. That had been random, he was sure. Random kidnappings weren't about ransom, and the victims didn't last long, usually. He forced his thoughts away from that outcome. "Here's Sean's plane, now," he said. "Holy crap, it's Air Force One! Gotta go."

Carter rushed outside to gape at the plane. Sean was the first one down the steps, but he was followed by a couple of the Executive Advantage people he'd met and a dozen or so others he didn't recognize. The President was not among them, which was only a surprise because they were exiting his plane. Every face was set in hard lines, some grim, some just determined. Sean's expression warmed as he recognized Carter and raised an arm in greeting.

As he greeted Sean, Carter said, "Who are all these people?"

"You know my guys. This is FBI agent Dan Simmons, our comms expert. His opposite is headed to Athens to join Dylan's team. They'll set up a link for instant messaging." He continued, introducing a cadre of four SEALs who would be guarding their underwater operations, a couple of CIA operatives to handle land-based investigations on Crete, and an administrative type from the State department.

Carter said, "I'm overwhelmed. Thank you all!"

One of the SEALs stepped forward. "I have kids, sir. This could have happened to any of us. We'll get your kids back, and that dolphin, too. We'll make the bastard regret the day he was born."

Carter snapped his fingers. "Sean, I've been thinking. Dylan's right. If this is related, he's going to deliver the ransom note for my kids the same way he did for Merrybeth's daughter. We've got to get out there."

Sean nodded. "Agreed. These guys have all been briefed, and they know what to do." He singled out one of the Executive Advantage men. "You're in charge in my absence. You guys get to work." To Carter, he added, "I agree with Dylan. You know what we always say. We don't like coincidences."

"They do happen, but I'm with you. I don't think this is one. And that gives me hope."

On the way to the coordinates where he always met Merrybeth, Carter noticed several dolphins trying to keep pace with the boat and had the captain slow down. He set up the translation device and hailed them. When they came closer, he recognized two of them as Merrybeth's sons, who were supposed to be looking for another entrance to the cave system.

"Have you found anything?" he asked.

One of the dolphins whistled, but the translation device didn't have a reference. Carter thought for a second it was a malfunction, and then realized the dolphin had given his name. Carter quickly assigned the whistle the name Jasper.

He said, "It's good to see you, Jasper. Have you found anything?"

"Not yet, Carter. Our mother said to tell you she is hunting. She will be with you soon."

"Thanks! I'll wait in the usual place."

With that, the dolphins peeled off and headed back in the other direction.

Sean asked, "Is that unusual? Getting a message from one dolphin by way of another?"

"Kind of. We don't talk to new dolphins that often, and it's always a stretch to discover again that they can understand us without the translation device. I envy them that. Wish we could still understand them without it."

"How'd you know his name was Jasper?"

"I didn't. You know each dolphin has a unique identifier. As unique as our fingerprints. Remember, the device records the sonogram – the sound's wave pattern – and we assign a name we can pronounce to it. Then the device uses the wave pattern when it translates our words. We think the dolphins then adapt to hearing the name we call them by, even though it sounds nothing like their whistle. But they're hearing both together – the translator's version of Dolphinese and at the same time, our words. Because their hearing is so much more sensitive to the uniqueness of their whistles, they're learning more of our language –stuff they've never been exposed to before – much faster than we're learning theirs."

"Oh, I see. They're still calling Mackenzie Sunhead?"

"That's just my doing. They call her that because of her red hair – you knew that – and it makes me smile when I hear it, so I didn't program the translator to convert it to her name. Of course, Merrybeth calls me by a unique whistle that's assigned my name. We all have whistle-names they've given us, just like we've given them human names. Land-human," he corrected himself again. "I had to hand-program the translator to coordinate them."

"Cool."

They'd arrived where they were to meet Merrybeth, and soon after, she arrived as well.

"Good hunting today?" Carter called to her.

"Enough," she said. "I did not hunt for two suns. But today we had news. Carmen is alive!"

Carter experienced an adrenaline rush. "Could you tell where she was?" He assumed the evidence was an ansible transmission.

"She is somewhere in the land," Merrybeth answered. "We heard her and used your triangulation idea. But we cannot reach her." She made a mournful sound that the translation device didn't recognize.

"If our theory is correct, Merrybeth, she's actually *under* the land. Remember Sean?" he asked, drawing Sean to the rail for Merrybeth's visual identification. He is a strong swimmer and a fierce fighter. Together, we are going to explore the cave and find Carmen. We think my children may be with her."

"She didn't say," Merrybeth answered. "But I will ask her. If she can signal again, I will tell you."

Carter experienced another adrenaline surge. *Of course! If they're in the same place...* But he knew that was a big 'if'.

Chapter Thirty-One

On the way to the coordinates where they met Merrybeth, Carter had checked his email for the first time in the past few hours. He'd almost forgotten his visit to Alan Connery, so he was surprised to see a reply to his email.

In it, he learned that there was a Labyrinth expert vacationing on Crete, by the name of Ahab Bashar. The name sounded vaguely familiar, but Carter couldn't place why. Connery had provided contact information, but before Carter could compose an email to Bashar, they'd arrived on the scene. The excitement of Merrybeth's news had driven the email out of his mind.

Then he'd taken Sean to the coordinates just beyond the tunnel entrance that led to the cave where Merrybeth had cautioned him not to get out.

"It's a long swim. Merrybeth towed me the first time, and even at her speed it took about fifteen minutes. I'd say we'll take two or three times as long, unless dolphins tow us. I'm concerned. We can get closer to the entrance now, so the tanks may be enough to get us in and back out of there," he explained, "But I ran out of air before we got back to the boat."

"Not a problem. I brought rebreathers for both of us," Sean answered. "We can get a tow if you want, but we'll be able to stay underwater for a couple of hours. Should be enough to get us in and out, if we dive from close enough."

"Some of the tunnel is pretty tight," Carter cautioned.

"Understood. I brought the most compact model that could support that amount of time. Could have bought us more time, but the tanks would have been bulkier. Dylan said you'd told him the tunnel was tight."

"I'm losing it, Sean. I know I have to be on top of my game, but there's only one other time in my life I've been this worried... I feel like my brain is wrapped in wool. Like I'm missing something."

"I know. I've got your back, buddy. You're still one of the smartest people I know, and you know that's saying something. Plus, you've got a whole lot of other very smart people on your team. We'll get them back."

"Are we ready to dive, then?"

"Soon as we gear up."

Inside the cave a little while later, Carter surfaced and pulled his helmet mask off. Sean surfaced behind him. They'd decided to leave the dolphins behind, since they weren't sure how long they'd be out of the water.

"You sure we can get back into this stuff?" Carter asked.

"One hundred percent," Sean answered confidently. "Let's see what we can find out about this place."

From the bag affixed to his dive belt, he pulled two headlamps and shoes more suitable for walking on the rough cave floor. From his, Carter pulled out his shoes, two bottles of water, and a sealed plastic bag with a couple of energy bars. They climbed out of the water, peeled out of their wetsuits and other gear, and sat on the rocky floor of the cave to have their snack before setting off to explore. Carter finished first. He'd practically swallowed his energy bar without chewing, anxious to make some progress after so many days and challenges.

Sean joined him a few seconds later, and they set out to determine how large a cave they were in. It didn't take long to discover it was quite small, and even more disappointingly, there didn't seem to be any other opening in the cave that would lead to where the river had been dammed. They checked where each other had been already, and then checked a third time, this time together at every step.

The third time, Carter saw something that they'd missed before. "Look. The rocks here look like they've recently been broken. What do you make of that?"

Sean bent to look, bringing his headlight closer and illuminating better what Carter had discovered. "This whole section has been brought down quite recently. What do you want to bet the bad guy did this to keep us from exploring further?"

Carter stood straight. "No bets. I think you're right, and it confirms to me that there's got to be another entrance leading to that river. Come on, we need to do what a colleague of mine suggested a couple of days ago. We need a geologist."

Back at the boat, Carter pulled up his email and saw a message was already open. He'd forgotten it. Before he ran a search for local geologists, he sent an email to the contact Connery had given him, asking for a meeting as soon as possible. He included a few details but left out mention that he was on the trail of someone looking for a live Minotaur.

A few minutes later, they were on their way back to

shore to meet with a geologist who specialized in mapping the voids and waterways below Crete's surface.

———————

Ahab emerged from the karst spring exit in the bay and swam to his yacht. He'd been to the cave where he was keeping his hostages and provided them with a little food and water. The dolphin seemed sick, so he was glad he'd had the forethought to secure the boy and girl. Although, if he'd known what a pest the boy would be, he'd have left him on the Acropolis and made off with just the girl.

It took all his self-control not to begin his experiments on them right away. Before he inflicted injuries, he needed their cooperation in a proof-of-life video, and they needed to be in good shape for the first one. He assumed if Devereux demanded one for the dolphin, he'd do the same for his own children. And Ahab was angry with himself for not remembering to take something to prove the date. He'd have to go back before he'd planned, to complete the task.

It had been several hours since he ate, so the first thing he did was prepare a large lunch of rice, steamed vegetables and lamb. The recipes called for slow-cooked sauces, but he patiently prepared his favorite foods, making enough to eat later in the day as well. He didn't especially enjoy cooking, but he did enjoy eating, so the cooking was a necessary evil.

While his sauce was simmering, he decided to check his email.

A moment later, his laughter was ringing out across the water. The great Carter Devereux wanted his help!

Ahab could not contain his amusement at the situation. His expertise about the Labyrinth was needed for 'a matter of extreme time sensitivity'. Devereux had been cagey in his details, but knowing what he did, Ahab understood that he was being recruited to help find and trap himself! It was too delicious.

From the tone of the email, it was clear Devereux didn't remember him. Ahab took a while to think through the implications of agreeing to work with Devereux. On the one hand, he might get plenty of warning if they were getting close. On the other, he wanted to be sure Devereux didn't see him face-to-face. He wasn't certain why he thought it would be a bad idea for Devereux to recognize him, but for some reason it was the way he felt.

In the end, he emailed back. 'Dr. Carter, I would be glad to be of assistance, were I still in the area. However, you are welcome to any insight you may get from my thesis, which you will find attached. Please do not hesitate to call upon me again if I can give you any further assistance.' He attached the thesis and sent the email, confident that he'd be able to outwit the man without knowing his exact moves anyway.

He thought it was particularly clever to indicate he was no longer in Greece.

Chapter Thirty-Two

Carter read with disappointment that the Labyrinth expert was no longer in the area. But the man had kindly attached his thesis to the email. Before he had a chance to read it, the boat had reached the harbor and he and Sean rushed to meet the geologist in his university office.

The geologist, who breezily told them in accented English to call him Theo, fit Carter's mental image of geologists to a 'T'. He was short and wiry, dressed in casual clothes consisting of well-worn jeans and a tee-shirt showing several boxes labeled 'favorite rocks', 'oversize rocks', 'pretty rocks', 'books' and 'sharp pointy things', with a caption that read *Never volunteer to help a geologist move*. To make it even funnier, there were several boxes of rocks labeled with their mineral makeup stacked in every corner of the office. Theo's warm brown eyes gave Carter a sense of his kindness, and his tousled, curly brown hair made him look young for a professor of geology.

"Thank you for seeing us on short notice, Theo. As I mentioned in my call, we're searching for another entrance to a cave system where we believe an underground river flows and exits here." He'd unrolled a map of the shoreline near the karst spring and pointed to an X that he'd drawn on it in as close an approximation of the coordinates as he could.

"Ah, yes, I know that area," Theo answered. He turned to a wall next to his desk and tapped his chin for a moment while studying several strings hanging from what looked like a stack of rolls. He selected one and pulled down a larger, more detailed map. He used an old-fashioned stick pointer to tap the map in the same place.

Carter and Sean leaned forward, then frowned slightly. The markings on the map were all in Greek. Carter flashed Sean a warning. If he said, 'it's all Greek to me'... But Sean pressed his lips together and didn't say it, though Carter could see his lips twitching.

Carter described his two dives into the tunnel and their suspicion that the cave had been sealed off recently. "Do you know of another entrance?"

"Understand, I'm not a spelunker. I haven't been in those caves," Theo answered. "But as you may know, there is a global effort to map below the surfaces of the earth to understand what happens above. I have Radio Frequency Identification data, and seismic imaging as well." He went on to explain at some length the science behind what he would show them.

Carter curbed his impatience, not wanting to get into the reasons for their interest, but he was aware of every passing moment and the urgency of their mission.

"...take me some time to trace the sub-surface route of the underground river you're interested in," Theo was saying. "But I could have it done for you in, let me think, perhaps one month?"

Carter slumped. A month was far too long. He was going to have to tell this man about the kidnappings, which would lead him into top-secret information about the dolphins, as well as revealing the reason for the dolphin's kidnapping.

Theo looked at him curiously. "Is something wrong, my friend?"

Carter took a deep breath. "Our request is urgent…"

As he explained that he thought his children and a dolphin were being held somewhere in the cave system, Theo's expressive face revealed surprise, shock, outrage, and then disbelief, in that order.

"A *Minotaur*? Are you playing with me?" He turned an incredulous look on Sean. What he saw on Sean's face must have convinced him they weren't joking.

"Bah!" he said.

When Carter opened his mouth to insist it was all true, Theo waved him off. "A Greek word," he explained. "It means I am shocked. Of course, I will set aside my work to help you. But it will still take several hours. Let me consult with one of my students who has done much of the mapping we have here. Why don't you enjoy an afternoon coffee for an hour, and then return? I will have something for you then; perhaps a better estimate of when I will have final results."

The last thing Carter wanted to do was cool his heels for an hour, but he was grateful the Greek was offering to put aside everything to work on his problem. He stood and took Theo's offered hand in both of his, thanking him sincerely. Sean also shook the professor's hand, and then they left, hopeful Theo would be able to help.

The time was past mid-afternoon, but a stroll along one of the main streets of the town revealed a sidewalk full of tables every few yards. People were drinking coffee and eating what looked like sweets while chattering away in a polyglot cacophony. Sean touched Carter's elbow and indicated an empty table at one of them. They took the opportunity to sit down. A few moments later, a waiter approached and took their order for iced coffee. "S*keto, metrio,* or *gliko,*" he asked. Both men looked at him with bewilderment.

"Surprise us," Carter said. It was the waiter's turn to look confused, but his brow was wrinkled for only a moment.

"And your dessert?"

Carter frowned again, but this time Sean answered. Pointing to something that looked a little like a muffin with dried fruit baked inside at the next table, he said "We'll have that."

"I didn't want to get into the Minotaur thing," Carter said, lowering his voice on the word *Minotaur* to avoid attracting unwanted attention from the tables around them.

"I know, but I agreed with your decision. He had to understand the urgency. I liked him," he added.

"Me, too. I think he's one of the good guys," Carter replied. "I hope so, anyway. I'm going to be in enough trouble for revealing top secret info about the dolphins to him. If he lets it slip to someone else..."

"I'm sure he understood what you meant by top-secret."

Just then, the server returned with their order. Carter looked at the frappé and muttered under his breath, "What the hell is this?"

Even so, the waiter heard him. "Your iced coffee, sir. I hope it is to your satisfaction. You did say to surprise you." Turning to Sean, he said, "Flaouna, sir. An excellent choice."

Carter looked at Sean and said, "Remind me not to tell anyone else to surprise me." Then he tasted his frappé. His eyebrows rose. "Hey, that's not bad."

With a mouthful of flaouna, Sean answered, "This is better than not bad. Try some."

Carter tried to relax, knowing that 'trying' and 'relaxing' were mutually exclusive. But he managed to enjoy a few bites of the dessert. He was just finishing his coffee when he felt the tingling on the back of his neck that meant someone was staring at him. He looked up quickly and scanned the faces around him. A tall, dark man who looked vaguely familiar dropped his eyes as Carter's gaze got to him. Carter stared frankly for a moment, but the man walked away.

"What are you looking at?" Sean asked.

"That man... I think he was staring at me. He looks familiar." Carter's voice took on a puzzled note. "I can't place him."

"Probably nothing," Sean said. "I've been texting my guys, and your A-Echelon team. No one has turned up anything about a couple of kids in the past twenty-four hours. You'd think someone would have seen."

"Unless the kidnapper took them straight from the boat to the cave system," Carter said. "I still think our best bet is the dolphins, or maybe Theo and his student. Has it been an hour?"

"Close enough," Sean answered. "Let's get back to him."

As they walked purposefully back to Theo's office, Carter's phone rang, and he answered even though it wasn't a familiar number.

"Dr. Devereux," an Oxford-accented voice said. "I understand you're vacationing on Crete. We'd like you to keep an eye out for one of the students we're trying to track."

It took Carter a moment to recognize the voice of the MI5 agent who'd been in charge of the murder investigation in London. "It's not..." he started, but the other man overrode his words.

"Guy by the name of Ahab Bashar. He's one of only two we haven't interviewed yet. It's a long shot, because he's been on Crete for a couple of months. But we'd appreciate it if you could track him down and interview him."

Carter started to explain that he was involved in something more important to him personally, but again the MI5 agent overrode him. "I'm texting you a photo of him. Get back to me as soon as you've talked to him." The call ended with Carter still trying to explain the situation. Frustrated, he stared at the blank screen of his phone.

A few seconds later, a ping announced the arrival of a text message. Carter opened it and nearly stumbled over a curb when he saw the photo. It was the man who'd been staring at him. And then he recognized the name. He'd emailed the same man only this morning, asking for help with the location of the Labyrinth. And the man had answered he wasn't still in the area. Why had he lied?

Chapter Thirty-Three

Liam woke disoriented again, but this time it took only a few minutes to remember. He got up, stumbled over two bottles of water and something else, and went to check on Beth. His eyes were adapted to the low bioluminescence now, so it took only a few seconds to find her, curled up on her jacket. She was unconscious, but he could feel her breath on his cheek when he placed it close to her mouth. Maybe she was just asleep.

He also went to check on the dolphin. It was lying in the net on its side, also asleep, it seemed. Liam reached out to touch its skin and withdrew his hand quickly when he felt how rough it was. He thought dolphins felt like rubber. That's what Mom had told him. He had a feeling this one was sick. He scooped up water in his hands and tossed it onto the dolphin's side. He thought it also needed to be underwater some of the time, but the net wouldn't let it get below the surface of the water. He tossed some more water on it, and then he heard Beth calling him.

"I'm here. I think the guy was here. There are two

bottles of water that weren't here before. And something in a sack."

"I'm thirsty, Liam."

He walked over to the bottles he'd tripped over and picked one up, along with the sack. Inside it, he found two energy bars. "Here, Beth. Drink this. And this is food." He handed her an energy bar.

"I don't like those," she objected, pushing away his hand that held the energy bar even as she reached for the bottle. She tried to open it but couldn't.

Liam took the bottle and opened it for her. "Take just a small sip, Beth. I don't know when or if he'll be back. And you have to eat this whether you like it or not. Just a bite."

"What if it's poison?" she asked.

Liam thought about it for a moment. "I don't think it is. If he wanted us dead, we'd already be dead. Go ahead and eat a bite. But save most of it in case he doesn't come back soon."

"You can have it. I don't like it," she repeated.

"Beth, listen. I'm in charge, and I say you have to eat. We don't know how long it will take Dad to find us, and we don't know when that guy will come back. So, quit being a baby and do what I say."

He regretted it a minute later, when she jumped up and flew at him, her little fists pummeling him. "Ow, Beth, stop it!"

"I'm not a baby! Who said you were in charge?" she screamed.

Liam managed to catch her wrists and stop her from hitting him. "Okay, okay. I'm sorry. Listen, you woke the dolphin up."

He could hear a weak whistle coming from behind him. Beth stopped struggling and listened, too.

"Beth, I'm in charge because I'm the big brother. Dad would want me to take care of you."

"Okay," she said. "But quit being so bossy."

"All right. Can I tell you something?"

"Okay," she said.

"People can live a pretty long time without food," he said, "But Ahote told me you have to have water. I want us to drink just a little bit, so if that guy doesn't come back, we can live longer." It made sense to him. He just hoped Beth would agree and cooperate.

"There's a lot of water," she said, pointing toward the river.

Liam hadn't tasted the water, but he assumed it was salt water, since the dolphin was in it. He knew they shouldn't drink salt water, but he couldn't explain why to Beth, and she'd just proved she was stubborn. So, he thought of another excuse. "That dolphin is probably pooping in that water."

"Ew," she said. "Okay. I'll save my water. But I still don't want those yucky energy bars."

Liam wisely decided not to argue. Maybe she'd eat it when she got hungry enough.

"We should see if there's any way out of here," Beth said.

Once again, Liam called on the knowledge Ahote had given him. "Ahote says if you're lost, you should stay where you are, so someone can find you." He would have said more, but nothing Ahote had taught him had prepared him for this kind of being lost. There were no trees, and they'd already been both upstream and downstream to see if they could follow the river.

In both directions, it flowed out of and into cracks that didn't have any way to pass except to swim. Liam might have tried it on his own, but he wasn't sure how far the river went, and he didn't think Beth could make it very far. The best thing to do, he was certain, was wait for Dad to find them, and try to fight the bad guy if he started to hurt them.

"I have an idea, Beth. Let's make a pile of rocks to throw at the bad guy if he gets mean."

"He's already mean," Beth pointed out with perfect logic.

"Well, I mean if he starts to hurt us."

Beth started crying. "I don't want him to hurt us," she wailed.

"That's why we need the rocks. Come on, let's find some you can throw and pile them up," Liam wheedled. If he could keep Beth busy, maybe she wouldn't be so scared.

Liam thought about everything Ahote had taught him. If he only had a shovel, maybe he could dig a trap for the bad guy. And if he had some sticks and a knife, he could whittle a sharp point. As he turned over every bit of woods lore he knew, he understood that they were virtually defenseless. It was up to him to think of a way for them to help themselves, since they weren't in the woods.

While Beth gathered a pile of small stones her little hands could grasp, Liam started looking for bigger ones, and a way to gain an advantage over an adult. There weren't many choices.

While he was thinking about it and piling up his own, slightly larger, stones, Beth whispered to him. "Liam, I think Akela is here."

Beth had named Keeva's female pup Akela, after a wolf in Rudyard Kipling's Jungle Book. It didn't matter to Beth that Akela was a male wolf. She liked the name, she said, and the little wolf had learned to respond to it. Beth and the pup had bonded, and everyone considered Akela hers, though of course no one owned the wolves.

The hairs on Liam's neck stood up, and he looked around involuntarily, though he knew it was impossible. "What makes you say that, Beth?" he asked quietly.

"I can feel her," Beth answered. "But I can't see her."

Liam remembered the time in captivity with his mom better than most kids his age would remember events from half his lifetime ago. He and his mom had only each other and Liu when Beth was born, but his mom talked about Keeva often. He thought maybe she and Keeva talked like the dolphins talked to each other across the miles.

"You can feel her in your head?" he asked, struggling to make his question understandable for his little sister, but designed to give him information he could use.

"Kind of." She placed her hand over her heart. "And here."

Relief flooded through Liam. He was right! The wolf pup was reassuring Beth, like Keeva had reassured his mom five years ago. "Beth, think about where we are. Think about how dark it is, and the river running through here, and the dolphin. Push the thought to Akela."

Somehow, the wolf pup would get word to his mom, and she'd get word to his dad. It had to help. He wished he had the same bond with the male. He loved Jeha with all his heart, but the dog wasn't a wolf. He didn't think she had any special powers. Liam believed the wolves did. They'd helped his mom in captivity, and they'd warned them all when the Russian guys had attacked the camp.

For the first time since they'd been captured, Liam truly believed they'd be rescued. He saw Beth sitting with her fists clenched and her eyes shut tight and went to her. "What are you doing?"

"I'm pushing my thoughts to Akela, like you said."

Liam felt a rush of affection for his prickly little sister. He put his arms around her and gave her a squeeze.

"Ew, quit it," she said, making him laugh.

Just to tease her, he squeezed her again. That earned him a sharp little fist in his ribs, and he backed off. He grew serious again. They still needed to prepare for the bad guy coming back. "Okay, keep gathering rocks, Beth. You can think while you gather."

Chapter Thirty-Four

Mackenzie paced as she talked with Irene on the phone. She was wild with worry, but her plans to get to Greece had been temporarily scuttled because of a Category Five hurricane racing up the East Coast. Airports up and down the coast were closed, and driving would have been impractical. Though they were safe on Freydis, miles inland, the same could not be said for anywhere she could reach with the transportation she had available.

Carter wasn't okay with her going, anyway, citing the danger if they were all located within a couple hundred miles of each other. Until they understood for certain why the children had been taken, he didn't want her nearby, though he understood her anguish.

"Wait for confirmation this is related to Carmen's disappearance," he'd insisted.

"What else could it be?" she'd countered.

"It could be random."

"You don't believe that, and neither do I," she stated

with passion. "And thank Heaven it is related. The alternative would be too much to bear."

Carter had been silent for a few seconds. "You're right."

Now, Irene had no better ideas. "Mackenzie, try not to worry. Our best people and Sean's best people are on it. Sean himself is on it. Soon they'll get the ransom demand, and then we'll be in a better position to do something. Meanwhile, don't make yourself crazy just because you can't travel. Go to the lab and work on your project. You'll feel better if you keep your mind occupied with something else."

Mackenzie wondered if Irene would be so calm if it were her kids. Then she chastised herself for the unkind thought. Irene was right. She should check in at the lab.

Minutes later, she was talking with the veterinarian again about Methuselah's behavior. She'd waved off his questions about news of the children with a shake of her head and gesture that indicated she didn't want to talk about it. So, he'd launched into a report that the old rat had stopped pushing the others away from the food dishes and off the exercise wheel.

"What do you make of it?" she asked.

"It's hard to say. Maybe the behavior was just him being grumpy about his surgery," the vet answered. "Or maybe we assumed too much about where the missing nanobot lodged, or that it was the cause. Maybe it *was* lodged in his brain but has since migrated. We simply can't make any assumptions."

"I agree. But we can do some experiments. Maybe you should implant respirocytes in a different subject's brain and see if the behavior repeats."

"I'd hate…"

"I know you would," she interrupted. "But this is critical. I'm afraid I'll have to insist. In fact, do it today. I'd like to see the results before I leave, if possible. And I'm leaving as soon as this storm lets me."

He nodded sadly. "Yes, ma'am. I'll do it."

Mackenzie felt terrible as she left the veterinary lab. She didn't like to be overbearing, but she simply had to get the vet's cooperation or replace him. And she was too kind-hearted to be willing to fire him. In a way, she reflected, it was the same weakness he had. She couldn't think of it as a character flaw. Kindness and compassion for animals couldn't be wrong – just misguided in this case.

The following morning, she got up with eagerness to check the weather. Her mood deflated as she saw it would be another twenty-four hours at least before she could get a flight to Greece. And if the hurricane didn't make landfall soon and lose momentum, it was going to tear all the way up the coast, potentially doing great damage to the airports along with everything else.

She called Carter, but her call went to voice mail. He must be underwater or underground already, she realized. With a seven-hour time difference, it was afternoon in Greece. She called her parents and interrupted their lunch. Her mom said it wasn't a problem. Neither of them was hungry anyway. After a few minutes, she ended the call. No news from Greece was disheartening.

Restless, Mackenzie decided to go for a walk, taking the satellite phone with her in case there was a call while she was in one of the areas of the ranch where cell phone reception was spotty because of the terrain. She headed toward her favorite spot in the woods, a small clearing where she'd first made contact with the wolves. Half a mile into her walk, Keeva joined her, with the pups following and

Loki ranging several yards behind or beside them, on constant lookout for threats to his family.

Keeva walked close to her, almost leaning on her. To Mackenzie's surprise, the female pup that Beth had claimed was just as close on the other side. Mackenzie strode confidently, knowing the wolves would not trip her. When they reached the clearing, she sat on a fallen log, and Keeva sat on her haunches, now leaning against her firmly. Once again, the female pup surprised her by climbing into her lap.

Even though the pups were only eleven months old by now, wolves develop rapidly in the first year of their lives. The animals Mackenzie was used to thinking of as 'pups' were about eighty percent of their adult size, so the female weighed perhaps sixty pounds. It was a lot of wolf on her lap.

"Akela, what is it?" she asked.

The wolf shifted so she was sitting on her haunches in Mackenzie's lap, echoing her mother's stance. Her paws dug into Mackenzie's leg, but she looked straight into Mackenzie's eyes, staring intently. Mackenzie stilled, her leg in agony, but understanding that Akela was trying to tell her something. The pup licked her face, and then lay down, her haunches slipping off Mackenzie's lap, but her front legs and paws still there, her head laid on them.

"Akela," Mackenzie gasped, "Are you trying to tell me Beth is all right?"

The pup raised her head and tried to lick Mackenzie's face again but couldn't quite reach. Mackenzie leaned over and put both arms around Akela. "Thank you! Thank you!" Tears started flowing, and Keeva grasped Akela's muzzle, growled a bit, and leaned into Mackenzie more. Akela submissively slipped to the ground and Keeva placed her head and one massive leg in Mackenzie's lap.

They were telling her she was part of their pack. She'd studied the face-licking and muzzle-grasping behaviors when Carter had been concerned about them early in her relationship with the wolves. But the lap-crawling was different. She was convinced that Beth had mentally reached out to Akela, or vice-versa, and that Beth was alive. She stared at the male pup, but he was chasing a grasshopper, paying no attention to what was going on between the females and Mackenzie.

She sighed. It might have been too much to ask that the male and her son have the same spiritual connection she and Beth had with the females. Mackenzie didn't pretend to understand it, and if someone had told her a similar story, she would have been skeptical. But she had experience with the comforting presence of her wolf friend in her mind and heart under terrifying circumstances. She knew how steadying it could be. She desperately wanted to believe that her little girl was receiving the same comfort.

She knew, too, that Liam was smart, both in intellectual ability and in survival skills. He'd had them drilled into him from early in his childhood. If any two kids were prepared for being kidnapped, hers and Carters were.

After sitting with the wolves for long enough to calm her emotions, she walked back to the house to call her loved ones again. This time, she had good news.

She was still unable to reach Carter, but she left the message on his phone. Her mother wept with her, this time in relief. There was still not much more to talk about, so once again Mackenzie ended the call after only a few minutes.

Then she went to the lab to distract herself again. The veterinarian met her a few yards outside the door.

"I was just coming to see if you would come by," he explained. "I tried to call, but your phone was busy."

"Yes," she answered simply, "I was talking to my mother." She might have gone on to tell him about her extraordinary experience with the wolves, but he was agitated about something. "What is it?"

"The young rat. The one I implanted a respirocyte generator in yesterday. He's exhibiting the same behavior."

"Already?" she asked, disturbed by the news.

"Virtually as soon as the anesthesia wore off. You know we don't need that for the implantation, right? The needle is so fine, we could do it without anesthesia. I only use it to keep the rat from struggling and making me miss the mark."

"Yes, you've explained that before."

"Right. Well, he'd barely begun to regain consciousness when it was time to feed them. He was waking up, so I put him in the cage with the others, and he rallied right away. He ran to the food dish and bared his fangs at the others!"

"Fangs?" Mackenzie asked, amused.

"Well, he snarled at them. He wouldn't let anyone else near. Even Methuselah couldn't get near it. The young one is already faster than Methuselah, and if you can believe it, more aggressive. I think we have our answer."

"Oh, no. We're nowhere near an answer. We must now learn why it has that effect and figure out a way to eliminate it or at least mitigate it. We can't unleash that on the world without trying to fix it. And I can't avoid reporting the successes to our sponsors for long."

Chapter Thirty-Five

Ahab was angry with himself. Devereux had spotted him. He'd only looked puzzled, so Ahab reckoned he hadn't recognized him. But he'd remember, sooner or later. Ahab should not have been walking around the town. He'd taken too big a risk, and now he was very worried about it.

He had no illusions that Carter Devereux wouldn't put his face and his name together eventually. And then he'd remember Ahab had told him he was no longer on Crete. Once he made that connection, he'd begin to ask questions, and then the game would be over.

Ahab's temper was never far from the surface. Now he took out his anger on the townhouse he'd rented, kicking the walls and the furniture, smashing dishes, and throwing anything he could put his hands on. Later, he'd regret it. It would also serve to call attention to him when the owners found their property wrecked after he left. His years of freedom would be over, unless he gave up his dream of making a mark on archaeology.

His only hope was to turn up the pressure on Devereux.

He'd intended to pick up a newspaper with tomorrow's date on it to use in filming his 'proof of life' video, then make his demand tomorrow afternoon. Now he'd need to get to the cave, make the video, and get back in time to make his demand tonight.

Gradually, he calmed himself, kicked listlessly at a pillow he'd torn in two before throwing it across the room, and resigned himself to making the swim again this afternoon. The children would be in better shape than he'd wanted them to be, but maybe their fright would be enough to convince their father.

Then, as soon as he had his Minotaur or its DNA, he'd kill the father. But he'd take his time with the children.

The thought cheered him. It would all turn out all right after all. He hadn't intended to kill Devereux, but the idea held its own appeal. Right now, Devereux was the most sensational news in the archaeology community. With him gone, Ahab's accomplishments would reign supreme.

———————

A few hours later, Ahab wasn't as confident of his success as he had been. Bruised and cut from the rain of rocks the brats had pelted him with, he was out of temper and barely able to restrain himself from damaging his hostages too soon.

He hadn't even emerged from the water when the first rock hit him in the head. The boy was standing with his feet spread apart, throwing with uncanny accuracy and hitting Ahab with every rock he threw. The little girl had smaller stones and a less accurate throw, but still managed to do some damage when one of hers caught him just under the eye and laid open his cheek.

With a roar, he'd charged the girl and tackled her. He'd come up with her trapped in one arm, the other extended toward the boy, with his finger pointed at him. "Throw one more rock and I'll snap her neck," he'd shouted.

The boy had stopped immediately, but he was still defiant. "Put her down!" he'd screamed.

Ahab had smiled and set her on her feet. "With pleasure," he'd said.

Moments later, both children were trussed like Christmas geese, the newspaper propped on the boy's lap, and the video equipment set up.

"Tell your father he must do as I say, or I'll hurt you," he commanded.

"Go to hell," the boy answered.

"You said a bad word, Liam," the girl scolded her brother. The boy just stared at Ahab.

Ahab got an unfamiliar feeling in his stomach. It was lucky the kid was so much smaller than he. "Liam, your sister is right. That isn't a nice way to talk. What's her name?"

Liam was silent, but the girl spoke up. "My name is Beth. What's your name?" she piped.

Liam kicked her.

"Ow!" she exclaimed. "Why did you kick me?"

"Don't talk to him," Liam answered.

"Now listen, you little brat," Ahab said. "You don't seem to understand your position. I am going to hurt your sister if you don't do as I say."

The girl started to cry, and Ahab could see that he'd made an impression on both of them. "Tell your father he must do as I say," he repeated. This time, the boy was silent. Ahab turned on the recording equipment.

"Now," he stage-whispered.

Liam straightened himself as well as he could. "Dad, we're okay, but this asshole says you have to do as he says, or he'll hurt us."

Ahab turned off the camera, walked over to the children, and cuffed Beth. "Let's try that again," he said.

He walked back to the camera and turned it on, then he nodded.

Liam's face was the image of outrage. "Dad, this *person* says you have to do as he says, or he'll hurt us. He just hit Beth. I'm sorry I made him mad."

Ahab considered whether he would hit the girl again and make the boy say what he wanted him to without the editorializing. Then he decided it was good, after all. Devereux would understand how serious he was, and he would comply. He turned off the mic but kept the video rolling.

"Now tell him he knows what he must do, or you die along with the dolphin."

"What do you want?" Liam asked.

"Your father knows. He must have been willing to sacrifice the dolphin. It's his fault you're in this position."

Liam knew the guy was lying. Dad would never sacrifice a friend, and he knew the dolphins were his parents' friends. He was genuinely sorry he'd called the guy an asshole. That was why he'd hit Beth, who hadn't said anything else since he'd hit her. Liam could hear her crying, so he knew she hadn't been seriously harmed. He also knew he wasn't big enough to do what he wanted to do to the man if he got free.

In fact, he thought, the whole rock idea had been a bad one. Or maybe they just didn't have big enough rocks. Now they were tied up, and if the guy left them this way, they'd have no way to get to their water and energy bars.

He hadn't heard the dolphin whistle in hours. For all he knew, it was dead. That made him sad, but not as sad as thinking about the bad man hitting his defenseless little sister. If he were a man, he'd kill the guy for that. His dad would, too, he was sure.

The light from the video camera was gone, now. It had damaged the adjustment he'd made to the darkness, so now he couldn't see the guy, but he didn't think he'd left.

Suddenly, hands on his ropes startled him.

"I'm letting you go this time, Liam. But if you hit me with rocks again next time I come, I'll kill your sister and make you watch me do it. Understand?"

Liam nodded, unable to speak. As soon as he was loose, he went toward where he'd last seen Beth. She was still tied up.

"You can set her loose when I'm gone. I'm watching, so I want you to count to one-hundred before you untie her."

Liam began counting as fast as he could. A splash behind him told him the guy had gone into the river, but he didn't dare touch Beth's ropes before he'd finished counting.

As soon as she was loose, she threw her arms around him. "I'm s-s-s-scared, Liam!"

"We'll be okay. Dad will rescue us, I promise."

"How will he find us?"

"I don't know, but he will. That bastard was lying. Dad's been looking for the dolphin. I know he has."

"Liam?"

"What?"

"Please don't say that word again."

Remorse flooded him. "I won't, Bethie. I'm sorry."

Chapter Thirty-Six

Carter was still puzzling over the Labyrinth expert's lie when he and Sean got back to Theo's office. They hadn't been gone quite the hour Theo had requested, but he was ready for them anyway. He introduced his student and together they traced the underground route of the river Carter was certain was the one he'd followed from the western end.

Carter put the mystery of the Labyrinth expert aside while he attended to the lecture, for that's what it felt like. Theo stood back proudly as his student expertly explained in English the theoretical origin of the river and traced it from the spring, closer to the western end of Crete than its center, to the exit at the tunnel Carter knew well.

He pointed out several voids along the way that might have pools big enough to keep a dolphin. "We don't really know whether there are pools or not," he explained. "The river could have carved a channel that's unobstructed, or maybe not. To the best of our knowledge, there is no land-based entrance to the cave system.

"You must understand that we have not mapped the entire system. As you can see for yourself, the interior of Crete is mountainous. Ground penetrating radar is not yet sophisticated enough to reach an underground river running under a mountain."

"What if we drilled into one of the voids you mention? And then we can explore from there," Sean suggested.

Theo and the student tried to speak at the same time, and then the student deferred to his professor. "The geology of Crete is complex, having been formed from different forces. Among them, plate tectonics. It's unstable. Drilling has been known to cause surface collapse. It would be dangerous to the hostages, and besides, it would require months' worth of red tape to get permission to drill."

The student added, "And many of them are under towns and villages. Permission to drill in those areas would be denied because of the danger of collapse or sinkholes forming."

Carter knew his disappointment and despair was evident in his body language when the student hastened to continue.

"But there is another way in."

Carter perked up, and noticed Sean doing the same.

"Unfortunately, I don't think it will help."

Carter disagreed. "It has to. Our suspect somehow got a dolphin in there, which means he had to have gone in from a different entrance. No man could carry a dolphin over that cave floor without mechanical help, and the tunnel is too narrow for him to have had that. That's what gave us the idea of another entrance in the first place." Sean's succinct statement seemed conclusive.

"Here's the issue, though," the student replied. "The other entrance is here." He tapped the edge of a bulge in the map of Crete's shoreline. "Here, inside a small bay, another karst spring emerges. We're certain its origin is the same spring as this one," he continued, tapping the entrance Carter was familiar with again.

"The distance is about twelve miles, you would say, 'as the crow flies'. A quaint expression." He paused, evidently thinking about the expression. Then he continued. "But the river does not flow in such a straight line." He traced a serpentine line with the pointer. "Harder rock here, here, and here deflects its progress before it eventually comes out here. And there are several voids along these curves, as well."

"I still don't see why it doesn't help us," Sean interjected.

"Because, here and here, the channel is completely full of water. And the distance is too great to swim it without SCUBA gear."

"We have SCUBA gear," Sean said.

"But I'm not finished. Here," he said, "Our measurements indicate the channel's tunnel is so narrow that you cannot pass both a person and large enough tanks to make it through the flooded portion. Believe me, many have tried. And before it gets to that part, the passage is too narrow to turn around. We have lost more than half a dozen divers who were too stubborn to listen and unable to back out of the death trap."

"Then how could the kidnapper have taken a dolphin in through that way?" Carter asked.

"That's what I'm saying. I don't think anyone could have. It's impossible."

"Is there any chance at all your imaging is incorrect?" Sean asked.

"It's been calibrated using underground areas we are

able to measure directly," the student answered. "I'm sorry."

Carter nodded numbly. He'd been wrong about Carmen's location, which meant he was probably wrong about his kids' location, too. They were at square one again, and it probably meant Carmen's death warrant.

Sean put his hand on Carter's shoulder. "There has to be a way." To the student, he said, "Is there anywhere else – any other cave system – where he could be holding the dolphin and..." he gulped and squeezed Carter's shoulder before continuing, "my friend's children?"

"None that I can think of. The children, yes. There are caves he could reach from the surface. But if they're with the dolphin, there's no other way to get to water under the surface."

Theo stood and faced Carter, putting both hands on his shoulders. "I am so sorry. Is there anything else we can do?"

Carter and Sean looked at each other, their bleak expressions signaling defeat. Then Carter's face changed, became harder. He stood straighter and Sean mirrored him. "We have the video of the dolphin. She's definitely in a cave. I have to believe there's a way in. We're missing something. Theo, will you write down the coordinates of that second entrance? I'm going to check it out for myself."

"Please," the student said, "do not risk your life." He was busy making marks on the map. "If you get to here," he said, making a large red X, "do not go further with your tanks. You will not be able to get through right here..." another X went on the map "nor will you be able to turn around."

"I'm a damn ex-SEAL," Sean answered him. "You'd be surprised what I can do. But thank you for the map."

Theo and his student wished them farewell and good

luck, but from the corner of his eye as they walked away, Carter saw them shaking their heads.

"Sean, you won't be the one to go in. They're my kids."

"That's exactly why I *am* going in. That and the fact that I've got a better chance than you. At least if I don't make it, the kids will still have a father."

Carter's voice broke as he answered. "But will the father still have any kids?"

"We'll get them, if I have to blow up that tunnel to get to them."

Carter's hope flared, and then died again. "You can't do that. Even if it were successful, that would cause an international incident. And you couldn't be sure you wouldn't collapse it instead of widening it. We have to get to the dolphins again and see what they can do to help. And I need to talk to Mackenzie. There's a chance she can help."

"Carter, what are you thinking? You can't mean…"

"They've had some success with rats. Maybe it's time for a human subject."

Sean shook his head. "Mackenzie will never go for it."

On the way back to the boat, they passed the place where they'd had coffee, reminding Carter of the man who'd been staring at him.

"I can't tell you why, but I know I've seen that guy before," Carter said. He gestured at the table where they'd been sitting.

"Probably just someone you've seen around here," Sean answered. "Maybe he waited on you at a restaurant or store?"

"No. To be honest, I wouldn't remember those faces. I've been too distracted." ,

"That will get you killed, my friend. You must notice and remember every face."

"Sean, I wasn't trained like you. And don't change the subject. I *know* that guy. And if I know him, then he knows me. Why would he recognize me and not approach?"

"Could be he was just intimidated by that look on your face, buddy." Sean said. "You've been pretty intense since I got here." He put his hands up and stepped back as Carter turned a fierce grimace on him. "With good reason! Or," he mused, "you said he's an archaeologist, one that the Brit authorities are looking for. Maybe he's worked for you. But he looked like a native of this region, didn't he?"

Carter shook his head slowly. "No. He looked Middle Eastern! The Nabateans?" A jolt of fear went through him at the thought that a member of the Nabatean conspiracy might have escaped the net and might have his kids. Then a worse thought bubbled up, as his brain found the last piece of the puzzle.

A crude four-letter word burst from his lips. "Sean, he's the murderer! The Brits sent me the picture because he's a murder suspect, and I'd bet my last dollar that he's the one!" Carter bent over and moaned. "Oh, God! Let me be wrong!" But he knew he wasn't.

However, one piece of the puzzle didn't fit well. He pulled out his cell phone and redialed the last call. Without greeting the man who answered or identifying himself, he asked with frantic urgency, "Have the victims' families ever received a ransom demand?"

His eyes met Sean's as he listened to the answer. Then he said, "I need to know everything Ahab Bashar's professors and fellow students know about him." He paused for a response. "No, I haven't interviewed him, but he's here, and it's a long story, but he emailed me this morning that he's *not* here. He lied for a reason, and I think the reason is my kids.

I'll have to fill you in later. Meanwhile, please, get me that intel."

Without taking another step, he ended that call and dialed Mackenzie. The call went to voice mail. He couldn't leave news like that on voice mail. After a moment, he knew the call was ill-advised anyway. He couldn't tell his beloved wife that a monster had their children, and that even if he did as the bastard wanted, Ahab would probably kill them in horrific ways.

But the only way for Carter to draw him out was to do as he wanted anyway. And the dolphins must be convinced to cooperate.

Chapter Thirty-Seven

One of Merrybeth's sons was with the boat all the time now. It was a more efficient way of communicating than meeting her at the entrance to the cave system where they'd already determined they couldn't get through. But Carter wanted to talk to Merrybeth personally, not have the message relayed through the dolphin's ansible method, which he still didn't entirely understand. Did they actually repeat what was said, or was it pictures? He thought the latter. The pictures in his mind were too gruesome to broadcast to dolphins world-wide. They didn't need the trauma his own brain was experiencing.

As soon as they returned and boarded, Carter went to the translation device, heedless that he was about to reveal to anyone near enough to hear their semi-secret method of communicating with dolphins. Naturally, it was an open secret on the Alboran dig, and it was too naïve to assume that some of the employees hadn't talked out of turn on their leaves at home. But it was technically still top secret. If anyone heard and the media got more than they already knew, Carter could be in real trouble with A-Echelon. It didn't matter. Nothing mattered but getting his kids back. He'd give his life for them if necessary. His freedom was nothing compared to that.

"Jasper," he called. "Are you there?"

Seconds later, the young male breached and hailed him. "I am here, Carter."

"I need your mother. Is she nearby?"

"I will call her. She will be here soon."

The answer wasn't responsive, but not all the dolphins understood relative terms like nearby. 'Soon' might also mean something different to a dolphin than it did to a land-human. Even then, it depended on context. Carter spoke to a crew member about dinner for the crew, Sean, and himself while he waited for Merrybeth. It was too early by Greek standards, but by the standards of cops, spies, and scientists on the trail of answers, you ate when you had the chance. He might very well be diving tonight despite the hour, and he'd need his energy if so.

Merrybeth's unique whistle called him back to the rail. "Merrybeth, I have news, and it is not good."

The dolphin's pleasant facial expression never changed as Carter told her his conclusions about the kidnapper. She could not show anything but the apparent smile on her curved mouth, but her keening whistles told the story. She was grief-stricken – for *him*.

"Carter, we haven't heard from my daughter for two suns. I believe she is dead. You must do whatever will save your children, and we will help if we can. I do not blame you for Carmen's death."

"Don't give up hope, Merrybeth. If you're right, I'm so sorry we weren't in time. But I won't give up without confirmation."

He then told her they were going to take the boat to the other spot where the underground river came out to the sea. "I will try to swim in and find them," he concluded.

"I agree we must explore that," she responded. "But my sons will go first. If they can't make it, you can't make it."

"I won't have you sacrifice another child, Merrybeth. The man who told us about this says there is no room to turn around. Your sons could be swimming into a death trap."

"I will tell them to be careful. We must go now, Carter. This bad man may hurt your children soon."

"If I'm right, he'll deliver another ransom demand. Merrybeth, this is very important. You must believe that we are better able to take care of ourselves now. If you know where the Minotaur may be found, you must agree to lead him there."

"We thought the Minotaurs were in the cave where we took you," she answered. "If they are not there, then perhaps deeper in the caves, where you could not get through. Or perhaps they have all died."

"Can you lie to him, Merrybeth?"

"What is lie, Carter?"

Carter gave only a moment's thought to the ethical dilemma. Was it right to introduce a vice among an innocent race? Did it matter, when his children's lives were at stake? Could he even explain it to a race that didn't know its meaning already?

"I will show you, Merrybeth." He thought desperately for an example that would be meaningful to her. He seized a bucket and held it up. "If I tell you there are fish in this bucket, do you believe me?"

"If you tell me there are fish in the bucket, then there are fish in the bucket."

227

"All right. There are fish in this bucket. Here, I'll give them to you." He tipped the bucket, which was empty, and pretended to throw them toward Merrybeth. "Catch!"

Merrybeth jerked backward, prepared to dive for the fish. Her 'smile' never wavered as she swam back to the boat. "Where are the fish, Carter?"

"There were no fish. That was a lie."

"That was not nice."

"No, a lie isn't nice. But sometimes we must do it. It would be a lie if you told the bad man you would lead him to the Minotaur, when you don't know where it is. Do you understand?"

"Yes. I lead him away, while you rescue your children. That is a necessary lie. I will do it."

Carter wondered if he'd opened Pandora's box for the dolphins, but Merrybeth had it right. It was necessary, for the greater good. He hoped his plan would not get Merrybeth killed as well.

"Follow the boat, Merrybeth. I have a feeling we'll find this guy at the other entrance."

Carter didn't know why he thought that, unless the guy had been following him earlier rather than just stumbling across him. He also realized he was pinning all his hopes and perhaps risking his life on a series of guesses. He'd found the library of the Giants and the Alboran Codex on less. Besides, he had no other leads.

The other entrance was inside a bay, perhaps twenty miles from the harbor where they were now. It would take about an hour to get there. Carter asked the crew to serve the light dinner he'd arranged for, and then checked his phone. He saw he'd missed a return call from Mackenzie and decided he must talk to her before going into the water, even if he had to break bad news. He hit the keys to return her call.

"Carter! We've been playing phone tag," she said by way of a greeting.

"We have, Mackie. I'm sorry."

"Any news?"

He searched for the words to tell her. "There's news, Mackie. I'm not sure it's good news."

He pictured her suddenly clutching the phone. "Mackie, hang up. I'm going to call back with video."

"Carter, don't you dare dis…"

He didn't give her time to finish the word. He hit the end call icon, waited thirty seconds, an eternity, and called back. Her face filled his screen, and she looked angry.

"Mackie, please. I had to look you in the face when I tell you this. First, know that I love you with all my heart."

Her expression turned to concern in the heartbeat before he went on, telling her in a rush that left no room for a response. "There's no way to soften this blow. I believe our children are being held by the same man who's wanted for murder in London. I know it's a huge coincidence, but I have a gut feeling, and some evidence. The other bad news is that he's somehow gotten them into a cave system that's said to be unreachable. We were blocked at one end, but we're going now to the other end, and I'm going to do my damnedest to get to them and get them out. The dolphins are going to help."

"Carter, what in the world are you telling me?"

"Local geologists tell me the way in is blocked on this end by flooded tunnels, that the distance is too great for an unassisted dive, and that a normal-sized man with tanks won't fit through. But if I'm right, the kidnapper found a way. Merrybeth is going to lead the guy away if he's where we think he is and wants what we think he wants. While he's gone, I'll go in and get the kids, and Carmen if she's still alive. Merrybeth thinks she's dead already."

"Oh, no!"

"Try not to worry, Mackie. This guy wants something, and until he gets it, I don't think he'd deliberately harm the kids. He may have just miscalculated with Carmen. He's got her in water, but Merrybeth says it's fresh water, and that's bad for their skin. I don't know if it's fatal right away. Merrybeth says Carmen hasn't communicated in two days."

"Carter, I may know something. The wolves were acting strangely earlier. Keeva's pup, the one Beth named Akela? She climbed right into my lap, and she licked my face. I think she knows Beth is alive but in trouble."

"How sure are you?" Carter didn't question his wife's bond with the wolves, so it wasn't a stretch to believe Beth could have the same bond. The question had to do with Mackenzie's interpretation of the wolves' behavior. No matter what, he wouldn't take that hope away from her. "Anything about Liam?"

"No," she said, her face falling again. "I don't think the mental bond is there with Liam. But Beth would have been even more frightened if Liam isn't with her, wouldn't she? I didn't get that much fright from Akela. Just a longing to be with me. With us," she corrected.

"That jibes with my logic," he said. "They're alive, and I'm going in for them. I have to go get ready for the dive."

"Wait, Carter. I have an idea. It's risky. Maybe too risky. No, let me think about it. Don't take unnecessary chances unless this guy threatens to kill the children. Then do what you must."

"Mackie, you're not making sense. Back up and start over."

"The respirocytes, Carter. They work. There's a problem, but I need to talk to my team to see if it can be overcome, if it's even feasible to get them to you. It would be a desperate measure, though. We haven't tested them on anything but rats."

Carter grasped the implications at once. "I'll take them if it means I can save the kids. The risk to me doesn't matter. Can you get here with them?"

"I'll call Irene right now. Please, Carter, I can't lose the kids and you, too."

"I know, Mackie, and you won't. I promise."

Carter ended the call. He looked up from the screen to find Sean staring at him. "How can you make a promise like that?" he asked.

Carter answered, "I've never broken a promise to her. I won't break this one. If it's the last thing I do in this life, I'll at least give her back our children."

Chapter Thirty-Eight

Once they'd steered the boat into the bay where the other entrance was said to be located, Merrybeth and her sons took point on finding it. By then it was too dark for Carter, Sean, or the crew to see the tell-tale ripples where the karst spring exited underwater. But the dolphins would sense it if they got close enough but didn't see the entrance.

While Merrybeth, Jasper, and his brother explored the shoreline underwater, Carter and the other land-humans searched visually and electronically for another boat nearby where Bashar might be hiding. However, because of the sun setting beyond the horizon or the boat being too far away, they saw nothing. That didn't mean he wasn't out there. He could even be patrolling with the individual vessel Merrybeth had described. Nevertheless, they kept watch to avoid being surprised.

After about an hour, Merrybeth appeared at the side of the boat. "We have found the entrance. My son 'unknown whistle' is exploring. Jasper is trying to find the bad man's boat."

Carter made the adjustments to the translator to assign the name Franklin to the whistle Merrybeth had used. Odd they'd never heard that one before. He assumed it was because Jasper had never referred to him by 'name'.

"Did you tell Franklin to turn back when the passage gets too narrow to turn around?"

"He will be careful."

Carter let it go, although that was not a responsive answer, either. He was beginning to believe that the dolphins didn't always listen to land-human advice, especially when it came to their realm underwater. He only hoped Franklin wouldn't go too far and lose his life also. The geologists had been clear about the dangers.

Another shape joined Merrybeth, and they dived without speaking to Carter again. In a few minutes, though, Merrybeth came up again. "Jasper has found the boat. The bad man wants me to come to him. I will be back soon."

"Merrybeth, wait!" Carter called, but it was too late. She'd disappeared under the waves, and they couldn't follow her in the dark if she didn't want them to. He spent the next half-hour worrying about his friends. Sean tried to distract him, but it did no good. He was not in the mood for jokes, and there was no point in speculating about what was going on.

At last, Merrybeth returned. Once again, she had something in her mouth, and Carter extended a pole with a net on the end, normally used for pulling in a catch of fish, so she could drop it in.

The plastic bag contained a note and a flash drive. The note said, "*The dolphin must lead me to the Minotaur.*" Nothing was said about the flash drive, but Carter knew the drill. He inserted it into his laptop and watched, certain he knew what was coming.

Knowing he'd see his children in captivity and vulnerable to the monster who'd butchered other children was nothing compared to the reality. He was proud of Liam for his defiance, but the video went black for a moment. When it began again, Liam's expression had changed, and now the children were tied up. Carter clenched his jaw to keep from screaming his frustration. His hands curled into fists, and a fierce desire to put them around Bashar's neck and squeeze the life out of him momentarily blinded Carter.

He fought to regain control of his emotions, and then backed up the video to the beginning, determined to miss nothing, no clue. He listened closely to Liam's words, also.

"Dad, this *person* says you have to do as he says, or he'll hurt us. He just hit Beth. I'm sorry I made him mad."

Bashar had made a mistake by leaving in Liam's first version of the threat. That meant the children must have rattled him. Liam's next sentence was delivered in a flat tone.

"He says you have to sacrifice the dolphins. There's one here with us. She doesn't look good, Dad. He gave her a few fish, but I think she's hungry. We're hungry, too. He's given us water and some energy bars, but Beth doesn't like energy bars, so she won't eat them. She's scared, Dad, he said it's your fault we're in this position, but I know you'll be here soo..."

Liam's voice was cut off, but the camera remained on his face as an adult male's voice interrupted. "Don't bother trying to find them, Devereux. You can't get here. When I have what I want, I'll bring them out."

The video ended. Carter waited a beat for more, but that was all. He now knew more than he'd known before, both good and bad. Bashar had confirmed what Carter had guessed. The kids were being held in the same place as the dolphin, and were in good shape, except for the cut on Beth's lip. He saw red for a moment but then forced himself to remain calm. It could be so much worse.

He also knew that if Bashar could get there, wherever 'there' was, then there must be a way for him to get there, too. The puzzle was how. How had he gotten the kids there, if it was impossible to use tanks and too far for them to hold their breath?

"Sean, help me think this through," he said.

Sean had been silent through Carter's viewing of the video. "I don't think he's bluffing, Carter. Any man willing to hit a little girl…" He trailed off.

"I get that. I can't focus on it, or I won't be able to be effective. If we find him before we find the kids, you have to promise to keep me from killing him until we know where they are and how to get them out." Carter took a deep breath.

"I won't let you kill him then. But afterwards…"

"No, if we can take him alive, he has to answer for the people he's killed in London. But let's focus on the kids. Do you think he's guarding the way in somehow?"

"I think he's acting alone. His note from before, this note, and his voice on the video all indicate a loner. And serial killers usually work alone."

"How do you know? That isn't your specialty."

"No, but it's an interest. As a SEAL and since, I've had to kill a few people. I had to know if I was one of them, because I've never regretted killing."

Carter looked his friend in the eye. "War and protecting your charges is different from killing for pleasure, Sean. You must know that."

"I do. But I've still done the research. I'm no profiler, but I think I know how these guys think. They're not crazy, but there's something missing in them. Compassion, concern for other people – it's all missing. And that's why most of them work alone. They can't get along with other people, because they only think of themselves."

Carter asked, "So what are our options?"

"I think we should wait for what's-his-name – Franklin? Wait for him to scope out the entrance to the cave system. Then both of us should go in after the kids. Unless you want to go after Bashar instead, and let me go in after the kids. Remember, I'm the ex-SEAL," Sean said.

"I agree with your first sentence. I'll take the second under advisement. But I'm going in for them. It's my responsibility. You heard what Liam said. It's my fault they're in there."

"Carter, you know he was only saying what Bashar told him to say, and only because he threatened Beth. Watch the video again. He knows it isn't your fault."

"I don't need to watch it again. Not sure I can and remain in control. And what Liam said was he knows *I'll* be there soon. What kind of man would sit back and let someone else rescue his kids? It isn't negotiable."

Before Sean could argue, they heard Merrybeth's whistle again, simultaneously with the translator's artificial female voice. "Franklin is here."

They rushed to the side rail. "What did he learn?"

"Your information was correct. Franklin went as far as he could without a breath. Ahead, he could see the passage was too narrow for him, and it was still full of water. We cannot reach our children, Carter. They will die."

"Thank you for telling me and please thank Franklin for me as well, for scouting it. But I will not accept that we can't reach them. The bad man, Ahab Bashar, got in there some-how. I will get them out, and they will not die."

Merrybeth didn't answer, but Carter had one more thing to say. "If Carmen is alive, I will bring her out, too. What do you want me to do if she has not survived?" He couldn't bring himself to say 'if she's dead.'

"I do not wish to see my daughter dead, Carter. If she is dead, leave her."

It was one more way in which these sentient beings differed from mankind, Carter thought. They apparently had no sentimentality about the physical shell, once life had departed. He would respect her wishes, though he'd have brought out the body if she'd asked. It remained his fervent hope that she would be alive when, not if, he found the cave where she and his own children were being held.

"Merrybeth, we need to think and plan. Would you ask Franklin if we can measure him? We will put something around him at his widest part, but it will not stay there."

Soon after the request was made, they had a measurement of the dolphin's girth. He measured fifty-eight inches around just behind his dorsal fin. Sean had another thought. "Would he have been able to get through if he didn't have his dorsal fin?"

"I don't have a clue how to ask that, Sean. I doubt they have that concept. It wouldn't be like a man losing a leg. A dolphin wouldn't survive without his dorsal fin, and I'm certain they wouldn't consider not having it before going into a hole where they might get stuck. To have a safety margin, let's assume he would not get through, even without his dorsal fin. That means the passage is less than five feet in circumference."

"I could get through a dry passage that wide. And you'd have a few inches to spare. But with tanks, no way. Listen, it's late — we need to get some sleep or we're going to be making mistakes. And mistakes in this kind of situation will cost you your life."

"Maybe. Now that I've seen the kids have at least some water and food, I feel we can wait for Mackenzie as she asked. But it may be too late for Carmen if we do." Carter shook his head, undecided.

Sean added, "There's one more thing. We don't have anything like what Merrybeth said the dude was using to get around faster underwater. We're going to have to go back to town to get one. I don't see any choice in that."

"Yes, there's that, too. Okay. We'll go back. On the way, I'll call Mackenzie and see where she is with the respirocyte idea."

"You can't seriously be thinking of trying that," Sean said, putting all the skepticism he could into his statement.

"If I can't get through that passage any other way, then yes, I am."

"Just remember, Bashar got through."

"And we have no idea how. Who knows, maybe he's some kind of freak. There's no time to try everything we think of. If that gets me in there without a bunch of false starts, then yeah, I'm thinking of trying it."

Chapter Thirty-Nine

With the help of A-Echelon, Mackenzie and her clinician were winging their way toward Crete before midnight on the same day she and Carter had last talked. In Greece, it was nearly morning on the next day, but Mackenzie had talked to him before she left.

Immediately after their conversation, she'd called Irene to tell her she needed to get to Crete as soon as possible. The good news was that the hurricane had veered off to sea, and most of the northern coast and Canada's coast had escaped damage. Irene promised transport to the nearest military base in the States and the fastest military jet she could commandeer.

Mackenzie's next move was to call an emergency meeting in her lab and float the idea of using the respirocytes on Carter to help him get to their children. The debate had raged for almost two hours.

At the end of it, everyone agreed. It was foolhardy to implant the respirocytes in a human being before testing them more extensively on animals. Furthermore, it might be illegal. And it might be fruitless. Even if Carter didn't get sick or worse from having the nanobots use his body's resources to make oxygen, what if he still couldn't get to the kids with enhanced ability to hold his breath? And what of the other side effects? Would he have antisocial tendencies afterward? What about the rejuvenation effects? People might think that was a positive outcome, but there were ethical and other issues they hadn't resolved yet. It was simply too soon.

But when Mackenzie asked if they would do it to save their own kids, everyone who had children agreed. Yes, they would.

Mackenzie, as the lead scientist, made the decision. They had a supply of the nanobots, and they were stable. Mackenzie asked the veterinarian and the clinician to calculate how many they'd need to give a human being the optimal dose.

She took a vial with enough to inject three or four people. It wasn't clear to her how the rescue would work, but she reasoned that preparing for the unexpected couldn't hurt. She asked the clinician, who'd observed the implantation method for the rats, if she would accompany her. The clinician, a woman of sixty who had raised three children, all grown now, agreed. But only if Carter would sign a waiver to absolve her of any responsibility for the outcome would she implant the nanobots in him. Mackenzie assured her it would be no problem.

Mackenzie and the doctor landed just after eight a.m. and Carter met them at the tiny airport, where the locals were agog at the VTOL military plane. Nothing that large had landed there, ever. Only its vertical landing ability allowed it to.

Carter thanked the Navy pilots profusely, but he declined their offer to wait to take them home. "I'll get them home when this is all over. Thanks for everything, guys!"

As glad as they were to see each other, concern for the children was foremost in their minds when Mackenzie hurried down the exit stairs and into Carter's arms. They were tripping over each other's words as each apologized for their role in putting the kids in danger, and then both tried to reassure the other that nothing could have prepared them for a madman who would do such a thing. Carter grasped Mackenzie's arms and stood back to take in her appearance. She looked tired and worried. He supposed he looked the same. "I see you've brought help," he said, smiling at the clinician.

Mackenzie clung to him, worry clouding her expression. "Have you tried every other option?"

"Not yet. We know the approximate size of the first narrow passage. I've got about seven inches to spare. It isn't enough room with a big rebreather or tanks, but tanks won't get me far enough anyway, without something to propel me faster. We're waiting for the shops to open to see what's available for that."

"Seven inches! Carter, what if there are narrower passages farther along?"

"I'll have to cross that bridge when and if I can get to it. With any luck, there won't be any. Turning back isn't an option. If I can't get to them, they'll die. Bashar has said he'll release them once he has what he wants. We don't even know if what he wants still exists, and if they do, Merrybeth doesn't know where. On top of that, this guy is a killer. I don't believe he'll release them, even if we did somehow get him what he wants. But Mackie, you must not give up hope." Summed up that way, even Carter could barely summon hope. It seemed impossible.

They left the clinician at the hotel to get some rest, while the others went shopping.

An hour later, there were no other options. Carter was excited to see a Sea-Bob in the shop, what Merrybeth must have been referring to when she described Bashar's machine. It was much smaller than even the smallest model of jet ski with which they were familiar. But at about sixty-nine inches in circumference, it was inches too large. The clerk didn't know of anything smaller on the island.

"Can't we get something here?" Mackenzie asked.

The answer was unacceptable – it would take at least a week. Going to the mainland, shopping, and back would take most of a day. Carter wasn't willing to risk Bashar's wrath for even a day's delay. "We don't know that he won't kill one of them to show he's serious. It has to be today."

"Carter, we don't know how long it will take the respiro-cyte generators to give you the boost in oxygen you'll need for this," Mackenzie warned.

"It doesn't matter. There's no more time. If we stall Bashar, he could very well harm the kids."

"Inject me, too," Sean said.

"What? No!" Carter and Mackenzie spoke in unison, as if they'd practiced it.

"If you don't get through, Carmen definitely dies if she isn't gone already. And your kids may die, too. We can only pull off this ruse once. From what you told me about Bashar, he'd probably go in and kill them if he's thwarted. Inject me now, and I'll find a way to follow Merrybeth as she leads him away. I'll also have more time to generate the respirocytes. If you don't come out, I'll make sure I get in before he does, and I'll force him to tell me how to get them out before I kill him."

Mackenzie's expression was dubious, but Carter considered the plan. "That could work. But what if I'm stuck? You wouldn't be able to get past me."

"We can't make plans for something like that. If that's the case, the game's over. But that Bashar guy is huge, didn't you say? If he can get in through there somehow, you won't get stuck."

"Yeah. I mean, compared to the other people on the street, he looked big," Carter answered.

"Wait," Mackenzie said. "Did you say Bashar? A big guy named Bashar? *Ahab* Bashar?"

It was Carter's turn to stare at Mackenzie. "Yes. But how did you know?"

"Carter, he worked for you at the Alboran site! Don't you remember him?"

Carter snapped his fingers. "I *knew* he looked familiar. I can't believe I didn't remember him. Must have been the stress of the kids being taken, or I would have. He was a loner, right? It's all beginning to make sense. I'd still like to know how he knew the family was in Athens. I'll ask him before *I* kill him."

Mackenzie huffed in exasperation. "Neither of you will kill him. You'll take him into custody and he'll stand trial."

Carter shook his head. "In an ideal world, we would. But no promises, Mackie. He's a sick and violent man. We may have to."

After a bit more argument with Sean, Mackenzie conceded the point. She admitted she'd known it might be necessary to inject more than one person. "I brought enough nanobot generators to do it," she said. "I'd just hoped it wouldn't be necessary."

"What's the big deal?" Sean asked. "They're safe, aren't they? Tiny, submicroscopic things, made of an inert material – how could they be dangerous?"

Mackenzie launched into a quick synopsis. "Correct, but they haven't been tested on humans. Here's what we're facing. We've tested them on rats. Both rats that have received them showed almost immediate increased strength, speed, endurance, and ability to perform feats of athletic ability. Over a short time, they also seemed to be rejuvenated, and the researcher who cared for them indicated their life span may have doubled. But both began to exhibit previously unobserved antisocial behavior. We're not sure whether that resulted from one or more of the nanobots escaping from where we injected them and lodging in the brain, or whether it's going to be a problem universally."

Sean summed it up. "So, we'll get stronger, faster, better at what we do, and the price is living longer and being mean sumbitches. I'm already the meanest sumbitch around, so I don't see the problem."

Carter grinned at Sean. "I think what he's saying, Mackie, is most of those side effects don't worry us. And we're not rats. We'll be able to observe and control any antisocial tendencies, *if* they happen. The good outweighs the bad."

"One last thing." Mackenzie said. "The generators use resources your own bodies store to enhance the red cells. We don't know long-term effects. You could get sick."

"Long term. We'll worry about that if and when it happens. Worst case, you remove the nanobots. We're doing this. It's the kids' best hope," Carter answered. His tone said his decision was final.

Mackenzie knew when it was time to stop arguing. "All right, then, let's go."

With that, they returned to the hotel and picked up the clinician. "We're out of options. It's time to inject us," Carter told her.

"Us?" the clinician answered. "I thought it was just you."

"Sean has said he'll do it, too. Inject us both, and then if I'm not able to get out, he'll have had more time for them to take effect."

"Does he understand all the risks?" she persisted.

"Yes. And you and Mackie can explain them again while you prep us. Do we need a clinic or a hospital?" Carter asked.

"Yes," Mackenzie answered. "But Irene has made arrangements. The local hospital has agreed to lend us what we need."

"Then what are we waiting for?"

Carter turned to the Executive Advantage operator Sean had called in from the other tasks the rest of the team were attending to. "Get to the boat and ask Jasper to get his mother there if she isn't already. Give her a plastic bag with a note in it to take to Bashar. Tell her to give him the note, and then lead him to the south side of the island. While they're gone, we'll get ready and I'll go in before they get back."

"Yes, sir. And may I say, the team's best wishes are with you."

"Thanks, man. We appreciate it," Carter said. He turned to Sean. "While you wait your turn, you'd better call Sam. In case, you know…"

"Good idea." Sean answered. There was no need to spell it out. He excused himself to make the call.

Mackenzie leaned into Carter. "If I thought for a minute I could do this…"

"Don't say it, Mackenzie Anderson Devereux. What kind of man would sit back and let his wife go into danger in his place? You know I love you and the kids more than my life. I'm going to do everything in my power to bring them back to you and get back to you myself. I promise I won't take unnecessary risks. Do you trust me?"

"You know I do. I love you, too."

Chapter Forty

Mackenzie watched anxiously from the operating theater balcony as her clinician used guided imagery to carefully thread a fine needle into Carter's lung. The magnified and color-enhanced image looked like pink chenille, with white lace edging. Beside her, her parents, Liu, and Dylan watched as well. They'd flown in that morning from Athens. Dylan had sent his team home, now that they were certain the kidnapper wasn't on the mainland.

Sean was being prepped for his injection in pre-op. As soon as the patients were released, shortly after the procedure, Sean and Dylan would coordinate with Sean's team to surveil the decoy operation. Merrybeth was standing by with Franklin in the bay, and Jasper was in communication with them from near the boat in the town harbor.

When Merrybeth signaled Jasper that she was leading Bashar away, Carter, the boat's crew, and a few of Sean's men would set out for the bay. Carter had asked Mackenzie to stay ashore, but she refused, saying she needed to be there when he got back to the boat with the children. But her parents and Liu would stay at the hotel and wait for news.

Mackenzie felt as if a tornado was wreaking havoc in her gut. Her entire future could be determined today. Between apprehension about the known side effects of the respirocytes and the unknown outcome of the rescue operation, she was experiencing an electrical storm along every neural pathway. Yet, at the center of it all, there was a calm space. That was where she knew that they had made the right decisions until now, and that the outcome was in God's hands.

The scientist in her pushed away her own anxiety to observe Carter's condition. He didn't seem anxious, but she didn't see how he could not. "Carter, how are you feeling? Any aftereffects of the anesthetic?"

He took her hand. "Mackie, it was a local anesthetic. I'm fine. I feel great, in fact, like I'm breathing pure oxygen." He took a deep breath to show her. "If I didn't know better, I'd say I feel like I could run up mountains, or swim to the mainland."

"That's the increased oxygen in your bloodstream. That helps my anxiety!" Mackenzie exclaimed. In response, Carter kissed the top of her head.

Determined to take Carter's mind off the stakes of today's task, put her anxiety aside, and spend what may be her last moments with Carter in some meaningful way, she introduced a subject she'd been thinking about ever since Merrybeth told her that Carmen had been kidnapped.

"Carter, are you thinking about your dive, or can we talk about something else?"

"Nothing to think about. I'm going to take a deep breath and swim into a tunnel. Keep going until I find the kids and bring them out. Since I don't know what I'll encounter in there, there isn't anything to think about." He gave her a lopsided grin.

She loved him even more for acting like it was no big deal. She grinned back. Then she said, "Okay, then here's what I want to talk about. Kidnapping is a crime in every civilized nation, if not every nation. But the dolphins have virtually no protection. I want to campaign to have them recognized as sentient and get some laws in place to protect their rights. If Bashar hadn't kidnapped our children, there would have been nothing to charge him with for taking Carmen."

"You mean, besides a dozen or more murders in London," Carter mentioned sardonically.

"Well, right. But I mean this incident. Carter, it's mind-boggling that this person we know is a serial killer. And because he has our children, I don't want to think about it. Can we just talk about the dolphins for now?"

"Of course, Mackie. I didn't mean to sidetrack you. So, let me understand you. You know that the extent of their intelligence has been a secret, touching on national security. But now you want to have that set aside and publish to the world that we are not alone in advanced intelligence? And that it isn't aliens among us, but dolphins?"

"Yes, Carter. That's exactly what I mean. They deserve to have their rights protected, don't you agree? Otherwise, we're tacitly saying they're less than human. The US has been down that road before. It wasn't pretty."

"I'll support whatever you want to do about that, Mackie. But just be careful about revealing top secret information. We're already skating on thin ice, and don't tell me you don't remember being wanted for treason just a few years ago."

"I'll negotiate to have the top-secret designation removed before I go public with my campaign, I promise."

"Then I'm behind you all the way. And speaking of all the way, we're here."

They'd been so focused on each other that they hadn't realized how quickly the shoreline was changing until the boat stopped.

"Are you ready, sir?" one of the crew asked.

"I was born ready," he answered, winking at Mackenzie.

"Aren't you going to wear any dive equipment?" she asked.

"I'll get on some flippers to help me swim faster, and a mask to help me see better, but there's no point in tanks or the rebreather. They won't go through the first narrow spot, and there's no place to take them off. Wish me luck," he said, kissing her goodbye.

She wanted to cling to him, tell him not to go. But she couldn't give up the hope of seeing her children alive and safe. "Luck," she whispered, as he went over the side.

———

Carter had only a few yards to go before he ducked under the water to find the flooded entrance to the underground river. He had an idea of what it would look like from his experience of the other entrance. He'd be swimming upstream of the current, and he had to remind himself that he'd have plenty of oxygen, and he should not to try to breathe. Land-humans' breathing is normally an involuntary function, but like dolphins, they can voluntarily control it – usually for a short time. Most people who learn to hold their breath for extraordinarily long periods do so with practice. Carter had not had the opportunity to practice, so a small part of his cortex was engaged in a rigid battle to maintain control.

Sean had told him that Navy SEALs must be able to hold their breath for two to three minutes, though trained divers could learn to hold it for about eleven minutes. While the average person can hold it for about one minute, a world record holder who prepared by hyperventilating for nearly twenty minutes was then able to hold his breath for an astounding twenty-two minutes and twenty seconds. He'd immediately followed up with the opinion that no one could go that long while also swimming as fast as they could, though the lack of a place to breathe in air might help them hold it longer than they otherwise could.

Carter's dive watch told him he'd been underwater about fifteen minutes when he sensed air above his head. He surfaced into a void that was just large enough to allow him to get his nose and mouth above water before he bumped his head on the rock above him. However, the distance was enough that his headlamp didn't extend to the end of the shallow cave. He turned on his back and breathed deeply while he swam toward the other end. Idly, he wondered how there was any air at all in the pocket, and whether he would use it all before he had to go underwater again.

Swimming on his back, using his arms underwater in a reverse breast-stroke pattern because his hands would hit the top if he used the normal technique, he wasn't making progress as fast as he could underwater. But he reasoned he should take advantage of all the external oxygen he could get. Not only would it replenish the supply in his blood-stream and brain, but it gave the respirocyte generators time to do their jobs if he wasn't constantly drawing down their product.

When he bumped into a solid wall, he took a last deep breath and dove under again, seeking the opening that would get him through. Immediately, he understood that this one was where Franklin had been forced to turn back.

Not normally claustrophobic, Carter had to draw on every iota of his will to force himself into the tight confines of the tube. And then he was forced to back out, remove his flippers, and push them ahead of him as he used one hand to pull himself through. To his astonishment and delight, the narrow opening was less than three feet long, and was barely underwater on the other side. He pushed the side hard with his free hand and popped out into a large opening, the top of which was easily ten feet above the surface of the water. Furthermore, there was dry land beside the water.

He climbed out to explore further, but soon realized this was not the place. No dolphin was in the water, no children on the rocks beside the river waiting for him. It was disappointing, but Ahab had warned him in the video that the children were inaccessible. He didn't really expect to find them right away. His dive watch told him he'd been in the water for nearly forty-five minutes. He figured he had four or five hours at most before Bashar started back for the entrance, and he'd know by then that he'd been tricked. Carter didn't especially want to meet him coming in as he was leading the children out. He wasted no more time on the empty cave, but instead he put his flippers and mask back on and headed farther into the cave system.

Chapter Forty-One

It was nearly three hours later when Carter swam through a narrow but tall crack into another cave. He'd encountered several in the meanwhile, but all were either too small or brief exploration had convinced him they were empty. His control over his breathing had gradually become almost second nature in the spots where the river had carved tunnels through smooth sedimentary rock, some only a few feet long, and the longest taking more than half an hour to traverse.

He was no longer surprised at the strength he felt, but he was astonished when he calculated his distance with the pedometer-type measurement function of his dive watch. He'd traveled more than twenty miles by that calculation, far more than he'd thought necessary to reach the children. He thought he must be near the other end of the cave system, a hunch borne out by the fact he'd been traveling *with* the current for the last hour.

He climbed out of the water, noting he felt as fresh as if he'd only just started, pulled off his flippers, and turned on his headlamp, which he'd been keeping off as much as possible to conserve the batteries.

"Dad!"

Carter's heart leaped. The shout had startled him, but it was the word that caused the irregularity in his heartbeat. "Liam?"

"Dad, over here!"

He turned toward where he thought the sound had come from. In the distance, almost at the end of his head-lamp's reach, a small figure stood waving his arms. Carter sprinted for the child, heedless of the cuts on his bare feet from several small, sharp stones.

When he got to Liam, he threw himself to his knees and swallowed his son in a bear hug. Liam returned it enthusiastically.

"Beth?" Carter asked, holding Liam by both arms and looking around wildly. A few feet away, Beth was holding her arms out to him. Both children had been tied by thin climbing ropes to boulders too big for them to move. They had enough leeway to reach bottles of water and still-wrapped energy bars, but they couldn't reach each other.

"That bastard," Carter mumbled.

"I guess we made him mad when we threw rocks at him," Liam explained. "He tied us up like this right after he made that video. I'm sorry I used a bad word in the video, Dad."

"He did! He used a lot of bad words to that man," Beth affirmed.

Her indignation over her brother's transgressions struck Carter as hilarious, given the circumstances. He laughed loudly and told Liam he got a pass this time but to watch it in the future. He was busy untying Beth when Liam said, "Uh oh."

Carter turned just in time to see a large figure rushing him. He stood to protect Beth from the charge and threw himself backward and sideways, his arms wrapped around his assailant. They both scrambled for purchase for a moment. Carter was a second faster. He swung a wild roundhouse just as Bashar got to his feet. Although he connected, it hardly delayed Bashar's response at all. Carter felt a solid blow to his solar plexus.

"Hit him, Dad!" Liam and Beth were both cheering him on. It would have been cute if it hadn't been such a desperate situation.

Carter drew on his martial arts training to regroup. Bashar was huge – at least a head taller than Carter, and his muscular body matched. Carter, though was in superb physical condition. His tai chi training, with its beneficial effects on pulmonary function and mental control had already been enhanced by the respirocytes. He could feel it. But his true advantage would come from his krav maga skills.

Carter counterattacked before Bashar could press his advantage. While Bashar threw awkward punches at Carter's body, Carter targeted Bashar's most vulnerable points – his eyes, neck, throat and face. Nor did he feel any compunction to follow Marquess of Queensbury rules. This wasn't by any definition a fair fight, so Carter targeted Bashar's groin, ribs, knee – anywhere where he could potentially cripple his opponent and end the fight as soon as possible.

The two men rained blow after blow on each other. Bashar was bigger, but Carter was faster. He got in three punches for every two of Bashar's. But it was a lucky one that knocked Bashar off his feet. His head connected with a rock with a sickening thud, and he lay still.

Carter staggered back and breathed deeply, waiting for

the other man to stir. He bent down and picked up a large rock, ready to brain Bashar before he got to his feet. But Bashar didn't rise. Carter approached him cautiously and felt for a pulse, finding a weak one. He sighed in relief. He needed Bashar to tell him how he got the children in here without drowning them. After that, the bastard could die for all Carter cared.

"Keep an eye on him while I get Beth loose," he said to Liam. "Let me know if he starts coming around."

"Okay, Dad. You need to check on the dolphin, too. I can wait."

The dolphin! Was Carmen still alive? Carter finished untying Beth and went back to the shoreline. Beth was right behind him. "She's over here," she said, taking his hand and pulling him farther along the edge of the river.

"How do you know it's a she?" Carter asked, smiling down at his little girl.

"I just know. I guess Akela told me," she answered. She didn't seem to think it was remarkable.

Carter saw Carmen lying on her side, held mostly out of the water by a fishing net. He approached slowly, reluctant to learn the dolphin was dead while Beth looked on. But when he put his hand on her side, Carmen whistled. Carter snatched his hand back. "You're alive!" he shouted. "Your mother is going to be so happy."

He could tell Carmen was in bad shape, but he felt there was one silver lining. She must have been difficult to get in through the narrows in the cave system, but he could tell she'd lost weight by the way her skin hung on her around her dorsal fin. "We'll get you out of here and fatten you back up in no time," he said, patting her gingerly. Then, not knowing if the tatters of skin were sensitive, he withdrew his hand. "I'll be right back."

He wasn't certain Carmen understood everything he said, and he had no way of knowing what she'd said with her one weak whistle, but he needed to release Liam, who'd been very patient for a boy of nine.

Bashar came around not long after Carter had used the ropes he'd removed from his children to truss the man securely. Carter was watching him for signs of consciousness when he did.

"Glad you could join us, Ahab," he said.

"I knew you recognized me," Bashar snarled. "How did you get in here? It's impossible for anyone but me."

Carter grinned a feral grin. "That will remain my secret for now. But if you want to get *out* of here, you'll tell me how you got my children and the dolphin in."

"Two can keep secrets, my friend. How long can your children go without food and fresh water? I'm betting I can last longer than they can."

"You'd be betting that I won't continue to incentivize you to tell me," Carter answered mildly. He looked around for a rock of just the right size. Finding one, he picked it up and walked over to Ahab, then casually dropped the rock on his shin. A sickening crack told the story.

Ahab howled in pain but bit off his cry. He glared up at Carter. "You're a monster."

"Oh, I think we both know who's the monster. Be quick. We… correction, *you* don't have all day."

"You would not torture me as your children looked on," Ahab tried.

"Try me. Better yet, I think I'll let my son drop the next rock. He's the one who was yelling 'kill him' a few minutes ago."

"Dad," Liam said.

"Quiet, son. I'm having a conversation with our guest."

"But Dad, Sean's here."

Carter turned around to see his friend climbing out of the water, a black tubular object in one hand. "Hey, buddy! What are you doing here? And what's that?"

"All according to plan, Carter. You've been in here over four hours. Coming up on five. I thought I'd better come and rescue you. And this," he said, brandishing the black tube, "is what he must have been using to get in and out so fast. It's a SeaDoo. Individual propulsion device. I found it tucked under an overhang just over there." He grinned, casting a significant look at the tied and miserable Bashar.

"You were supposed to follow me five hours later, and it took me four to get here."

"So, I swim a bit faster than you. And I figured if it was much of a distance, I'd better follow as soon as we knew the respirocytes were working. I knew that in an hour."

A gasp from Bashar turned both their attention to him. He'd turned a bit green, or maybe it was the bioluminescent organisms on the wall that gave him that color. "Do you have something to say, asshole?" Carter asked.

Beth said, "Daddy, that's a bad word."

"Yes, it is, sweetheart. Unless the person is a bad person. And then it's the perfect word. But I won't say it anymore." To Bashar, Carter said, "What's your problem?"

"Respirocytes. That… that is impossible. The research was destroyed."

"What research?"

Bashar spilled it then. His life story. Algosaibi's research, all the failed experiments. His extraordinary abilities. "But you have not been genetically altered. You cannot have respirocytes."

"Wrong again. My wife happens to be brilliant. I have them, Sean has them, and soon they'll be saving the lives of hundreds of thousands of people with respiratory illnesses. But that's beside the point. Tell me how you got the children in here, and you'll live to stand trial for the murders you've committed."

Bashar must have thought he could beat the murder charges, or perhaps he thought he could escape somehow, or that a few more months or years of life were worth hoping for. He explained the makeshift dive equipment he'd used for the children as well as the drugs he'd used to slow their respiration, so their tanks would last.

It was all Carter could do to stop himself from choking the life out of the man who'd put his kids at such risk. But he knew he'd have to do the same to get them out. There was just one problem. The tanks were empty, and there were no more drugs. He thanked God that Sean hadn't waited for the full five hours. Someone was going to have to go out to resupply the tanks and get a safe dose of something to put the kids to sleep during the return trip.

And the SeaDoo would have to be recharged at least once, to get the kids and the dolphin out safely.

"Kids, if I stay here with you, are you okay to wait until our dolphin friend, Carmen, gets out? She's really sick."

"I'm hungry," Beth said. "But I will eat the yucky food if Carmen needs to go first."

Liam agreed.

"Tell us how you rigged the dolphin's air, and I won't break your other leg," Carter said to Bashar.

"It doesn't matter. There isn't enough left to get her back out," Bashar said. His indifferent delivery made Carter want to go back on his promise and kill the bastard right then.

"I have an idea," Sean said. "We've got extra oxygen in

our lungs, right? I'll give her some of mine, and I'll tow her out with this thing." He gestured to the SeaDoo.

"Mouth to mouth?" Carter asked.

"Mouth to blowhole," Sean said. "It looks to me like her only chance. I don't see her lasting another eight hours, do you?

"No, you're right. Go for it."

They had to 'persuade' Bashar to reveal where he'd hidden more rope, water, and food. But in short order, Sean had Carmen turned in the right direction, fastened to him by a rope, and he'd breathed into her blowhole to test the theory. She moved a bit better, though she was still in bad shape. Carter had explained to her what they were going to do, and she hadn't fought them. It was now up to Sean to get her out as fast as he could, and then return with the SeaDoo and full tanks for the kids.

Carter didn't give a second thought to what would happen to them if Sean failed to return. He knew his friend, and he knew his wife. Someone would be back, and then the ordeal would be over.

Chapter Forty-Two

Sean made it back in a little over seven hours. He'd used the SeaDoo going out, and he reported it had been a harrowing experience when the charge ran out before the last long stretch of flooded tunnel. But the mouth-to-blowhole scheme had worked well, and he was happy to report that Carmen was expected to survive her ordeal.

"You know, I didn't think about it before," Carter said. "I knew she'd fit through, because he got her in here. But what about that first, short stretch, where Franklin didn't fit? How'd you get her through there?"

"Oh, she's quite a bit smaller than Franklin. Her dorsal fin got a bit scraped again, but we got her through."

"I'll bet Merrybeth was happy," Carter remarked.

"Was she ever! I never saw her jump so high out of the water. And you'd better brace yourself when you come out. I think she's standing by to give you a big kiss."

Beth giggled. She'd been awakened by the men talking, though it was after midnight. Liam woke up then, too, so

Carter decided they might as well start back. But first, the kids had to go back to sleep, this time under sedation.

"Bethie," Carter said. "Can you be a brave girl? I need to give you a shot, so you can sleep through the trip back out to the surface."

"I don't want a shot, Daddy," she answered.

"Let me try, Dad," Liam urged.

"Okay."

"Beth, if you let Dad give you a shot, I'll bet Mom will never make you eat broccoli again."

"Okay!!! But Daddy, I don't want it to hurt."

"I'll do my best not to hurt you, sweetheart. Tell you what. I'll give Liam his shot first. He can tell you if it hurts." Carter hoped his son would get the message. He had no idea if the shot would hurt, but he didn't want to force his daughter to submit to it. She'd had enough trauma for one little girl's lifetime. More at his hands was not acceptable.

Liam took his shot like a man, not even a grunt of pain. Then he said, "Beth, it didn't hurt. It was a piece of cake."

"Can I have some cake, too, Daddy?" she asked.

"All the cake you can eat, once we get out."

She bravely held out her little arm, and to Carter's surprise, she didn't even say 'ouch'. A few minutes later, both kids were unconscious.

"Okay, get going. I'll deal with this piece of trash," Sean said, indicating Bashar. His leg had swollen to twice its normal size.

"I can't swim like this," Bashar complained.

"I'll tow you, but the least bit of funny business, and I'll cut you loose to fend for yourself," Sean said, showing Bashar his knife.

Carter had gently carried each child to the shoreline while Sean and Bashar were talking and was now quickly rigging their makeshift dive equipment and putting on the harness he'd fashioned from the rest of the rope. He called out to Sean that they were ready. Sean went to help get the kids in the water behind Carter and wished them Godspeed. Carter gave a hasty salute and then started the SeaDoo.

Bashar would not have a comfortable journey to the water's edge, nor a safe one through the cave system. Carter didn't much care. The man would be sentenced to life in prison for his crimes, since Great Britain didn't have capital punishment anymore. As far as Carter was concerned, death was too good for him. If he drowned being towed out, Carter wouldn't mourn his passing.

A little less than three hours later, he carefully handed each sleeping child up to their mother, who passed them to the clinician. She was standing by to bring them out of the deep sedation she'd calculated would give them their best chance to survive the trip through the flooded tunnels Sean had described.

After examining them, she pronounced them slightly dehydrated and in need of nutrition, but otherwise in great shape considering their ordeal. Liam told his mother what he'd promised Beth, and Mackenzie solemnly swore not to make Beth eat broccoli ever again.

Carter also underwent a physical exam. His respiratory capacity had already expanded to double its previous measurement, and he felt as fresh after his three-hour swim towing the children as if he'd just awoken from eight hours' sleep.

He had just one regret, he told Mackenzie. He hadn't asked Bashar if there'd been any evidence anywhere that Minotaurs had ever really existed.

Everyone aboard waited anxiously for Sean to appear.

He'd been due to set out as soon as he could rig up a harness for Bashar. But to do so, he was going to have to untie the man. All the other rope had been used for Carmen and the children. It was a calculated risk. Sean was certainly as capable of defending himself as Carter, and Bashar was injured. But Sean was overdue. It was nearly dawn.

Carter was preparing to go back in after them, when Sean's head finally broke the surface. Bashar was not with him.

"Don't tell me the bastard got away," Carter called.

"He's still in there. I had to cut him loose. What do you want to do?" Sean called back.

"We can't take the risk that he makes it out of there. You up to go back in?"

"Hell, yes. I feel like I could swim around the world," Sean answered.

Carter gave Mackenzie a swift kiss, then dropped one on each of his precious children's heads. "I'll be right there. I have a question for him, anyway."

He dropped into the water and together the two friends swam to the point where they needed to dive to get to the opening. "Where did you lose him?"

"He attacked me in the last big cave before the one where he was holding the kids. Pulled the rope I was towing him with around my neck and was trying to choke me. I managed to cut the rope like I told him I would. That must have been his goal. My headlamp failed before I found him in there. He could be anywhere by now, except out. That leg has to be slowing him down."

"Okay," Carter replied. "How are you thinking we do this?"

"I say we go as far as that cave, then one of us guards

the passage on this end of it, while the other searches the cave. I doubt he'll go back in any farther."

"Sounds like a plan. But wait, your headlamp is out of juice, right? Let's get you some fresh batteries, and I'm thinking we need weapons. What do we have?"

"We'll take the Glocks. Hope we don't need them, especially underwater. They're not accurate at any distance underwater, and shooting underwater will probably blow out our eardrums. But better to be prepared." Sean waited and rested, though he didn't seem to need the rest, while Carter went back to the side of the boat to get what they needed. When he returned, they set out with strong strokes and reentered the passage to the cave system.

The cave where Sean led was the one Carter had explored before, so when they got there, it was Sean who stayed in the water to guard Bashar's escape route, and Carter got out to explore the cave again. With his 6000 lumens LED headlamp turned all the way up in all three bulbs, he examined the cave floor for any clues where Bashar had stepped. It was mostly rock, though a few footprints in sand showed up between them. Then Carter caught a break.

Enough sand for Bashar to have taken two steps showed one foot dragging. Carter couldn't believe the man was walking at all, but he had enough respect for the strength of the big man that he looked up frequently to avoid an ambush. Coming upon a couple of large boulders with a narrow passage between them, Carter cautiously leaned forward just far enough to see around them without losing his balance. Crouched behind one of them, Bashar lunged at him.

Carter had just enough time to jump back and withdraw his weapon before Bashar was within a couple feet of him. "Stop right there," Carter commanded, leveling the Glock at Bashar.

Bashar stopped, an expression of hate twisting his face.

"You can either come out of there with your hands up, or I'll shoot you where you stand," Carter stated calmly. "But before you decide, I have a question for you. Did you ever find any evidence the Minotaur was real?"

"As a matter of fact," Bashar said, keeping his hands above his shoulders, "I did. It's back here."

Carter didn't trust what he was hearing. "Sean," he called out. "I've got him. Come over here, please."

Carter and Bashar held their standoff while Sean got out of the river and made his way to where they were standing.

Carter said, "He tells me there's evidence of the Minotaur's existence back behind those boulders. I don't trust him, but I have to know."

"Okay, that's easy." Sean sidled forward, grabbed Bashar by one upraised wrist and snatched him out from between the boulders. Bashar landed on his face with a snarl. Before he could get up, Sean put his foot on Bashar's back and pulled his own Glock. "I've got him. Go see if he was telling the truth."

Carter moved between the boulders and looked around. In an alcove along the side of the back wall of the cave, he could see a pile of large bones. He approached. When his light struck the bones, he recoiled. In the alcove were the bones of a huge skeleton that looked human, except for the head. Long, curved horns stuck out on each side of the skull, and an elongated jaw suggested a bovine head rather than a human. Yet, the spine of the skeleton disappeared into the back of the skull.

"I'll be tarred and feathered," he said.

He went back to where Sean and Bashar waited. "What were you going to do with that? he asked. "I assume you put it together. Were you going to claim you'd found the Minotaur? How did you expect to get away with a fraud like that?"

"It's no fraud," Bashar grunted. "I didn't put it together. I only just found it. And if I had to guess, I'd say there's probably a way to get out of here that leads to the Labyrinth. The real one."

"You're lying."

"I'm not. You can explore for yourself. But you'd better give me credit for the find, or I'll expose you for an artifact thief."

"We'll see about that. For now, we're going to leave it right there and take you where the families of the people you killed can get some justice. Let's go."

As Carter looked down to make sure of his footing, Bashar twisted and grabbed Sean's foot, making him lose his balance and fall with a heavy grunt onto a small boulder that knocked the wind out of him. Bashar grabbed for his Glock, and Sean held onto it in desperation.

Carter drew his weapon again, but he couldn't get a clean shot at Bashar without risking the bullet going right through him and wounding Sean. Sean was on the bottom of the fight, and he was having a hard time gaining an advantage. Carter felt he had just one choice. He jumped on Bashar's back, threading an arm around Bashar's neck, and grabbed his own wrist with his other hand. Then he squeezed, and kept squeezing as Bashar thrashed, trying to throw him off.

When Bashar slumped, Carter kept the choke hold firm until Sean rolled out from under him. "Thanks, buddy. He almost had me." Sean picked up his Glock and pointed it at Bashar. "Okay, I've got him covered. You can let go."

Carter let go, and Bashar collapsed to the ground. Carter nudged him with his foot. "Get up, asshole." There was no response.

Sean raised his eyebrows. Carter bent and put his fingers on Bashar's pulse point behind his ear. "Uh oh."

"What?"

"I think he's dead. Shit," Carter said.

"That's exactly what he was, and it's not your fault. You were trying to defend me. Justifiable in anyone's book."

"I know. I don't regret killing him myself. But his victims' families won't get their day in court, now."

"I'll bet they won't care. Come on, we've got to get this excrement out of here, before his body pollutes the entire cave system," Sean said. "Do you think he was telling the truth about the Minotaur?"

"Only if his lips weren't moving. But there's only one way to know, really. I'll have to organize a new expedition. I'm sure it isn't going anywhere while we get Bashar out and wrap up this business. I'll think about the new expedition afterward."

"To quote you, that sounds like a plan," Sean said. "And don't blame yourself for what happened to him. He brought it on himself. If you hadn't killed him, I would have, as soon as I got control of the Glock."

Chapter Forty-Three

It was still early morning on the day after Carter and Sean had rescued Liam, Beth, and Carmen, when the A-Echelon boat entered the town harbor with a dead man on board. Liam and Beth had been sound asleep when Carter and Sean got Bashar to the boat. With as little commotion as possible, the body was brought aboard and covered with tarps, so the kids wouldn't see him. They'd had enough trauma.

Mackenzie and the doctor hustled them off the boat and back to the hotel for baths, clean clothes, and a big breakfast. Meanwhile, Carter and Sean had the authorities to deal with. It took most of the day to unsnarl the various jurisdictions' concerns.

Chief among them were MI5 and MI6, who weren't happy that they couldn't close their case with anything more than supposition. To everyone's disgust, Bashar had never admitted the killings in London. The case would grow cold, and the news media would have a field day. But because Bashar's death hadn't happened on British soil, there was nothing they could do but grumble. Secretly, the MI5 detectives were relieved that a serial killer was gone forever. Some of them still advocated the death penalty for monsters like that, and they resented the expense of keeping them in prison for the rest of their lives.

Carter and Mackenzie debated whether to stay and let the kids enjoy their planned vacation, but finally decided another time would be better, after they'd had a chance to get over their ordeal. Besides, Mackenzie needed to get back to Freydis with the results of their unplanned experiment, and she needed both Sean and Carter there for examination and study.

The wrap-up was going to take several days, as Greek authorities wanted to debrief everyone on both the Athens team and the Crete team. Mackenzie, her parents, and the children took the jet home, with the pilot who'd been pressed into service to fly it before and a few of the Tala-based Executive Advantage team who'd already been debriefed by the time the plane got to Crete. The family members were exhausted and slept the entire way back.

On Crete, Carter and Sean were being grilled by police, who were baffled at their ability to do what they'd done. It was a tricky situation, because Irene had given them a gag order about the respirocytes. Without being able to talk about them, Carter and Sean couldn't explain their advantage. Carter had also cautioned Sean not to talk about the Minotaur skeleton, if that's indeed what it was. He wanted to verify it wasn't a hoax first. So, they both had markers of deception in their debriefing. Fortunately, though, no guilt indicators. Greek authorities were bewildered.

On the evening of the second day of questioning, Carter got a call from Theo and an invitation to dinner that night. He accepted, and at ten p.m., he and Sean met Theo in what turned out to be a popular restaurant. They had to wait for a while to be seated. In the meantime, they chatted idly, but Theo seemed to be barely able to contain his questions.

Finally, they were seated in a secluded alcove of the restaurant that Theo had requested when he arrived. Part of the wait was because that was the only table he'd accept. They placed their orders, and when they were finally alone, Theo leaned forward conspiratorially.

"Tell me, please, how you did it. My student believed you would perish in the attempt, or that it was a fairy tale you told us in the first place."

Carter and Sean looked at each other, questioning the wisdom of disobeying Irene to explain everything to this man, without whose help they would not have been able to effect the rescue. An understanding passed between them, and Sean gave Carter a slight nod.

Carter fixed Theo with a serious gaze. "What we're about to tell you is top-secret, and we could be prosecuted for telling you. Your having the knowledge will be dangerous. Do you still want to know?"

"I'm not sure," Theo said honestly. "Do I?"

"If you want to know how we did it, then yes. But you can't tell your student, or anyone else. If this gets out, your life may be in danger."

"From whom?" Theo asked.

"From our government, for starters," Sean growled.

"Then no, I think I do not want to know still," Theo said, grinning. "But it's true? You did what they are saying in the newspapers? You rescued your children from below ground?"

"It's true," Carter answered. "I'm sorry we can't tell you

how. If it is ever declassified, I'll let you know and tell you the whole story."

"I would appreciate that," Theo said. "And now, let us enjoy our meal."

"Only if you'll let me buy it," Carter answered. "We owe you."

"In that case, I would like to order a bottle of wine to go with the meal, and a round of ouzo for right now," Theo said. He winked and summoned the server. "Your finest ouzo for my friends," he requested.

A few moments later, he raised his glass with the cloudy liquid, diluted with just a splash of ice-cold water, and declaimed, "*stin uyeia sou!*"

Carter chuckled at Sean's baffled expression and raised his own glass. "And to your health as well!"

Sean's expression cleared. He raised his own glass. "Down the hatch!" Then he shuddered at the strong anise taste as he took the first sip, following Theo's lead. Given his choice, he'd have 'shot' it – swallowed it in one gulp. But when in Greece…

A few days later, everyone was released to return to their various duty stations and homes. Carter had summoned the plane back to Crete and put the pilot on a commercial flight back to Spain. Before the flight back to Freydis, he inspected every inch of his favorite toy. There wasn't a speck of dust to be found. The galley was fully stocked, and everything arranged as it should be. His pre-flight routine revealed all systems were go. With the plane full of A-Echelon and Executive Advantage team members, Sean in the co-pilot's seat, and Carter at the controls, they took off for home.

Chapter Forty-Four

Mackenzie was eager to get Carter and Sean into the lab to do some evaluations. Only then could they make any decision about whether to remove the respirocyte generators from their bodies until further animal testing could be done.

Carter and Sean both objected. Neither wanted an invasive surgery, which would be required to remove the mesh cage containing the generators. Both were enjoying the effects of increased oxygen uptake – a feeling of euphoria that Carter attributed to increased strength and vigor. And neither liked hospitals or anything resembling them.

"In other words," Makenzie explained to her team, "typical men."

The team laughed dutifully. There was nothing typical about either of these men, even before they were enhanced with respirocytes.

A week had passed since Carter had brought the team home, and still he and Sean, whom Irene had insisted remain at Tala until the decision about the surgery had been made, balked at coming in for their evaluations. They were too busy training, they claimed. Mackenzie had heard from Dylan that each was outperforming the rest of the team put together. That was one way of evaluating them, she supposed, but she wanted measurable data.

On the Monday morning following their week of excuses, she used the ruse of needing to see Liam's teacher about something to accompany Carter to Tala. After they went their separate ways inside the gate, Mackenzie went a different route to the training grounds to secretly observe.

Today, the entire group was doing obstacle courses. The object of the exercise was to hone their abilities to go over, around, under, or through any barrier to their objective. To Mackenzie, it looked like a dirty and exhausting game, but every face she could see was smiling. Evidently these young men thought it was fun.

As she watched, Mackenzie realized the trainees were vying to be the fastest at getting through the course. She began to time them as they raced to the first obstacle, a ten-foot or so wall, and scrambled over it. She couldn't see the entire course, as it was laid out in a circle. She could see the starting point and as the first group came around, now muddy and some limping, she saw it was also the end. They had to scramble back over the wall to the finish line. But in the ten minutes in between, they must have had some challenging obstacles, because no one got back over the wall with the same ease they'd gone over it in the beginning.

The trainees were taking the course in groups of four. Mackenzie had missed timing the first group until she realized it was a race. That group came back around spread out by nearly thirty seconds, and the last man endured a good-natured shoving back and forth between the other three when they were done. That's when Mackenzie started timing the next group. The second group also took about ten minutes, and each of the groups after that took a little less time. She surmised that they'd been grouped by speed and ability, the newer recruits going first, and then the more experienced or more athletic coming afterward.

Then she recognized Carter and Sean in the last group, matched with Dylan and one other man she didn't know. This was going to be interesting. She knew Dylan to be highly competitive in everything he did. Her money, though, was on Sean. She felt no disloyalty to Carter in thinking that. It was Sean's job to be in top physical condition, and he had the musculature developed over long years to attest to his excellence. He was also highly competitive. Carter, on the other hand, was more likely to compete against his own personal best. He wanted to excel, not because it was his job – or not all the time – but because he drove himself hard, believing that the gifts of intellect and wealth he'd been given obligated him to make a difference in the world.

The starting gun fired, and the three men she knew well hit the wall within a split second of each other. The fourth man was already a second or two behind. Carter and Sean almost leaped over the wall. With their arms extended, they had no trouble catching the top, but where Dylan caught the top and then used his feet to propel him over, Carter and Sean both simply pulled strongly, pushed off when their upper bodies cleared the top, and flipped to land on their feet on the other side.

Mackenzie wasn't sure what to make of it, until she noticed the fourth man stopped on the ground, his mouth hanging open as he stared at the disappearing backs of

Carter and Sean, with Dylan trailing yards behind. Then he dispiritedly began to trot away from her, evidently determined to finish the course, but knowing he'd be last no matter what.

Five minutes later, Sean and Carter came back into view. They were as muddy as the others had been, but still moving fast. Sean took the wall one second ahead of Carter, but because he was heavier she suspected, Carter made up half the second before they made the finish line. They were high-fiving for two minutes before Dylan appeared. He finished a full three minutes after them – still the best time for a non-enhanced man. Carter and Sean absorbed him into a circle of three and slapped him on the back. Mackenzie surmised he'd just beat a personal, or maybe a camp record.

She turned away, smiling. Pleased that Carter had acquitted himself well against Sean, she wondered if she could bring herself to take away what he was clearly enjoying. But the ethical issues her team had wrestled with since the old lab rat had shown early indications of the side effects remained. And they still didn't know whether Sean and Carter would be affected with the worst of them – the antisocial behavior. She understood intellectually that Carter hadn't meant to kill Bashar, only keep him from killing Sean. But emotionally, she wondered if he hadn't squeezed just a little bit too hard because of the respirocytes.

Without letting them know she'd been there, she went back to the school, spoke to Liam's and Beth's teachers to learn if they were showing any signs of maladjustment after their ordeal, and then went back home. She called her dad and asked him to take the children hiking or fishing after school, so she could have a serious and private conversation with Carter. And then she went to her lab. It was time to sacrifice Methuselah to learn what they could about his change of temperament.

_____

When she got to her lab, she had several requisition orders to sign, and a few of the scientists wanted her opinion of this or that. It was nearly noon before she had a chance to talk to the veterinarian. She asked her research assistant to busy herself elsewhere and gave her mother the rest of the day off. Then she called in her tender-hearted veterinarian for a consultation she thought would be difficult.

"How is it going?" she asked him first.

"Well! We have been experimenting with the number of generators needed to achieve optimal results. They've improved the mesh cages. I don't think we've had any more mishaps with roaming nanobots. I've been constructing more and more complex mazes, and there seems to be no limit to the subjects' capacity to learn them within hours. For my money, it's an unqualified success," he answered. But his eyes shifted away from hers as he uttered the last sentence.

"Truly? How are Methuselah and your second subject doing? Have any of the others showed similar signs of anti-social behavior?"

He couldn't look at her as he answered. "Well – I can't say for sure. Maybe the others are just reacting to Methuselah's treatment of them."

"Pushing back against a bully, now that they can match him physically?" she asked, genuinely curious.

"Something like that," he answered.

"You know," she said gently, "we still need to understand

what happened with Methuselah. And now maybe with the others. I'm afraid it's time for that examination we talked about."

"I understand. I appreciate your delicacy, but I've come to realize I've been valuing the lives of non-sentient animals over humans. I still wish there were a way to test the safety of new drugs and procedures without harming animals, but I can do what you need me to. I'll do it this afternoon."

Mackenzie sighed in relief after he left. She would have hated to have to fire him, but his previous attitude had made her wonder if he was up to the job. Now she knew why he was available. As a brilliant researcher, he should have been in great demand. No one had warned her in her background checks on him that he was too sensitive for the work. But now it seemed he'd work out.

She went home for lunch, as did most of the workers on Freydis. It was one of the perks of working in a tight-knit and geographically close community. But unlike in a big city, they had the rural ease of living and beauty of the surroundings to enjoy as well. Mackenzie thought of it as heaven on earth, and as far as she knew, their employees did, too.

At home, she found a freshly showered Carter fixing lunch for them. "Hi, honey!" she said, standing on tiptoe for a kiss. "Do anything interesting today?"

"Had some fun at Tala," he answered. "Did you enjoy the performance?"

"How did you know I was there?" she asked, amazed but disconcerted. She'd concealed herself well, she thought.

"My vision seems to be improving, as well as everything else. I caught sight of you watching from the trees when I went over the wall."

"You bum! You didn't give any indication," she said. She punched him lightly.

"Didn't want to spoil your fun. So, what did you think?" he asked.

"I think you and Sean need to quit stalling and come in for your evaluations. It's important, Carter. I'm concerned about a few things, but even if my concern turns out to be unfounded, we can still find out valuable information for the later human trials."

"I'll talk to Sean, and we'll be in tomorrow. But can you tell me what you're concerned about?" he answered.

"There's still an indication that the respirocytes might be responsible for some degree of antisocial disorder," she said. "To be honest, I've been concerned about what happened in that cave." Seeing Carter opening his mouth to protest, she held up her hand. "I'm not very concerned, Carter. I haven't seen anything since that day to worry me. But we're examining the first rat subject's brain this afternoon for evidence of changes. If we see anything to indicate it's more than just a nanobot lodged somewhere it shouldn't be, I'm going to want to remove the generators from you and Sean. I'm sorry if that spoils your fun."

Carter frowned. "It isn't just fun, Mackie. I can't tell you how amazing it is to feel like this. Like I could be like Superman. You know, 'faster than a speeding bullet, more powerful than a locomotive, able to leap tall buildings in a single bound.'"

Mackenzie felt a thrill of alarm. "That's a problem, Carter! Don't you see? You *can't* do any of that, not even with the respirocytes. It worries me that you may try to do something that will get you killed, just because you *feel* like you can. Now I think we need a psych evaluation, too."

Carter's jaw dropped. "You can't be serious!"

"Please, Carter. For me. Just to make sure you can trust your own judgement."

He shook his head. "All right. If it will make you feel better. But I'm sure your fears are unfounded."

"Then there's no reason not to undergo the tests, right?" she said.

Chapter Forty-Five

Mackenzie observed methuselah's euthanasia. The vet was dry-eyed as he injected the sedative that would put the rat humanely to sleep, then suppress his respiration until he expired. Mackenzie considered it a good sign.

When the rat had quit breathing a few minutes later, she also observed the preparation of its brain tissue for electron microscope examination. They were looking for the missing respirocyte generator. If they found it in the part of Methuselah's brain that corresponded to a primate's prefrontal cortex, specifically that part responsible for social behavior, then it would be arguable that the nanobot's presence there could account for the rat's behavior. However, then they would have to examine other rat brains to verify it was the diamondoid fullerene, rather than the generated respirocytes, at fault.

Mackenzie found herself periodically holding her breath and consciously remembering to breathe as the veterinarian prepared each slide for examination. For what seemed like hours, he carved impossibly thin slices of frozen brain matter, stained them with the dyes that would help differentiate structures, and transferred them meticulously to dozens of slides.

Sometime during the afternoon, Irene unexpectedly joined her. "Hey, Mackenzie. Did you get my message?" she whispered.

Mackenzie looked up, startled, and shook her head to bring herself back to a broader focus. "I guess not. You mean the one where you let us know you were coming?"

Irene shook with silent laughter. "Yeah, that's the one. Carter let me know you were here, and what's going on. Want to fill me in a little more?"

Reluctantly, Mackenzie left her post. She knew she didn't need to supervise. It was only the stakes of the examination that had kept her there. She quietly told the veterinarian she was leaving but would be in her office, and then left him to his work.

As they walked down the hall, Mackenzie asked, "So, what did Carter tell you, exactly?"

"Something about you thought he might turn into a serial killer if you left those nanobots in his body," Irene said. She laughed, which Mackenzie took to mean she was exaggerating.

"Well, maybe not a serial killer," she said, with a little less humor. "But yes, there's a concern about antisocial behavior. What brings you here on a Monday?" she asked.

"Three-day weekend in Washington. When Carter called to see if there was anything urgent on the horizon, he told me you might be doing surgery on him and Sean. I had to come see for myself. You can't seriously mean to deprive the guys of their superhuman powers, can you?" This time she winked.

They'd reached Mackenzie's office, and Mackenzie

decided it was time to give Irene a full run-down on the research progress they'd made so far. When she'd finished, Irene was no longer joking.

"That would be a serious setback, wouldn't it?" she observed.

"Yes. We'd have to go back to the drawing board to figure out how to offset that side-effect, before it would be useful to DARPA or anyone else. And there are other ethical issues involved." She explained the longevity issue, but Irene waved it off.

"I don't see that as quite as much of a problem as you do," she said. "Other medical advances have extended the average lifespan of humans. Why not double it?"

"Well, because this would do so artificially, not as a result of better genetics, better food, medicine, and medical care. We'd essentially have to give everyone the nanobots to be fair. And then there's the question of how sustainable our standard of living would be, if everyone lived twice as long. The resources of the planet are already strained as it is."

Irene nodded slowly. "I see you've given this quite a bit of thought. But let's table that discussion for another time. If you determine the antisocial behavior is caused by the extra oxygen to the brain, then that becomes the first obstacle to overcome. After that, you can discuss the longevity issue with DARPA. But I suspect they'll want you to continue anyway. There's probably a solution."

Mackenzie answered, "I sincerely hope so. I was so encouraged when Liu found the schematics for the respiro-cyte generator nanobot. That put us months ahead of our projected timeline. And then when we had to use that desperate experiment to find our children, and it actually worked… Well, I guess I don't have to tell you that I thought a breakthrough was possible this year."

"It still is, Mackenzie. Let's think positively. When will you know?"

"What we'll be looking for is the area of the rat's brain where the missing nanobot lodged, if indeed it's even *in* the brain. How much do you know about brain function?" Mackenzie asked.

"I know mine doesn't function before my first cup of coffee in the morning," Irene quipped.

Mackenzie laughed. "I hope you've had yours today, then, because you're about to get a crash course, though it will be oversimplified. So, here's how what we're concerned about works. In humans and other primates, social behavior, among other things, is controlled by the prefrontal cortex." She tapped her forehead. "That's the bulge in the brain right behind here. It is a structural feature of our brains that controls function. Are you with me?"

Irene smiled. "I think so. That's why they used to perform prefrontal lobotomies for certain mental issues."

"Yes, well. That's for another discussion. Getting back to rats and other non-primates. There has been scientific debate over whether they have a structure comparable to the PFC, the prefrontal cortex. Because they don't have the physical structure that we do. If they did, they'd look like that cartoon character evil genius rat, with the high forehead. But because they seem to have some of the *functions*, for example, altruistic social behavior, quite a bit of study has gone into what brain structures in rats mediate those functions that are controlled in primates by the PFC."

"I get it. Where in the brains of rats do their social behaviors originate, or where are they controlled? Yes?" Irene summarized.

"Precisely. And the answer seems to be the function is divided among several structures, chiefly the anterior cingulate cortex and the dorsolateral prefrontal cortex. The ACC is responsible for motor control, perhaps cognition, and a relationship with the arousal or drive state of the animal. The DL-PFC isn't an anatomical structure at all, but a functional one. And its function in rats seems to be associated with rats' medial PFC."

"Wait... What's the medial... Actually, never mind. You can draw me a picture later. So, what's the bottom line?"

"Bottom line, we expect... No, that's wrong. We *hope* to find the missing nanobot lodged in either the ACC or preferably the medial PFC. The latter would strongly suggest that the first subject's antisocial disorder was caused by irritation or blood clotting in the anatomical structure we believe responsible for social rule encoding. The former would suggest it originates in the area responsible for decision-making in situations where cognitive conflict arises." Mackenzie got up to find a book in her library. "Here. This shows a rat's brain, compared to a human's."

Irene looked closely. "Okay. I think I get it. So, it isn't our minds that control our socialization, but our brains."

"Well, there you are getting into an area where medicine becomes philosophy. No one actually knows how consciousness – what we call our minds – arises. Whole different subject."

"Gotcha. So, back to my question. How long will it be before you know for sure?" Irene repeated.

"For sure? Maybe months. But enough to make the decision whether to immediately remove the nanobots from Carter and Sean, as soon as the slides have been examined. I believe he intends to start with those from the medial PFC, then the ACC, and then if he doesn't find it there, he'll examine the rest of the brain. If it isn't anywhere in the brain, we'll have to remove them from the guys as a precautionary measure, until we can inject more rats and develop a statistical profile." Mackenzie rubbed her head. She recognized her own gesture as a subconscious desire not to have that conversation with Carter.

"Let's hope they find it in the medium PFC, then," Irene said.

"Medial," Mackenzie corrected automatically. Then she apologized. "Sorry. You aren't one of my students."

"No, it's all right. Medial."

An ugly suspicion she didn't want to voice slipped into Mackenzie's mind. "Irene, why are you so interested in the mechanics? Are you here on DARPA's behalf?"

Irene's expression wavered between surprise and hurt. "What? No! You and Carter are like family to me, Mackenzie, not just employees, but dear, dear friends. And Sean, Dylan, all the EA guys I know are friends as well, not just colleagues. I'm concerned about them."

Mackenzie apologized immediately. She wouldn't use the excuse of stress, though she had that in plenty. But Irene went on.

"I'm going to put that down to stress, 'Kenzie. I know it's been tremendous for you. Have you considered taking a real break?"

"I can't. Not when we're so close. But thank you for understanding. I don't know what I was thinking," Mackenzie said, ignoring the new nickname. If she let that take hold, she wouldn't know what to answer to before long, Mackie, Sunhead, or 'Kenzie.

"I do understand DARPA's position, though," Irene continued. "The world has become a very dangerous place, and for the first time in history there's a serious threat on our turf. Your research could make an incredible difference in our favor."

"And that would present us with a different ethical dilemma. You know I started this research because of its promise for medicine. To make a difference in our favor, it would have to be kept secret. Once its benefits were proven and its existence known – I mean a practical, working solution, not just theory – it wouldn't take long for our enemies to reverse-engineer it." Mackenzie leaned forward to emphasize her seriousness.

"And what's wrong with it being secret?" Irene asked mildly.

"That would mean withholding it from people whose lives could be saved."

"Just a few minutes ago, you were worried about the world becoming overpopulated because of it. Now you want to save people who would die without it. Your positions are inconsistent, Mackenzie."

"Did you ever take an ethics class in college, Irene? Do you remember the impossible situations they put up for discussion? The sinking lifeboat, where one person's sacrifice meant the others would live? How do you choose? Or how about this...a maniac is using a little girl for a human shield while spraying a crowd with an automatic weapon. The only way to stop the carnage is to shoot him *through* the little girl. What's the answer? Let dozens of people die because you can't shoot the child? The use of this technology comes down to the same kind of ethical dilemma." Mackenzie had risen from her chair again, and was pacing back and forth in her office, her face the picture of misery. "I only wanted to do something good for humanity. And now I'm not sure if I should even continue the research."

Irene got up and caught the younger woman in her arms. "Mackenzie, honey. You're working yourself into a frenzy. You don't have to solve these issues yourself. We're here for you, Carter, me, Sean, and I'd be willing to bet POTUS will want to be involved. Stop thinking for a moment before you give yourself a nervous breakdown."

Mackenzie nodded, and to her surprise, burst into tears. "I'm so torn about Carter!"

"It will all work out," Irene assured her.

As if on cue, the veterinarian ran into the office at that moment, yelling, "I found it!"

Mackenzie's mood lifted instantly as she remembered the picture Dylan had painted of Liu dancing around in the wee hours of that morning a few weeks ago, yelling "Eureka!" The vet was grinning from ear to ear, and she grasped immediately that it was good news.

"Tell us!" she urged.

"It was in the medial PFC," he said in a rush. "Lodged along a primary neural pathway. It must have confused the hell out of poor Methuselah. But I'm confident it's what caused the antisocial behavior."

Both women sighed in relief. "Wow," Irene said. "I had no idea it would be so dramatic!"

Mackenzie wiped a lingering tear from her cheek, drawing a fleeting frown of concern from the veterinarian. "What is it?" he asked.

"Nothing." She waved him off. "That's great news! What do you propose as a confirmatory study?"

"I'll inject several more of the rats of both genders with the nanobots and observe their behavior. We should see the antisocial tendencies almost immediately if I'm wrong. I'd like to keep the second subject alive to see if his disappear now that Methuselah's behavior won't be a trigger."

"That sounds like a good plan," Mackenzie answered. "I'd like you to confer with the doctor and come up with an opinion on whether it's safe to leave the nanobots in my husband and his colleague for now. Can you have an answer for me by end of day?"

"I think so. Even if it's 'we can't decide', I'll report back by then."

"Thank you. And good job," she praised.

He left her office whistling a jaunty tune, and Mackenzie turned to Irene. "Looks like I was a baby for nothing," she said sheepishly.

"Not at all," Irene assured her. "It had to have been nerve-wracking to let Carter do it in the first place. Which reminds me, I have other news. I know Carter saved some of his debriefing information for us. Specifically, the information he got from Bashar about the experimentation that was done on him. I've had a report from the Greeks that Bashar's autopsy revealed some unusually large red blood cells. Would you like to have the report?"

"Need you ask? Of course! Even more, I'd like some of the samples," Mackenzie said.

"I thought you might say that. Consider it done. Do you think Algosaibi had the same information Liu discovered?"

"No, I don't. But there are often many paths to the same destination. From what Carter has told me, it seems Algosaibi was experimenting with DNA splicing," Mackenzie said. "But if I can examine some of the samples for myself, say, brain, lung, and blood, maybe I can figure out what was done to him. You know, I almost feel sorry for him," Mackenzie added.

Irene was incredulous. "Sorry for him! A serial killer! The man who kidnapped your children and would have killed them?"

Mackenzie nodded. "I know. And we may never understand it completely, but what if the same experiments that gave him his super strength and athletic ability also robbed him of his humanity? He was not to blame for being a victim of the Nabateans. In a way, it's like Methuselah's antisocial behavior, only on a human scale."

"You'd better hope not, because now you're back to blaming the respirocytes, not the misplaced generator," Irene pointed out.

"I suppose you're right. Only time will tell."

Chapter Forty-Six

With the approval of the doctor, subject to a retroactive
ethics review under US Common Rule regarding human
subject experimentation, Carter and Sean were allowed to
keep their respirocyte generators in place. She also required
them to submit to weekly physical and mental evaluation.

After a month of getting clean bills of health, Carter
asked when he could go back to Crete to examine the
skeleton Bashar had discovered. The doctor released him
and Sean from the weekly exams, then, but asked them to
come back monthly. By that time, Mackenzie had navigated
the complexities of the governmental restrictions. She had
agreed with the doctor about US Common Rule, because
the project was government funded. But the fact that they
were in Quebec created an issue.

Canada had its own equivalent to the US Office of
Human Subjects Research, popularly known as the Tri-
Council, comprising the Canadian Institutes of Health
Research, the Social Sciences and Humanities Research
Council, and the Natural Sciences and Engineering

Research Council of Canada. The Tri-Council Policy Statement governed human research in Canada, and when the US government funded research projects at Canadian institutions, the rules of both countries applied. Quebec itself added an extra layer of ethics review, with its requirement for ethics review of *all* research taking place within its borders.

The top-secret requirement DARPA had placed on the research made it tricky to navigate the regulatory requirements, but she finally had permission to fast-track the human trials, mostly based on the data the doctor was able to provide for Carter and Sean. DARPA had finally conceded that democratically-advanced allies could be let in on the research, so long as they also kept it under top-secret wraps.

Mackenzie's team was preparing to welcome observers from Canada, the US, Great Britain, and Australia, who would monitor the studies and make the ethical decisions that had troubled Mackenzie so much. She privately reserved the right to make her own as well, but she confided to Carter that she understood it would be of little consequence if she disagreed with the ethics team. The decisions were above her pay grade, Carter teased her.

Now that he'd been released, Carter's desire to get to the bottom of the Minotaur legend had him planning a new archaeological expedition. In practical terms, only Sean would be able to accompany him, since the cave was unreachable by ordinary human means. But he hoped to find the passage to the Labyrinth that Bashar had surmised would be deeper in the cave, so the entire area could be excavated scientifically and the age-old argument of where the real Labyrinth had been could be put to rest.

Sean agreed to go with him, saying it would be like a

vacation for him, although his agency was still charged with Carter's safety. A week after the doctor released them from weekly evaluations, they took off in Carter's jet for Crete.

Carter's first visit was to Alan Connery, who'd been generous with him before. Connery was winding down his dig for the season, but he greeted Carter and Sean enthusiastically. "I'm so glad you dropped by," he said. "I've been meaning to email my congratulations that you recovered your children safely."

"Thank you," said Carter. "I'm here to wrap up a discovery we made in the process. We may need some help, if you'd like to participate next season. I can't guarantee we'll find what we're looking for, but you'd be welcome if we do."

"I'll take it under advisement, my friend. Good luck," Connery answered.

His social obligations behind him, Carter dropped Sean at a hotel and went to charter a boat to take them to the eastern entrance to the cave system. They could have swum there from the beach at the park, and they discussed doing so. But Carter wanted to bring out the skeleton if they could, so they decided having the boat would be more prudent.

"Are you going to give Bashar the credit for finding it?" Sean asked.

"Depends on what it is," Carter said. "If it's a hoax, then I doubt I'll even publish it. But yeah, on the doubtful chance that it's real, I think I'll have to, distasteful as that might be. I certainly can't take credit for it."

"Understood. Let's go get it, then."

Carter knew he couldn't bring out the whole skeleton. If it turned out to be genuine, the destruction of the provenance would be shameful. But before he went to the trouble of looking for a passage through the subterranean strata, he wanted to verify it was a hoax, even if it wasn't Bashar's hoax.

The two men made the now-familiar trip through the cave system to the large cave where Bashar had died. Carter half-expected the weird skeleton to be gone, but it was right where they'd left it. With his and Sean's headlamps illustrating it, he could see that the upper part of the human spine seemed to be fused with the bovine skull, but he couldn't tell whether it was a recent hoax or an ancient one. Reluctantly, he confirmed he'd have to get it out and examine it by x-ray and other means before disarticulating it. However, he had no compunction about separating the upper spine, clavicles, scapula and sternum from the rest, so he could leave the rest of the skeleton in place.

Fortunately, he had anticipated just this problem. Though he had originally thought Bashar must be lying when he said he hadn't created the skeleton, Carter had decided there was no reason for Bashar to have lied. He knew Carter would come back to make some sense of it, and that he would never be free again. Unless he was simply messing with Carter's head, there was a chance he was telling the truth. So, Carter had brought a portable x-ray machine in the jet's cargo hold. Once he and Sean had wrestled the partial skeleton out of its resting place, they put it in a fine-mesh net they'd brought for the purpose and towed it out of the cave system to the boat under wraps, so the crew wouldn't see it.

From there, they transported it to the hangar where Carter had arranged to store the jet while in Crete. There, they took the x-ray machine out of the jet and hooked it up to a portable generator Carter rented. At last, they'd be able to get to the bottom of the mystery.

When they turned on the machine, the built-in screen showed something they couldn't make out. Carter made some adjustments, and the picture resolved to show them the truth. Sean said, "What the hell?"

Carter shook his head. "It must have been excruciating."

Sean said, "But I don't understand. What is it?"

"I'd have to have a doctor or a veterinarian examine it to be sure, and I know just the ones to do it. We'll have to take it home. What I think it was, is a human being with a bull's head grafted onto the spine, but it could be a thousands-of-years old hoax. I'm not sure how long it takes for bone to become fossilized in this environment. Maybe we should talk to Theo. I'll bet he could answer that."

"Go ahead. He already thinks we're insane," Sean joked.

A quick call to Theo confirmed that mineralization of the bone could have fused two unrelated species' skeletons together within a minimum of ten thousand years. The myth of the Minotaur was about the right age. So, they still didn't know whether they had a hoax or a medical anomaly on their hands. Carter said as much.

"But we couldn't do that even today! How…" Sean stopped speaking. Carter had turned up more unusual findings than this. It didn't matter how, not until it had been proven one way or the other.

"I can surmise, but I don't know if we'll ever be able to prove it." Carter said, answering Sean's unspoken question. "I can say one thing. If I'm right, then Bashar may also have been right that the back of that cave is hiding a passage to the surface. We're going to have to go back and search."

"You're the boss. Want to go ahead and do that while we're here?" Sean asked.

"Might as well. But I'm eager to get this back home and find out how it was done."

"I'm up for another swim today. Shall we?" Sean grinned.

Carter understood. He hadn't felt this energized in years, either, if ever. "Let's go!"

They took water and food this time, in case the search and exploration of the passage took longer. They asked the baffled boat crew, who couldn't understand how their charges could stay so long underwater, to take them once again to the bay.

Climbing up through the boulders that concealed the remainder of the skeleton, Carter looked ahead rather than at the alcove where the skeleton lay. Sean was right behind him. By unspoken agreement, Carter went left, and Sean went right. The cave was narrower back here than at the underground river's shoreline. If a passage was here, it wouldn't take long to find it, and it didn't.

Carter spotted the opening first and called Sean over. It was narrow, but tall enough that Sean could enter it standing up. He deferred to Carter but cautioned him to watch out for unstable rubble. Carter moved forward cautiously. He slipped sideways through a pair of stalactites that drooped almost to the floor of the cave, and into a larger room that had been partially sealed off by the formations.

"This may not be as quick as we thought," he called to Sean, who had been forced to crawl at the bottom of the stalactites to fit his larger body through.

Another hour passed while they divided and conquered the larger room. This time, Sean found the way through.

They had walked in a tunnel-like passage that led steadily upward for another half hour, when it opened again into a larger room. There, Sean called a halt and insisted they eat some of their provisions. They sat and discussed whether it was practical to keep going, when the route they'd been following could lead anywhere and take days to fully explore.

Carter pointed out that there was little chance of getting lost, as they hadn't found more than one passage in any cave room they'd passed. He argued that they could reasonably expect to go for hours more before tiring, thanks to their respirocytes. Sean agreed to explore for two more hours, but he pointed out they still had to return the way they came if they didn't find an opening to the surface soon, not to mention an arduous swim. And they hadn't explored the limits of their abilities. Carter agreed to the restriction, knowing there was nothing to keep them from returning on another day if they didn't reach the limit of the cave system on this trip.

"Do you have a sense of how long, total, we've exerted ourselves today?" he asked.

Sean replied that he thought they'd been on the move for at least twelve hours, with a couple of periods of rest of at least an hour during that period. He promised to keep track from then on. "This time, since leaving the boat, it's been about six hours," he estimated.

"Okay. That's important to know," Carter answered. "Are you ready to continue?"

"Go for it."

Carter was beginning to feel discouraged that they weren't going to find the answer before he had promised to turn back, when he noticed something on his hand while reaching for a handhold to pull himself up a six-foot shelf with a void beyond it. He stared at the spot for a while, before it dawned on him what he was seeing.

"Sean! There's a beam of sun on my hand!"

"Impossible. It's only about four a.m.," Sean said. Then he looked at his watch. "Damn, it's nearly eight! How did I miscalculate that badly?"

"Time flies when you're having fun," Sean quipped. "That's sunlight. There's an opening somewhere above!" He kept climbing, but when he found the opening, it was a mere crack between big rocks. There was no way to climb out. While he and Sean searched for an exit, their time to turn back came and went. An hour after that, Carter conceded temporary defeat.

"What if we could mark this spot on the surface?" he suggested. "How would you do it, with the resources we have?"

"It may not do any good, because it would be hard to spot from the air," Sean answered, "But that ridiculous red bandana in your go-bag might be the way to go. Can you poke it up through the opening you found?"

"I guess I could sacrifice it," Carter said. "But you're right. I doubt if it would do any good." He opened the bag that was suspended from his dive belt and took out the red bandana, a relic of his desert archaeological digs. It had traveled many miles with him. He extended his arm as far as he could through the opening, bandana in hand, and suddenly felt it snatched out of his fist. He gave a startled yelp.

"Who is that? Where are you?" a familiar voice demanded.

"Connery? Is that you?" Carter couldn't believe his ears.

"Yes. Who… Devereux?" Connery replied. "What are you doing down there, man?"

"Long story. Do you think you could help us widen this hole?" Carter asked. "Otherwise we have a long journey back. And we'd like to know where we ended up."

"You're safe?" Connery asked.

"Yes."

"Hold tight, then," Connery said. "I'll get some help."

Carter and Sean retreated from the hole, in case the help consisted of heavy machinery. While they waited, they found perches and took turns sleeping. Three hours later, the rumble of machinery told them Connery was back. A wider swath of sunlight attested to one of the larger rocks blocking the exit being removed. The roar of the engine shut off, and Connery's voice floated down to them. "Is that big enough? I don't want to disturb more of the area than I have to."

Carter climbed back up and found he could get his head and shoulders through the newly-widened hole. "It's big enough for me. Pull me out, and we'll see if Sean can get through." He took Connery's hand, and with a boost from Sean from below, popped out through the hole like a groundhog. Then he turned and helped Connery pull Sean up.

Connery stepped back and put his hands on his hips. "Want to tell me how you got down there?"

"It's a long story," Carter said. "But yes, I think you deserve an answer. Where are we, by the way?"

"After you came around asking about the Labyrinth," Connery answered, "I decided to poke around a bit after my dig shut down."

"But we must be miles from Knossos," Carter objected.

"No. About fifty yards from the Palace, give or take," Connery said. "It's right through those trees there." He pointed.

Carter gave Sean a significant look. There was no other way to account for the distance than that they'd traveled about sixty miles as calculated in a straight line from the cave where they'd started. Considering the passage hadn't been straight, and that they'd been underground for a little more than nine hours, one of them spent combing the immediate area for an opening, it was a feat only possible because of their respirocytes. That meant they couldn't tell Connery how they'd gotten there, without obfuscating the details.

"We were spelunking," Carter said carefully. "I guess we lost our bearings. It was damn lucky you were there at the right time."

"Remarkable," Connery answered. "Well, I'm glad I was. And I'm glad the local authorities let me remove this rock. Now I have to put it back, or we'll all be in trouble."

"No problem, Alan," Carter responded. "I hope you won't mind if we hail a taxi to get back where we started."

"Oh, no need for that. I'll give you a lift."

"Really, we couldn't impose," Sean said. It wouldn't do for Connery to know how far they'd come. That would create questions they couldn't legally answer.

"Suit yourself, then," Connery said cheerfully. "I'll just finish up here. But you'll have to hike about three miles to Heraklion, unless you can persuade a tour operator to let you tag along. Tours should just be starting."

"Thanks, we'll manage," Carter said, suppressing a grin.

Chapter Forty-Seven

Back at Freydis, Carter and Sean landed with little fanfare. They weren't expected for another few days, but they'd done what they went to Crete to do. So, there was no need to linger there. Carter was anxious to have the partial skeleton he'd brought back examined by Mackie's team.

To avoid startling Mackenzie by walking unannounced into her office, Carter called her from the runway. "Hi, honey, I'm home!" he said, in a singsong voice.

"Carter! What are you doing home so soon? Where are you, at the house? I'll be there in five minutes…"

Carter laughed. She sounded as excited to see him as she had been when they were newly in love, and he was just as excited to see her after only a few days' absence. He was a lucky man. "No, we just landed. Listen, stay there. I'm bringing something for your team to examine. It's beyond my expertise."

"You found it? The Minotaur?" she asked.

"I found something. Darned if I know exactly what it is, but I have a theory. But I don't want to influence your team

– specifically your doctor and veterinarian. I'll just bring it and see what they have to say."

"Okay, I'll see you in a few minutes then?"

"Give me half an hour."

Carter was so anxious to get the partial skeleton in the hands of the scientists that he barely took the time to shower and change clothes after the long flight. Twenty-nine minutes after his call to Mackenzie, he wheeled a small crate on a dolly through the front door of the lab building. Mackenzie met him at her office door.

"Where shall I take this?" he asked.

Mackenzie led him to one of the examining cubicles in the clinician's lab, where she and the veterinarian were waiting.

The clinician greeted him. "Good to see you again, Carter. As soon as we're done here, I'll want to examine you and Sean and debrief you on what you did in Crete."

"Sure," he said. "But this is going to take you a while, I think." He slipped the dolly's lift plate out from under the crate, opened the crate's lid, and gestured for everyone to have a look inside.

Mackenzie peeked in, but left room for the veterinarian and clinician to get closer. A full ten seconds passed before anyone said anything. Then the veterinarian whispered, "What the hell is that?"

Carter chuckled. "I was hoping you could tell me. This is only part of it. I left the rest of what looked like a human skeleton in place, but I have pictures."

"This can't possibly be one, er, individual," the clinician said.

"I also have some interesting x-rays, if you want them. But I figured you'd have more sophisticated equipment."

"What do they show?" the clinician asked.

"I'm going to let you tell me," Carter said again. "I don't want to influence your examination. I will say this. The upper part of the spine is fused to the skull."

"Impossible," the doctor said again, shaking her head. "Let's get it on the table. Carter, your examination and debriefing will have to wait. I'll see you at eight a.m. tomorrow. Bring Sean with you."

Carter felt like he'd been dismissed, but he was happy that the two scientists were as eager to get to the bottom of the mystery as he was.

"Mackie, can you leave work early today? I'd like some time with you before the kids get home."

Mackenzie blushed and nodded. She sneaked a look at the two scientists who were carefully lifting the partial skeleton from the crate onto the table. Neither was paying any attention to Carter's words.

"I have an item or two to clear off my desk, and then I'll be home. See you in half an hour?" she said.

"Make it twenty-nine minutes," Carter deadpanned. He walked out of the lab, confident his mystery would be solved by the next morning.

Carter and Sean presented themselves at the clinician's lab promptly at eight a.m., with Mackenzie tagging along. She wouldn't stay for their examination, but like Carter, she expected a report from the clinician on the unusual skeleton Carter had left there the afternoon before.

To everyone's surprise, the doctor said nothing about it. Instead, she had Carter and Sean sit down in chairs she'd arranged in front of her desk and told Mackenzie she'd be awhile and not to wait. Mackenzie threw Carter a puzzled look as she left. He responded with a shrug.

For the next half hour, the doctor questioned Carter and Sean about their physical exertion inside the cave system, asking about the time they spent there, distance traveled, and what they'd consumed. She seemed satisfied with their answers, even though most of them were vague because neither man had thought to keep precise notes at the time.

She seemed most interested in the distance they'd managed to travel in the ten or so hours they thought they'd been in the cave, and what they'd eaten when they got to town. After notating their answers in both files, she lifted the phone and spoke to someone else, asking them to come in and join them.

Carter recognized the psychologist who'd been brought on board just a month ago. *What's he doing here?"* he wondered. It soon became apparent.

Carter and Sean both stood, accustomed to talking with the psychologist alone, but he asked them to sit down. "This won't take long," he said. His first question was whether they were comfortable talking about Bashar's death together. He'd talked to each of them separately about it, and this wasn't the first time he'd circled back to that fight.

Carter didn't have an objection. After all, Sean was there. And he didn't think Sean would have an objection either. *He* hadn't killed Bashar, Carter had. The psychologist asked a few questions that Sean had answered before, and then the conversation took an unexpected turn.

He began to ask about how they'd found the skeleton, when they'd first seen it, and why they'd brought out only part of it. Sean seemed content to let Carter answer the questions, finally answering when the psychologist asked him directly if Carter's answers were accurate according to his recollection.

"Of course," he said.

"They're telling the truth," the psychologist said to the doctor. Then he left with no further comment.

Carter was astounded. "You thought we'd *lie* about this?" he asked the doctor. "If you did, then that shrink should have talked to us separately."

She answered in a calm voice. "No, I didn't think you would, but I had to have documentation for when the media gets hold of this story."

"What do you mean, the media? The media isn't going to hear anything about it," Sean said, jumping to his feet. "This is top-secret."

Carter nodded. "What story? What did you find?"

"I think it's time to call your wife back in, Carter. And my colleague. We have some disturbing conclusions."

Carter waited impatiently while Mackie and the vet were summoned. Sean seemed calmer, but he never seemed to get ruffled. When they were all assembled, the doctor led the way back to the cubicle where the skeleton still lay on the examining table.

"We worked all night on this, and we're prepared to offer our conclusions, though we have a few tests still running that should confirm them," the doctor began. "First, these bones are not fossilized, though some mineralization has begun. We didn't want to subject them to strong X-rays, because the literature we were able to find on examining sub-fossilized bone indicates that it damages the DNA in the marrow. And the... unusual... nature of this specimen dictated that we run DNA tests on the skull and the other portion of it to confirm that they don't match. That is the test we're waiting for." She paused and gestured for the veterinarian to continue.

"Our hypothesis was that this was some clever hoax. However, the apparent age of the bone led us to believe that the hoax was manufactured at some time in the past. We're also waiting for carbon-dating of the bone to determine how long ago. But once we had the DNA and bone samples for those tests, we ran the skeleton through the CT-scanner."

He stopped for breath, and it was the doctor's turn to take up the narrative again. Carter was about to jump out of his skin, waiting for the punch line. What had they seen in that scan? He made an impatient noise, and Mackenzie put her hand on his arm to calm him. The doctor suddenly smiled at him.

"I'm sorry this seems so dramatic, Carter. But you can't imagine what we found with the CT-scan." Her expression darkened. "What was done to this man was monstrous, and hardly believable. What we found inside the bull's skull was a partial skull of a human being. Several of the facial bones, to be exact." She crossed the room to another cubicle, where she drew out an articulated plastic skeleton and rolled it across to the open cubicle where they were gathered. There, she pointed out the lower portion of the skull's front, naming the bones as she touched each of them. "The mandible, maxilla, and zygomatics are all visible inside the bovine skull." She turned the skeleton, so they could see the back, and pointed out the cervical axis, the spinal bone that connects directly with the skull. "This bone, the cervical axis, connects directly with the skull in both humans and cattle." She pushed the plastic skeleton aside and turned the bovine skull on the table slightly. "You can see that the same bone here is oriented in a different direction. In a human, it's only slightly off parallel with the ground. This supports our skulls with their heavy brains on top of the column of the spine. Now, in cattle, it's perpendicular to the ground, as the spine itself is more or less parallel to the ground, with the exception of the neck, which rises only slightly. Does that make sense?"

Carter, Sean and Mackenzie all nodded. The doctor continued.

"This is a human cervical axis, but it has been turned about forty-five degrees and fused with the bull's skull. If the facial bones had not been left intact *inside* the bull's larger facial bones, we would have had a different conclusion. But, although we don't have the soft tissues to prove it, we believe this was somehow done to a living human being. Whoever did this essentially *grafted* a bull's head on the poor soul."

Carter slammed one fist into the palm of the other hand. "I knew it!" He raised his stinging palm to meet Sean's high five.

Mackenzie was horrified, but her scientific curiosity won over her distaste for the mental image. "Why do you think the human was living?"

"Because," the doctor answered, "the bone has completely knit. The creature lived at least for some time in this condition. Don't ask me how. I can't imagine how it could operate the bovine jaw to open and shut it to eat, for example. That would have required neurosurgery on a level we can only imagine now."

Carter had settled down, the horror of the situation catching up with his excitement over the find. "So, you're saying this *thing* is not a hoax. The monster they created actually lived."

"For a time, yes. There's no way to tell how long, precisely. And we can't explain how. I believe it would have been quite insane, though. Imagine waking from anesthesia to learn most of your skull had been removed and your face, your whole head, being replaced by that of a bull's skeleton."

"Could it have been more than the skeleton? Could the skin, hair, and tongue have been intact?" Sean asked.

"After what we've seen, I won't ever doubt anything again. I suppose it could have been," the doctor answered.

"Like the images of the Minotaur of Crete?" Carter asked.

"Why, yes, I suppose it would have looked like that."

The veterinarian spoke slowly. "I remember learning about that when I was in school. Elective class," he added, embarrassed. "That thing was supposed to have torn people apart and eaten them."

"Which an insane creature might be forgiven for doing," Mackenzie offered.

Carter looked at the skeleton in awe. "We found... correction, *Bashar* found the true Minotaur!"

Mackenzie looked at him, distressed. "You aren't going to publish that, are you?"

"No, I don't think I can. And I don't think I can excavate to learn how it got from the Labyrinth in the Knossos Palace into that cave system, either. I'd have to explain how we got to the place where Bashar found this thing, and that's a secret. And I can't claim the discovery as mine, but I don't want to credit him, either. I think I'm going to have to put this back where I found it and forget we ever saw it."

Chapter Forty-Eight

Seven months later

Mackenzie couldn't decide whether spring was trying to come early, or winter was hanging on late. She always had trouble adjusting to Quebec's seasons, as it was colder here in March than it was back home in Boston. A chill rain was falling, so she took an electric cart to the lab rather than walk and arrive soaked. It looked like they might even get snow, as the forecast called for temperatures to drop later in the day.

Today was the conclusion of a six-month study of half a dozen human subjects who'd received the respirocyte generators, three men and three women of various ages. The last experiment to be conducted with them was to be a run on the same obstacle course at Tala Camp where she'd observed Carter and Sean not long after they'd received their nanobots. She didn't envy the subjects the run on a day like today.

In fact, though, she'd be observing the run. As miserable

as the weather was, she felt it was her duty to suffer along with them. Carter and Sean were going to be running it as well, and she wanted to see if their times had improved. Once the run was complete, she would finish writing up the study for DARPA, and then she'd have some time off before her sponsors decided what to do with the results.

In the beginning, she'd felt she'd possibly made a deal with the Devil. A peaceful person by nature, she was concerned about the potential for keeping the research for military purposes, though she was fine with it saving the lives of young soldiers on the battlefield. But in the months since her children had been kidnapped, she'd come to terms with the idea that national security would dictate the uses. If Carter and Sean hadn't had the advantage of respirocytes, the children would probably be dead by now, and with them, her heart.

She still hoped DARPA would agree to release the technology for medical purposes, however. It was why she'd begun the research in the first place. And although she was grateful for the funding, the truth was she could have done it, though perhaps more slowly, without that. Nevertheless, what was done was done. She supposed her melancholy came from the dreary weather and the approaching end of the project.

They'd done it. They'd perfected the manufacture of the nanobots as well as the ideal method of injecting them. No more unfortunate incidents with straying 'bots had occurred, and she was confident of the durability of the mesh cages they'd devised now. Both rat subjects and human subjects were thriving, with no sign of antisocial behavior to mar the results. Mackenzie felt the project was an unqualified success.

Furthermore, the early predictions of a doubled lifetime

seemed to have been premature. It was true the rats were rejuvenated, but older rats injected with the generators lived only an extra few months, not double their ordinary lifetimes. Humans exhibited a relative rejuvenation as well. Carter said he felt ten years younger. Based on his grandfather's life, since his parents had died in an accident rather than old age, she thought Carter might live to be one-hundred and fifteen or twenty. Perhaps, if it seemed warranted, she would get an injection as well. But that was for later. Her genetics would give her a long lifespan on their own, and she was too young to worry about it now.

Her ruminations took a back seat in her mind as she arrived at the lab and convened the staff meeting. Today's was a special one. Normally, the weekly meeting took place on Mondays. She'd receive reports from each department, and the week's work would be laid out. Today was Thursday. After the run, only the doctor would remain at the lab through tomorrow to complete the statistical reports on the last obstacle course run. Everyone else was taking an extended vacation after their long, intense project had ended. Some would return for the next phase, and others had accepted contracts elsewhere, their part complete. The three engineers anticipated being hired on directly at DARPA to handle development of the manufacturing facility for the military's supply of respirocyte generators. Mackenzie would miss those who weren't returning, and she said so.

They'd considered a farewell party for the previous weekend, but then the week would have been an anticlimax. And a couple of the scientists wanted the three days because they were to report for duty at their new jobs on the following Monday. So, instead of a party, Mackenzie and Carter had invited them all to dinner the night before. This was the last time she'd see three of them, who would be leaving before the obstacle course run was finished later that afternoon.

"What's next for you, Mackenzie?" someone asked.

"A lot depends on what DARPA wants," she answered. "We haven't yet tested the limits of how many generators humans can tolerate, and before we can even start on that, we have to work up to it with chimps. But we all know the wheels of government grind slowly. Carter is between assignments, so he's been making noises about buying a boat and sailing around the world with the kids."

"A yacht," Carter corrected from the doorway.

Mackenzie looked up in surprise. "Carter! What are you doing here?"

"Just wanted to say one last thank you to your team for their work. Without it…" he stopped. Everyone knew what would have happened without it. "Anyway, I wanted you all to have a token of our appreciation." He stepped forward with envelopes and began to pass them out. The first person to open his was the vet, whose eyes widened in amazement.

"Th-th-this is too much," he stammered. He was looking at a cashier's check for ten-thousand US dollars.

"On the contrary, it isn't enough," Carter said. "It's just a small bonus for a job well done."

Sean's voice now sounded from the doorway. "Say thank you and shut up," he advised in a droll tone. The resulting laughter broke up the consternation in the room, and everyone chorused "Thank you!"

"You're welcome. You know Mackenzie and I are grateful for the work you did giving me the ability to rescue our children. And Sean thanks you…"

"For my awesome new lease on life," Sean interrupted. "I was getting old and decrepit, and…"

He couldn't finish because the room erupted in laughter.

"Well, on that note," Mackenzie said, trying to control her own mirth, "I guess we're dismissed. You guys have a wonderful life. And keep us in mind when you're ready for a vacation, or to come back and work with me. You're all welcome back at any time. And those who are returning, I'll be in touch with a date.'"

The scientists filed out the door, shaking hands with Carter and Sean and hugging Mackenzie as they left. The clinician hung back, since she wasn't leaving until after tomorrow. The vet was the last to leave otherwise. He stopped and thanked Mackenzie for inviting him to come back early, in just a couple of weeks, to work on the wolf study he wanted to do.

"I'll see you then," she said.

When everyone else had gone, the doctor stepped forward. "I'll see you at Camp Tala," she said to Mackenzie. To the men, she said, "Don't eat too large a lunch." She grinned and left.

Chapter Forty-Nine

Everyone on Freydis except for the translators, who were not involved in any way, turned out for the afternoon's entertainment. They'd set the test for two p.m., which should have been the warmest part of the day. Today, though, the high temperature had come at around eleven in the morning, and it was now dropping rapidly. The school-children were bundled in snow apparel up to their eyes, and they bunched up for mutual warmth. Mackenzie, her parents, Ahote and Bly as special guests, and the doctor stood in a group. Mackenzie and the doctor were both holding timepieces and electronic notepads in gloved hands. If it hadn't been for the test being scheduled months ago, Mackenzie would have suggested they postpone it.

First to run were the Tala trainees. Ever since Carter and Sean had bested them on the first obstacle course run, they'd served as a control group. Some had improved their time, but most had already been at their peak conditioning back then. Each person's times was recorded carefully over the past six months, when the human trials of the respirocyte generators began, along with their weight, age, various measurements of body size, and other physiologically relevant data.

The trainees all wore Gortex skiwear – light, thin, and supple, but water and windproof. The weight of their clothing had been carefully recorded also. At the starting gun, they raced toward the first wall and scrambled over, as they'd done every time Mackenzie had watched this ritual. Their times were perhaps a few seconds faster. Mackenzie attributed it to their desire to get through and get on something warmer than the Gortex.

Next were the three women from the experimental group. They ranged in age from twenty-four to forty-seven, with a thirty-something in the middle. All had been in good condition, typical for their ages, when they volunteered for the study. All were military but had desk jobs when they volunteered. And all had told Mackenzie that they were motivated to volunteer because they had experienced gender-discrimination in their military careers – some subtle, some not so subtle. They wanted to be able to compete with the men in their units with no gender-based accommodations. Mackenzie knew they probably had good cause, although she thought progress had been made in the past few years.

When they'd run the course the first time, all three women had made it through, but their times were worse than the Tala trainees, largely because of that wall. Two of them were quite a bit shorter than any Executive Advantage recruit. One was taller, but still shorter than the average EA recruit. Each time they'd run, though, their times improved. Seeing them take the wall at a leap and vault sideways, their feet swinging over the wall a split second after they'd heaved themselves above it with sheer arm strength, Mackenzie was confident they'd beat most of the EA men, if not all of them.

Less than five minutes later, her predictions came true, as the last of the women beat the first of the EA men's time by a full two minutes. The women clustered just beyond the starting line, laughing and giving each other high fives. Their faces were flushed with pride, and they showed no sign of being cold. The doctor waved them over to blow into a breath analyzer for evidence of drug enhancement, which she never found but had to document anyway, and respiratory by-products of exertion. While they were doing that, the men waited impatiently for their turn.

The men were also military desk-jockeys. Wanting age-based comparisons as well as gender diversity, they'd selected a thirty-five-year-old male and one who was forty-six. The third was fifty-four, but he had statistics like the forty-six-year-old. Mackenzie felt they should have had someone who wasn't in tip-top shape, but this man had been the only person older than fifty to volunteer. None of them had been told that they could expect rejuvenation. It had been a happy surprise for all of them, but especially for the oldest man.

When the doctor finished with the women, she signaled the EA instructor with the starting gun, and he had the men line up. Their expressions took on a glint of determination, and the oldest pointed at his next younger companion with a gesture that said he was going to win. The other two grinned and got into a starting position like runners, crouched with one leg extended on the starting block and the other bent, their arms lightly supporting them in the awkward position. The gun went off, and the men literally exploded off the blocks.

The youngest one took the wall in a flip, landing at the

top with his hands extended and pulling his entire body over to drop lightly to the other side. Mackenzie admired the move while at the same time hoping Carter wouldn't try it when it was his turn. It looked like a good way to get injured to her. The other two took it in the same way the women had. As they disappeared around the curve, Mackenzie noted they were already ten to fifteen seconds ahead of the women's times at that point.

They came back into view with the youngest and oldest neck and neck, the middle guy lagging two steps behind. They'd beaten the women by only about thirty seconds average, but the middle guy did come in last. They rushed over to the doctor without being prompted, laughing and pushing among themselves. As they came into hearing range over the cold breeze that had begun blowing, Mackenzie heard the oldest say to the middle guy, "I told you not to carb load. That just makes you sluggish."

'Sluggish' wasn't a word Mackenzie would have applied to any of them. The doctor completed the same measurements she'd done on the women, and once again signaled to the starter. Carter and Sean were already lined up at the starting line, so all they had to do was get in position. Mackenzie admired Carter's trim physique as he did so. He'd never been soft, always fit. But now he could have been a model on one of those romances Liu was always reading, she thought.

Carter and Sean had developed a friendly rivalry over this obstacle course. At first, Sean had won, though not by much. But Sean had heavier muscles, a different body type. And gradually, as the respirocytes and Carter's desire to train had sculpted his body to a near-perfect specimen, he'd gotten faster. For the past three months, he'd been the one to finish first, and he'd pioneered the wall vault that everyone else now emulated. *Except for that flip guy*, Mackenzie thought.

The gun sounded, and Mackenzie's breath caught in her throat as a split second later, Carter's body executed a perfect flip over the wall. He dropped to the ground as Sean's legs cleared the top of the wall. Only three minutes later, Carter came back into view alone. It was the first time that had happened. Mackenzie was used to a photo finish, but for a split second she wondered if Sean had injured himself. Then he came into view, five paces behind Carter. Carter was going to win, handily!

Mackenzie couldn't believe her eyes when Carter slowed a few yards from the wall, and Sean caught up with him. They both sprinted the rest of the way and went over in the original vault move, and they crossed the finish line together. They threw their arms over each other's shoulders and walked together to the doctor, who was *tsking* in irritation. "Carter, you did that deliberately. And it's screwed up my stats," she said.

Carter winked at her. "I think those are *my* stats," he said. "And we're not officially part of the trials, are we?"

Chapter Fifty

In June, Carther, Mackenzie, the team clinician, and Irene O'Connell traveled together in unmarked cars from A-Echelon headquarters to DARPA headquarters, not far from the Pentagon and Fort Myer. They were there to present the findings of the first phase of the respirocyte research. Mackenzie hoped to receive permission to continue her independent research into medical uses for the technology. The delicate business of how to help people all over the world with it, without revealing US military uses, was on her agenda for the meeting as well.

The project fell under the auspices of DARPAs Biological Technologies Office (BTO), Battlefield Medicine division. Led by a medical doctor with a distinguished military background, BTO had been conceived in 2014 to overcome the logistical obstacles of delivering needed medical interventions in war-torn areas. Dr. Bradley Stevensen had seen the potential in Mackenzie's research immediately upon hearing of it and was eager to hear of her progress.

At his invitation, several of his top researchers were on

hand for the meeting. Some had known of the research. Others were just now hearing about it, as it had been need-to-know previously. Mackenzie was a little nervous. Although she and the clinician had what she considered to be spectacular success to show for the project funds, this would be the first time Dr. Stevensen, who was the embodiment of her sponsor and client, would hear of the unauthorized use of the respirocyte generators on Carter and Sean.

At the time, Irene and everyone else she'd consulted had advised it was better to ask for forgiveness than permission. If permission had been denied, Carter and Sean would not have been able to rescue the children. And in any case, permission, even if granted, would have taken too long. Everyone on her side of the decision believed that consequences would be at most a slap on the wrist, given the successful rescue. But revealing the project to those who'd had to know to get the job done had constituted illegal release of top-secret information. It could result in a treason charge.

As Mackenzie prepared to introduce her clinician to give the details of the report, she stood and cleared her throat. She took only two or three seconds to calm and center her mind. Longer would have constituted an awkward pause. Her outwardly calm demeanor and the few seconds of silence served to focus everyone's attention on her. This was like lecturing at her former University post. She could do this.

"Gentlemen, thank you for your attendance. We are here today to announce the successful completion of The Respirocyte Project." She gave the name of the project sufficient vocal weight to convey the capital letters, and she noted the puzzled expressions of the attendees who had not previously heard of the research.

"Briefly, it has been a dream of mine for several years to bring to fruition a concept from the nineteen-sixties, and now known to have been described in ancient times. The concept is that increased oxygenation of the blood can provide medical benefits ranging from increased athletic ability to improved health for respiratory and cardiac patients, as well as improved longevity.

"By successful completion, I mean that we have found a way to provide these benefits via non-invasive injection of nanobots that then use the body's available resources to self-assemble what a layman might call red super-cells."

Seeing several people's mouths open slightly to ask questions, she went on. "Please hold your questions until after the detailed report, and then we will answer them, and we will have a demonstration of some of the named benefits."

A susurration of quiet responses, mutters, and release of held breath followed. After introducing her clinician with a very brief bio and recitation of her qualifications, Mackenzie sat down and prepared to listen to the presentation she and her clinician had worked out. She noticed several people giving Carter puzzled looks, but his presence there was part of the surprise she hoped would carry her argument that the technology must be released for general medicine.

The clinician crisply detailed the facts of the human trials, without mentioning the experiments that had gone before or the manufacturing process for the respirocyte generators. She kept her presentation to the progress of the six men and women who were the first wave of human trials. It took about ten minutes to show with charts that she passed to each participant, that the six subjects had all, without respect to varying ages or gender, improved in their strength, endurance, athletic ability, and general health.

The latter included respiratory and cardiac efficiency, and surprisingly, achievement of ideal weight. This she had originally attributed solely to the exercise the subjects got in the trials, but closer measurement revealed the fat was being broken down to supply much of the oxygen the supercells needed. In other words, oxygen was being stolen by the nanobots from the triglycerides in adipose tissue, creating a sort of reciprocal loop where more was oxidized, releasing CO^2 and water.

Over the six months of the trial, the subjects had to eat more and more to replace the raw materials of the lost fat, but all stabilized at a healthy 15% body fat for the men and 21% for the women. Their appetites eventually stabilized as well, and two months after the end of the trial their follow-up exams revealed a natural ability to eat what they needed, no more and no less, to maintain their healthy weight without tracking or feeling deprived. If released to the public, it would be the first weight-loss plan that ever worked indefinitely to stabilize weight.

At this revelation, the assembled scientists broke out into excited chatter. Many of the most intractable health problems of modern life resulted from improper diet. Solve that, and you solved a high percentage of so-called lifestyle diseases, from Type II diabetes to COPD.

The clinician sat down, her part finished, and Mackenzie stood again to ask for questions. One of the first was about the demonstration she'd promised.

"Oh, yes," she replied. The question had played into her plans perfectly. "Carter, would you please stand?" She introduced Carter as her husband, and he endured the smattering of applause that followed. "Nine months ago," she continued, "our children were kidnapped in Athens by a man who believed my husband could assist in leading him to the answer to an ancient mystery. The details don't matter, except that this man had somehow secreted our children in an inaccessible cave. Inaccessible to ordinary people, that is.

"We have since learned that this man was genetically engineered to have the same red super-cells, or a very close approximation, as our respirocyte generators provide for our subjects. At the time, we didn't know how he'd done it, only that he had. The situation was desperate, and Carter had, with the help of a remarkable assembly of human resources, exhausted all options. Except this," she said dramatically, pointing to a diagram of the respirocyte generator the clinician had queued up in the slide show. "We made the difficult decision to equip Carter and a member of his team with the generators, to allow them access to the deep caves where our children were being held. That decision led to our children being rescued, the kidnapper apprehended and later killed in an attempt to escape, and the discovery of his capabilities."

Vocal expressions of surprise and dismay had begun with Mackenzie's first admission of using Carter as a human experiment, and by the time she'd finished her last sentence, she was having to shout to be heard over the din. No sooner than she fell silent, Dr. Stevensen's booming bass voice rang out.

"Am I to understand that you revealed *top-secret* information to your husband and his teammate?"

Irene intervened at that point. "Carter and his colleague both have top-secret clearance. I was aware of the decision and supported it. Carter and Mackenzie are my employees, and if you have something to say about our decision to *save their children*, say it to me." Her chin lifted and her jaw set, she stared Stevensen down.

Wisely, he backed off. "You considered it a necessity?"

"I did."

"Then we'll let it go, assuming it has not leaked beyond the people required to effect that positive outcome," he said.

"It hasn't."

Mackenzie now took up the narrative again. "Two things, Dr. Stevensen. First, Carter is here to provide demonstrations if you or your staff require them. His colleague is on assignment, or he would be here as well. Second, I would like to explore the possibility of releasing this technology for medical purposes to the public, or at least to selected institutions. The benefit to mankind is unquestionable. To keep it a secret is to condemn millions of people to unnecessary poor health and death."

"Thank you, Dr. Devereux. Both doctors Devereux," he amended. "I'm sure my colleagues will wish to avail themselves of the offered demonstrations. However, your request to release is something I'm going to have to take under advisement. I'm not unsympathetic to your position. But the final decision is above my pay grade."

"Fair enough," Mackenzie said. "When can I expect an answer?"

"I can't say," he replied. "But I will take it to my superiors immediately."

Chapter Fifty-One

Within a month, Mackenzie had a new contract with DARPA to develop a way to provide the first-generation respirocytes in medically significant quantities while designing a second-generation type that would give US military personnel a miraculous healing advantage. She had managed to retrieve most of her crew, and where it was impossible to buy out contracts for some, she had replaced them. The three engineers were now employed directly by DARPA, but they would be collaborating with her new engineers in the second part of the project.

By August, she had authored and published a paper, with DARPA's blessing, and by September, the breakthrough was receiving worldwide attention. That's when a doctor at the world-renowned Mayo Clinic received an invitation from the Nobel Committee to submit a nomination for the following year's Nobel Prize for Medicine. He could think of no greater medical breakthrough than Mackenzie Devereux's respirocyte generator.

The wheels of the Nobel Committee's evaluation

process grind slowly. Nominations are by invitation only, to qualified persons who cannot nominate themselves, but must nominate someone whose discoveries have changed the scientific paradigm and are of great benefit to mankind. Their nominations are due back to the committee by the following January thirty-first. During March through May, the committee invites international reputable experts to evaluate the submissions, and during June through August, the evaluation work is in progress.

During the year when, unbeknownst to her or anyone outside the Nobel Committee and their evaluators, Mackenzie's nomination wound its way through the process, her team found more and more economic and efficient ways to manufacture the generators. The procedure became affordable for everyone but the poorest patients in the US, whose access to it was hung up in Medicaid regulations. In countries with one-payer systems, access was universal.

Some industries developed terminal illnesses as newly-healthy people gave up smoking, voted with their wallets for more nutritious fast food, and stopped buying fad diet books. Others, like gyms, outdoor recreation gear manufacturers, and health food stores, flourished.

A year after her nomination, Mackenzie's recommendation made it through from the Nobel Committee to discussion in the Nobel Assembly. On the first Monday in October, a majority vote of the Assembly awarded her the coveted prize. Early that morning, Mackenzie received an international call from Sweden. She and Carter were enjoying a last cup of coffee before going to their separate offices, Mackenzie's in her lab and Carter's in the translation building.

After saying hello, she listened, and her eyes grew round. "You're kidding!" she exclaimed. Her eyes went to

Carter's face. He appeared mildly curious. Then she burst into tears. "Oh, my God! Thank you! Thank you!"

Carter got up and crossed to her, his face a mask of concern. "What is it?" he mouthed.

She shook her head. Then she said, "Yes, I understand. Yes, I will be there. Is my family welcome?" And then, finally, "Thank you again. Goodbye."

She looked up at Carter, who was hovering over her as if to protect her from some threat from above. "Come on," she said. "We have to get to my office in the next five minutes."

"What are you talking about?" he said.

"I'm not allowed to say, not even to you, until the press conference. It will be streamed live in ten minutes. Hurry!"

Wearing a mystified expression, Carter followed Mackenzie at a leisurely trot for him. She was running as fast as she could. They arrived at the lab door in three minutes and she threw herself into her chair and woke up her computer, while telling him to get on the intercom and summon the rest of the team there.

Four minutes later, everyone was assembled, and she turned her monitor to the room where everyone could see. Then she rolled her chair around to watch as well, as the link she'd been given displayed "*The press conference will begin in ___ minutes.*" A countdown timer counted seconds in the underlined spot.

"Mackie…"

"Shh, they're starting," she whispered.

The screen message disappeared, and in its place, an image of two gold coins, or rather both sides of the same coin, appeared. The assembled team and Carter gasped as they recognized the profile of Alfred Nobel on the left, and the Genius of Medicine, an open book on her lap and a bowl collecting water to quench the thirst of a sick girl in her right hand. The inscription circling the edge of the medal read *Inventas vitam luvat excoluisse per artes*, loosely translated from a passage of Vergil's Aeneid as "And they who bettered life on earth by their newly found mastery."

The room went utterly silent as the press conference began, announcing that Dr. Mackenzie Devereux had won the Nobel Prize for Physiology or Medicine. Then it exploded.

Questions rained on her from every side. Had she known of her nomination? Who else had been nominated? When was the presentation ceremony scheduled? Was she going?

To the first question, she answered, "No." To the second, she couldn't say. Someone mentioned they thought that information could only be revealed after fifty years. To the third, in December, and to the fourth, looking at Carter, she said, "I believe we will. It will be fun for the kids."

Later in the day, Carter congratulated her as he'd wished to at the time but couldn't because of the witnesses. Holding her in his arms after a lengthy and smoldering kiss, he told her he was so proud of her.

"I couldn't have done it without my team," she said. "It should have been awarded to the team."

"The concept was yours, Mackie. The honor goes to the right person."

"But we don't need the money," she said. "Would you care if I divided it among the team?"

"It's yours. You do what you want with it. But I hope you'll keep the medal to pass down to the kids someday."

"Of course," she said.

Chapter Fifty-Two

On the tenth of December, Mackenzie accepted her prize at the award ceremony. In the stands to observe were her husband and children, her parents and brother, and an assembly of their closest friends, including Irene O'Connell, former President Samuel Houston Grant, James Rhodes, Sean Walker and his bride Sam, Liu and Dylan Mulligan and their toddler. Ahote and Bly had been invited, but they elected to stay and care for the ranch while everyone else was gone.

Also missing were the research team. Mackenzie had already told them that they would be receiving a share of the financial prize, and to a man and woman they had elected to remain at their posts to continue the work. However, they did assemble in Mackenzie's office to watch the live stream of the ceremony as it took place.

Watching at DARPA headquarters, Dr. Stevensen reflected that the decision to release the technology had been the right thing to do. Any time an American won a Nobel Prize was a feather in the cap of the US. He was aware that the Devereuxs had requested an extended leave of absence from A-Echelon, but he had full confidence the research and development of the respirocyte technology would continue without Mackenzie overseeing it daily.

Communications technology would allow her to maintain contact with her team as she and her family sailed around the world, a well-earned break for Dr. Carter Devereux.

Because it was not in his office's mission, Stevensen had not been informed that the sailing trip was also the cover for more extensive research into the dolphin ansible communication. Nor did he know that little Beth Devereux would be in constant touch with a young wolf at home on Freydis, with her mother recording the interactions.

All the Devereux's still had questions they wanted to explore, from Carter and Mackenzie, to Liam and his little sister.

"There are more things in heaven and earth, Horatio, than are dreamt of in your philosophy."

More by JC Ryan

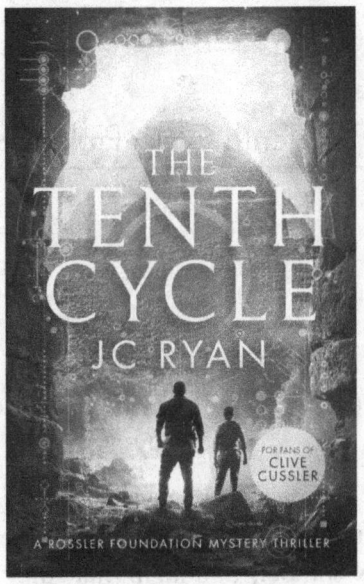

vinci-books.com/tenth-cycle

Unraveling the truth buried in the Great Pyramid may come at the ultimate price.

Daniel Rossler and Dr. Sarah Clarke race against time to decipher the secrets hidden within the Great Pyramid of Giza. As they uncover a truth suppressed for millennia, they find themselves in the crosshairs of powerful adversaries, including the enigmatic Orion Society, the CIA, and even the President. With danger lurking at every turn, they must navigate a treacherous landscape of deceit and violence to expose the reality of human history.

Turn the page for a free preview…

The Tenth Cycle: Prologue

10th Cycle year 25,990, a city near the present site of Giza, Egypt

The Supreme Council of Knowledge had been in session for more than two hours and the mood between the twenty-one elders was somber, although what they heard excited some.

Aleph, first among the members, listened attentively as Zebulon, their youngest, made his request. The nineteen Chosen who ranked between the two listened in various mental states, some supporting, others dismayed. Zebulon, a genius and excellent orator, was making a compelling argument, succeeding in convincing the elders that he had a worthy cause.

Concluding, he said. "We have made our world a better place since we received it nearly 26,000 years ago. Why should we not pass the benefit of our knowledge on to Those Who Come After? Our world will end soon, in about ten years if my calculations are correct. We have nothing more to prove or achieve, our time has come and gone. Let us be gracious about it. A new civilization will be built on the ruins of ours. Why should we not give them the best chance to build it even better than ours? A chance to break the cycle of destruction? They are our children and descendants. We owe it to them. I beg you to consider wisely." Zebulon bowed and sat down.

All eyes were on Aleph as he made his answer. "Why would we undertake this task? It has ever been so, God has decreed it. Civilizations are born, they live and grow and they are destroyed. This is the tenth Cycle. Those Who Come After in the eleventh must once again learn wisdom in their own Cycle and in their own way. You defy the natural order!"

"With respect, Aleph, show me in the holy writings where God has decreed we may not reveal our knowledge to Those Who Come After." A gasp went up as nineteen pairs of eyes flew to Aleph expecting to see his rage. Instead, they saw him in deep thought.

He looked at Zebulon. "Very well, you have spoken well, and have convinced me. If the rest of the members agree, you may gather the information and build your Library of Knowledge of the Tenth Cycle." The nineteen members nodded their heads in agreement.

Aleph looked around, confirming he had the support of everyone, and continued. "The Council will bear the expense of what you described to us. But there is one very important condition. You must devise and encode the message in such a way that it is time-locked to Those Who Come After. They will first have to achieve a high measure of intelligence and civil behavior before they can read it. Only when they have advanced to the point where they can read and understand the message will they be ready to make use of the information you will leave for them to improve their world. If you fail to do so, it might cause them much more harm than the good you intend for them."

The other nineteen members nodded their heads in agreement again.

"Thank you, Aleph and learned elders. I will follow your wise counsel with great care and precision."

Zebulon bowed in affirmation and turned to leave the conference chamber. There was no time to waste. According to his calculations, the Cycle would end in less than ten years. Despite the engineering capabilities of a 26,000-year-old civilization, it would take at least eight years to build the massive structure he planned, a pyramid, shaped and constructed to withstand any natural disaster he could imagine. Within its measurements and placement would be a sign for those who could see it, that a great accumulation of facts, history and scientific discovery was contained within. In turn, the key to unlock the treasure-trove would be encoded, requiring both intelligence and persistence to locate and read it. In this way, he would cleverly time-lock the knowledge and wisdom of the Tenth Cycle of humanity.

The Tenth Cycle: Chapter One

NEAR KABUL, AFGHANISTAN, JULY 2009

Daniel Rossler and two of his friends from ISAF headquarters in Kabul, Afghanistan set out early in the morning on Daniel's birthday, July 8th, on the A1 toward Jalalabad some one-hundred and fifty klicks and three hours or so to the east. IEDs, or Improvised Explosive Devices had made this stretch of road one of the most dangerous places in the world.

Daniel, an irrepressible 26-year-old journalist embedded with the Marine unit, matched his comrades' skill for skill except in armed combat. As a journalist, he was neither expected nor permitted to carry a weapon, though his upbringing in the North Carolina Mountains had included skill with a hunting rifle. Now, his preferred physical activities were hiking, swimming, and the occasional impromptu wrestling match with the two friends in the Jeep with him today or other opponents from their unit. At six-foot-three, his wiry frame was perhaps a little lighter than most of his heavily-muscled Marine opponents, but his quick thinking and unconventional moves allowed him to win more often than he lost.

"Hey, Sarge," Rossler yelled over the noise of the vehicle on the highway. "Isn't this the road that the Taliban keeps bombing?"

"You afraid of a little rebel IED, Rossler?" the sergeant retorted.

That effectively shut down any further discussion on the matter. The one thing Daniel couldn't allow was his Marine friends thinking he was a wuss. Traffic was unusually light this morning, which should have warned the three friends, especially the Marines. Instead, they were elated to be making such good time during the early hours before the heat of the day set in.

Seeing the well-populated area on both sides of the road for the first fifty klicks, Daniel wondered at the logic of the Taliban rebels who harassed travelers along this road without regard to loyalty. Anyone could be killed by an IED, even Afghan citizens making their way to market, or children.

He was aware of the joint task force squads that had been specially trained to sweep for and dispose of the deadly items, though. Daniel felt as safe on this trip as he did anywhere in Afghanistan, which was to say, not very. Nevertheless, today's mission would provide good background for his next column. It was important work, and Daniel was good at it.

Daniel didn't realize he had stopped watching the road ahead until he heard Sgt. Ellis shout, "Look out!" He found himself in mid-flight as the Jeep swerved violently, and then overturned beside the road, pinning Ellis and the driver, Sgt. Pierce, and throwing Daniel clear. He was trying to sort himself out to stand when shots rang out from further up the road.

"Shit!" Daniel cried, hunkering down into a rapid belly crawl toward the Jeep where his friends lay injured a couple of yards away. With bullets kicking up the sandy dirt all around him, Daniel reached the relative safety of the Jeep more in rage than in fear. Finding Pierce conscious but injured, he said, "What the hell?"

"IED," Pierce answered, wincing in pain. "Didn't see it until Ellis hollered, had to swerve to miss it."

"Who's shooting at us?" Daniel asked.

"Oh, I don't know. The Taliban maybe?" Even in pain, Pierce was acerbic, causing Daniel to wish he hadn't asked such a stupid question.

"How are you doing? What hurts?" he asked.

Pierce said, "Think my arm is broken, maybe leg too. Mostly I'd like to get this hunk of metal off me."

Daniel surveyed the way the vehicle had come to rest on Pierce's leg, noticing that a fortuitously-placed rock had kept the vehicle from resting heavily on the leg, though it would still need a couple more inches to clear the leg and foot. Sgt. Ellis was unconscious, his head resting on a larger but flatter rock, and both legs pinned by the frame of the windshield. One looked bad, like the frame had acted as a cleaver. Daniel couldn't tell if the lower part was still attached to Ellis' body.

"Where's your weapon, Pierce?" Daniel asked anxiously. While he and the two Marines were relatively sheltered by the bulk of the vehicle, sporadic automatic weapons fire told him the rebels were still out there, and would probably come looking for anything they could pick up unless they knew someone would shoot back.

"Racked between the seats," Pierce ground out between clenched teeth.

"Hold on. I'm going to try to get you and Ellis out from under this thing, and then I'll grab the weapons."

Daniel quickly surveyed what they had in the Jeep that could be used as a lever, or at least a prop, without finding much that he thought would be useful. They did have a large metal lockbox, which Daniel found a few feet from the rear of the vehicle. Retrieving it, he shoved the box under the center of the vehicle to prevent it shifting further - he hoped. Bullets were flying overhead and hitting the Jeep sporadically. If the Jeep crushed the box, they'd be in worse shape than before. Then, with no other choice, he asked Pierce if he would be able to scoot out from under the vehicle on his own, if Daniel could lift it a few inches.

"I'll try," Pierce answered.

Daniel wormed his way into the gap, shoving his head and shoulders under the frame and pushing until his body was lifting one side of the Jeep, while dragging the box in with him to solidify his gains. He had managed to lift the vehicle only a couple of inches when Pierce said, "I'm loose."

Leaving the box in place, Daniel backed out, hoping to find that he'd also made enough progress that he could drag Ellis out. When he went to look, he paled at the damage he could now see. Though he swiftly used his belt as a tourniquet, it appeared Ellis could be in trouble if help didn't arrive soon. However, there was nothing else he could do but pull him out from under the vehicle before it shifted again and finished the job of severing Ellis's leg. With little more to be gained in lifting the Jeep higher, Daniel stood, then half-crouched to get purchase on the injured man, pulling him to safety as bullets flew by his now-exposed head.

Both of his friends now released but too injured to help, Daniel retrieved their Colt SMGs and fired a few shots back in the general direction of the gunfire just to let the bastards know there would be hell to pay if they dared to come closer. He could only hope that a friendly military patrol would come along before he exhausted his ammunition. With that in mind, he quickly reconnoitered to see if he could determine the exact location where the shots were coming from. About three hundred yards away he could see a structure, and nothing in between. Well within *their* effective range, but to his advantage was that if they were to attack him and his friends they would have to approach over open terrain with no protection. He would have the cover of the Jeep and would be able to pick them off one by one. He fired a few shots toward the building to scare them and let them know that he knew where they were. He would wait until they approached before firing more shots, and just hope there weren't too many of them coming at the same time. With adrenaline pumping through his system, he waited.

Half an hour passed, during which time he'd been forced to fire a short burst to keep two insurgents off them. Then, a rumble that signaled a vehicle approaching from the direction of Kabul caught his attention. It was followed shortly by automatic weapons fire and the gun fire from the building going quiet very quickly.

The sound of American voices, yelling out "Yo, jarheads, you all right?" brought him up from his post.

"Got two wounded here. Who are you guys?"

"Task Force Paladin. Looks like you started to do our job for us out here. Who the hell are you?"

Daniel didn't take offense. He wasn't in uniform after all. He stood to his full height and walked toward the Army squad to explain what had happened.

Grab your copy…
vinci-books.com/tenth-cycle

About the Author

JC Ryan is a bestselling author renowned for his intricate espionage, archaeological thrillers, and conspiracy mysteries. With over 30 acclaimed novels, including the popular Rex Dalton K9 Thrillers, Rossler Foundation Mysteries, and Carter Devereux Mystery Thrillers, Ryan has captivated readers around the globe.

Drawing from his diverse professional background—as a military officer, lawyer, and IT manager—Ryan creates compelling narratives that skillfully blend historical accuracy with thrilling adventure. He is celebrated as a master storyteller, known for crafting riveting plots, meticulous historical details, and engaging, multidimensional characters. Ryan's meticulous research lends authenticity and depth to each story, immersing readers in richly constructed worlds filled with intrigue, suspense, and adventure.

Fans of David Baldacci, Lee Child's Jack Reacher, Tom Clancy's Jack Ryan, Nelson DeMille's John Corey, Vince Flynn's Mitch Rapp, Mark Greaney's Gray Man, Gregg Hurwitz's Orphan X, Robert Ludlum's Jason Bourne, Daniel Silva's Gabriel Allon, Brad Taylor's Pike Logan, Brad Thor's Scot Harvath, James Rollins' Sigma Force, Steve Berry's Cotton Malone, and Dan Brown's Robert Langdon will find JC Ryan's novels equally compelling and unforgettable.

When not writing, Ryan enjoys spending time with his college sweetheart, whom he married in 1978. They are proud parents of two daughters, have two sons-in-law, and are grandparents to two grandchildren.